CAUGHT IN THE AFTERMATH

JAMI GRAY

Cover Art: Deranged Doctor Design, www.derangeddoctordesign.com

Publisher: Celtic Moon Press Revised edition, 2021
ISBN: 978-1-948884-56-3 (ebook) ISBN: 978-1-948884-57-0 (print)

First edition, February 2019, Escape Publishing - HarperCollins Australia
ISBN: 978-1-4892-770-22 (ebook)

sign up for free reads from jami!

Join Jami's newsletter to be the first to hear about new releases, free books, special prices and other nifty events.

Sign up at: https://www.subscribepage.com/jami-gray-books

also by jami gray

ARCANE WONDERLAND

Last Call

Bitter Spirits

Rune & Tonic

ARCANE TRANSPORTER

Ignition Point (*Prequel Novella*)

Grave Cargo

Risky Goods

Lethal Contents

Collision Course

Blind Spot

Terminal Drift

THE KYN KRONICLES

Shadow's Edge

Shadow's Soul

Shadow's Moon

Shadow's Curse

Shadow's Dream

Shadow's Fall

Tangled in Shadows (*Short Story Collection*)

FATE'S VULTURES

Lying in Ruins

Beg for Mercy

Caught in the Aftermath

Fear the Reaper

PSY-IV TEAMS

Hunted by the Past

Touched by Fate

Marked by Obsession

Fractured by Deceit

Linked by Deception

BOX SETS

PSY-IV Teams Box Set I (Books 1-3)

The Collapse: Fate's Vultures (Books 1-4)

The Kyn Kronicles Box Set (Books 1-6)

Arcane Transporter Box Set I (Books 1-3)

Arcane Transporter Box Set II (Books 4-6)

To my personal Knight in Slightly Muddy Armor and his ever-faithful sidekicks, the Prankster Duo—you guys make my heart smile every damn day!

acknowledgments

Contrary to popular belief, writing is not always a wildly fun adventure. There are days when you wonder why the hell you thought you could tell a story. For those days, you find yourself reaching out for like-minded others who understand this strangely weird creative world that dominates your life. For all those times when I was tempted to throw in the towel, thank you for listening, for kicking my ass back in line, and for being the loving, supportive friends and readers who know much more than I ever will: Joanna Clayton, DeAnna Browne, Dave Benneman, Camille Douglass, Mona Karel, and Amber Kallyn.

one

Under the obscuring curtain of night-blind skies, Math released his grip on the lifeless form of the last of his tormentors. With the immediate threat eliminated, his adrenaline levels crashed, and his battered body protested the abuse leveled against it. The howl of a distant wolf snared him free of his pain-addled daze that left the edges of his mind frayed.

He dragged the body to the narrow ditch hidden among the shrub-infested wasteland. At the crumbling edge, his strength flatlined and he sank to his knees. He reached deep and found enough energy to shove the corpse over the edge. It tumbled down leaving a trail of dirt and gravel in its wake. He pushed back to sit on his heels, dropped his head like a man in supplication, and considered his recent re-education in an old lesson.

Never let your ego coldcock your brain.

This time the bait proved far too tempting to resist and once his arrogance and fury gained center stage, he willingly stepped into the role of the reluctant guest of the four men sent by the queen bitch herself - Greer.

Her name alone was enough to cause his simmering rage

to boil over. For nine years he tamped the lid down, even as escaping steam scorched his hand, but at this particular point, when the stakes were so high, he couldn't afford to let it to blow. Because Math craved more than simple vengeance, he dreamt of restitution, the sweet, lethal, bloody quid pro quo type.

Unfortunately, one of his people, Cam, was trapped in the traitorous woman's claws, and thanks to the talkative idiots now lying in the nearby ditch, he might have a lead on where Cam was stashed. And that was the only thing that kept the faint kernel of hope in his cynical heart alive.

The organ hadn't always been a diamond-hard lump, it once thundered for his family, one created by bonds of loyalty so deep the scars still ached. They were named the Strix, a tightly woven assassin clan that rose from the ashes of the Collapse. Their creation stories varied from being the remnants of covert government operatives so dark as to be invisible, to being the descendants of crime families whose reach spanned every corner of the grimy underworld. No matter the truth of their beginnings, when society fell into chaos, the founding members took their lethal skills and carved out new profit arenas.

If the price was right and the situation doable, the Strix would clean up the messes created by the emerging powers.

Still reeling from the loss of his blood family, a young Math stumbled into the welcoming arms of the Strix and found a home. His new clan recognized his natural ability in all things clandestine and honed them to a lethal edge until he was one of their most skilled. It was a position he enjoyed, until the day the power shifted.

It started when Greer slithered in on the coattails of Michael's name and wound her lethal coils around the Strix's leadership. Math didn't know if Greer had been acting under Michael's orders, or furthering her own personal agenda, when she slaughtered nearly all the Strix. Only a combination of luck and skill ensured Math, and a scant handful of others, escaped the brutal, nightmare-inducing massacre. When they regrouped, Math became the de facto leader, and in return, he vowed to make Greer pay.

But responsibility made for a ruthless mistress, and Math's resolve to protect the remnants of his family was a liability for Greer to manipulate. To be an effective operative meant cultivating a buffer of detachment. When Greer took Cam, she blew Math's buffer straight to hell and his carefully plotted long game disappeared in a puff of smoke.

Cam was the one person who managed to slip into the ragged hole of Math's heart labeled brother and to get him back, Math would do whatever it took, including spending the last couple of days at the not-so-tender mercies of the men currently taking a dirt nap. He thought about ending his stay earlier, but once the entertainment of torturing Math had faded, Greer's men did a lot of drinking and talking as they lounged around the fire. So, Math held on and in the end, his obstinacy paid off. When they thought he was out cold, his captors spilled their guts, first figuratively, and in the end, literally.

Despite having a possible location, he waged an internal war as his brain demanded he go to New Seattle and hunt down Greer, while his heart dictated he go after Cam first. No matter which choice he made, he had to play it just right because instinct warned if he didn't, Cam would be the one to pay the price. Once Greer realized that Math was on the hunt again, she would make sure there was no one and nothing left for Math to save.

Since there was no way he would chance that shit happening, he needed back up. The question was, who the hell could he reach out to?

With the echo of a timer counting relentlessly down in his

head, he braced his hand on the ground and forced his body to move. Once upright, instincts and training kicked in. It took precious time, but he gathered the scattered items that belonged to the strike team. He kept a few essentials—a knife, a half-filled canteen, some dried nutrition bars, and a marked-up map, but tossed the rest in the ditch. Better not to keep anything that could be traced back to this scene.

He choked down a bit of food and water to offset his lagging energy and studied the map's notations and landmarks under a match light. He scanned the surrounding terrain and eventually recognized the droning noise in the distance as a waterfall. Armed with that bit of information, he bent back over the map. Starting at where he encountered Greer's fumbling minions, his finger traced a path until he found his location, and his harsh laugh cut through the night.

Someone up there hates me.

His closest option for help was the furthest thing from a friendly asset he could imagine, but with Cam's life in the balance, it didn't matter, he'd make a deal with the devil, no matter how much it chafed his ass. It was a good thing his soul was used to dirty bargains, because this one was bound to get nasty.

two

"Simon is an ass." Vex mumbled, staring into the amber depths of her drink.

"Mmhmm."

Vex lifted her gaze at the noncommittal hum from her dark-haired drinking companion. "Mmmhmm, what?"

"Nothing." Mercy stared back with wide-eyed innocence. "I'm just agreeing with you."

Uh-huh, sure she was.

Vex narrowed her eyes as Mercy tried and failed to stifle her grin, and then raised her glass, and tilted it in the other woman's direction. "Agreement, my ass." She drained her beer, set it on the table, and then used a single finger to nudge it in line with the other empties. "Go ahead." She propped her elbow on the table and set her chin in her palm. "Share your infinite wisdom with me."

Across from her, Mercy paused, her drink halfway to her mouth, and arched a brow. Shrewd darkness shoved the fake innocence aside and revealed the assassin's pragmatically ruthless nature. "You sure you can handle it?"

Vex waved her hand in the air, knocking the beaded ends

of her multiple braids out of her face as the alcohol ran warm and loose through her veins. "Hit me."

Mercy shook her head and took a drink. After she set her bottle down, she folded her arms on the table, and leaned forward. "Fine." She pinned Vex with an exasperated but knowing look and waved her finger in Vex's face. "When the man who supposedly holds your heart tells you you're better off as friends, the traditional reaction is hurt, which then leads to plotting creative payback." She dropped her finger and sat back. "It's not heartache I hear in your voice."

The other woman's words struck like darts, straight and true and Vex braced before asking, "What do you think you're hearing?"

"Relief."

"Nope." Denial whipped through Vex and left her voice sharp. "That's called anger, my friend."

Mercy's lips twisted into a doubtful knot. "Maybe," she admitted before dipping her head in acquiescence, but not before something perilously close to sympathy swept through her hazel eyes.

"No fucking maybe about it." Unable to handle Mercy's too perceptive insight, Vex shoved back from the table. "I'm grabbing another. Want one?"

Mercy picked up her bottle, rolled her wrist, and eyed the liquid's level. "Sure, this one's almost out." She looked to the bar and then back to Vex, speculation adding a dry edge to her voice. "You sure you can make it back without starting a fight?"

"Who me?" Vex adopted an affronted look and rocked back on the heels of her biker boots. "I don't start fights."

The noise Mercy made was somewhere between a giggle and a snort. "That's not what I hear."

"Then you best get your ears checked." Vex turned and

strolled across the bar's floor, dodging chairs, hands, and indecent innuendos. *See? Not starting a thing.*

She gave Derek, the barkeep, her order, then half-turned, elbows braced on the bar's edge to watch the crowd. It used to be, people went to bars to blow off steam, to see and be seen, and if they were lucky, to find someone to mess up the sheets with. Then the world went to hell and survival became the new normal.

After seventy plus years of living under the law of the jungle, humans were only now getting back to enjoying the few pleasures they could find in life. Like hanging out after a long day, savoring a cold drink, and enjoying a decent meal. Or in tonight's case, listening to live music from the band who played for their drinks as they headed northward. The addition of the live band made for a crowded evening at the Tipsy Shrew.

What was that old saying about popular places? Location, location, location?

Whatever it was, the Tipsy Shrew had it. The bar claimed a prime location as it sat outside of the settlement of Pebble Creek and perched on the main travel route between Salt Lake and New Seattle. Its location managed to snag a variety of entertainment options and patrons.

Tonight's crowd contained the typical eclectic mix—rough riding road rats, weather-beaten farmers, traveling merchants, and the regular settlement joes looking to while away the hours with a night out. She spotted a couple of military types, trying hard, but failing, to blend in as they scanned the patrons with an obviousness that screamed they were on the hunt.

She let her gaze slip past them as her brain mulled over their presence. Guys like that stuck to the larger, urban centers like Salt Lake and New Seattle that were protected by the powers that be, and rarely found their way down into the smaller towns like Pebble Creek that fell under the dubious protection of others.

Pebble Creek was under the—*what was the word Havoc used that she loved?* —aegis of Fate's Vultures, the four nomadic arbitrators—*read mercenaries*—that currently called the settlement home. Which begged the question—*who was so important the city soldiers would voluntarily waltz into the Vultures' territory?*

Don't borrow trouble, a little voice in her head warned.

But as one of those Vultures who had more than enough trouble to handle, she had to wonder. Still, she set her curiosity aside and made a mental note to mention their presence to Reaper, the Vultures' inscrutable leader.

Then she turned her attention to more pressing matters. Like why the hell she thought hanging out with Mercy was a good idea. Maybe, instead of drowning her sorrows with Havoc's girlfriend, she should have stayed with Havoc and Reaper as they discussed how to ensure the next supply run made it through without disappearing into thin air.

But those sorrows needed drowning. Like image of the pint-sized brunette wrapped around Simon down by the market square this afternoon. Granted, Vex and Simon parted ways over a week ago, but would it have hurt him to wait until she was, say, not anywhere near Pebble Creek, before replacing her ass? Since Simon's answer was *"obviously not"*, she was angry. Angry at Simon, angry at herself, and angry at the whole fucked up situation in general. Hence her need for alcohol.

On cue, a thick glass hit the bar top. "Order's up."

"Thanks." She tossed the credits on the bar, nabbed the two chilled bottles, and headed back to her table.

The heavy beat of the music sank into her blood and rocked her hips. She let it drown out her troubles as she wove her way through bodies and chairs. Appreciative whistles followed her and earned a small smile, instead of her normal scowl. After Simon's clumsy handling, her bruised confidence could use the little salve.

She caught sight of Mercy and their table but was brought up short when a sadly misguided arm wrapped around her waist and dragged her into a barrel chest covered in cotton. With her hands full of the local brew, she had no choice but to come face-to-face with a dust-laced road rat. At five foot nine, she had no trouble meeting the bleary eyes of the idiot stupid enough to touch. Male sweat and alcoholic fumes hit her full in the face and her nose wrinkled.

Dear God, how did he stand himself? "Wanna let me go, pal?" She tried for civil, but it emerged on a growl.

"Nah." His thick arm tightened, pressing her close as he ground his negligent bulge against her. "I'm liking where you are."

Oh, for the love of— "Yeah, I'm not." She shifted her weight and without losing her grip on the bottles, brought her knee up in a sharp, debilitating move, taking his negligent package to microscopic.

A high-pitched yelp sounded and the arm around her waist disappeared. He bent over, cupping his abused bits, red suffusing his face, and stumbled back into one of his giggling friends. The impact sent them both crashing to the floor and knocked over a couple of bottles on a nearby table. When the drinks' owners rose with pissed off shouts, Vex cleared a path to their unknowing targets and stepped around the writhing bundle of limbs.

As the fight broke out in earnest behind her, she set the bottles in front of a laughing Mercy. "There, not a drop spilt."

She dragged her chair around to Mercy's side, spinning it so its back was to the table, and straddled it. She sank down, rested her arms on the back with her bottle hanging from one hand, and aimed her attention on the show unfolding in front of them.

Bruised balls or not, the wanna-be Romeo got to his feet and with another bull-like bellow, charged a wiry male who had finished laying out Romeo's giggling buddy with a solid right hook. Romeo's hit took them both into another table that collapsed under their combined weight. The brawl gained momentum and sucked in more participants. Fists flew and grunts interspersed with curses rose above the music while a few feminine shrieks played counterpoint.

Now this was what Vex called entertainment. "I give it another minute before Derek pulls out his shotgun."

Mercy winced when one of the younger customers delivered a particularly brutal hit to the burly drunk. "I don't think he'll get the chance to use it."

"And why's that?"

"Because." Mercy motioned with her bottle at the man wading through the room, "My favorite brawler just arrived."

Heading directly to them with a dark scowl was six feet of wrapped muscle. Thick, unruly dark hair was held back by a bandana, and a small, curved scar bisected his right eyebrow was joined by another scar high on his stubble-covered cheek. In his wake the fights petered out and like a bunch of cowed, unruly kids, the combatants busied themselves straightening chairs and tables.

"Oh goody, Havoc's back." Vex took a drink and kept her body relaxed even as she mentally braced for the approaching storm.

A look passed between Mercy and Havoc just before the moron who initially grabbed Vex stumbled into Havoc's path. Without pausing, Havoc introduced the road rat's head to a support timber. Introductions complete, the idiot slumped to the floor and stayed down.

An appreciative hum sounded from Mercy.

Vex rolled her eyes and stifled a beleaguered sigh.

Havoc grabbed a nearby empty chair, dragged it over to Mercy's other side, and dropped into it. "I leave you two alone for what? Fifteen minutes?" He draped an arm over Mercy's shoulders and snagged her beer. "That's got to be a record."

Vex leaned around Mercy so she could see him. "Did you not notice we are sitting right here, enjoying our drinks?" She wiggled her bottle. "Just minding our own business. Why would you think we had anything to do with it?"

"No 'we' here," Mercy corrected with mock innocence as she threw Vex under the proverbial bus and leaned into Havoc's shoulder.

"Traitor." Vex squashed her niggle of jealousy at the couple's obvious affection. Simon's words rang in her ears. "*Love you, Vex, but I can't keep hitting my head against that wall around your heart. If I haven't even made a dent in it by now, I'm never going to.*"

Just like that, he gave up on her. *Story of her damn life.*

"What a shocker," Havoc drawled.

Startled, Vex surfaced from her pity party and met his raised brow and pointed stare but said nothing.

He took another drink and handed the bottle back to Mercy. "Seeing as Reaper's in a pissy mood, if Derek hits him up for repairs, it's your ass, Vex."

"Isn't it always?" She shot back, an unusual bitter bite in her voice. It bothered her to hear it, so she shoved up from her chair and rapped her knuckles against the table. "Time to call it a night."

Havoc frowned and Mercy's humor disappeared, replaced by worry. "Vex—"

"Look," she cut the other woman off, not wanting to deal with it. "I'm just in a shitty mood. I'm going to drink my beer and head out. I'll see you two tomorrow, yeah?"

"Vex." This time it was Havoc, and he packed a world of questions and offers in her name.

It wasn't easy but she met his concerned gaze. Other than her twin brother, Ruin, Havoc was one of the few males in her life she hated to disappoint. A situation she seemed to find herself in more and more often lately. Tight bands wrapped around her chest, and she cleared her throat. "Just need some alone time, get my head on straight. That's all."

He studied her for what felt like forever before his slow nod released the chains on her feet. She turned, threw back the rest of her beer as she crossed the floor, and left the empty bottle on the bar's top, before heading into the freedom of the night.

VEX PULLED under the protective overhang, shut off her bike, and eased it into position next to Reaper's metal darling. She sat there, feet braced against the ground, and listened to the engine's rumble fade and she fought back the echo of Mercy's words in her head. *"Traditional reaction is hurt... I hear relief."*

Here, in the dark, with no one around, Vex admitted what she wouldn't dare at the bar. Mercy was right. And didn't that make Vex a total bitch when she whined about Simon giving up on her, even though his rejection felt more like a reprieve than the end of a possibility.

She got off her bike with a soft curse and stood in the shadows staring at the softly lit entrance of Grave Hall. If she walked in there and ran into Reaper, the eagle-eyed bastard would know her shit was a mess. *Well, messier than normal.* And pushy ass that he was, he'd make her spill, whether she wanted to or not, and she certainly did not.

If luck was paying attention, she might make it to her room without being spotted. Unfortunately, sleep was the last thing she wanted. Her chaotic emotions were scattered to hell and back, and after the scene at the bar, she needed a release of some sort.

She eyed the night shrouded streets and considered the distraction they might offer. Decision made, she started to walk. It didn't take more than ten minutes to leave the illusionary safety of the town's center behind and find the narrow paths that twisted through the more questionable areas. Like most of the large trading towns, Pebble Creek was built on the bones of what used to be. In this case, the bones belonged to a southern Idaho university town.

In the aftermath of economic collapse, pandemic rampages, and Mother Nature's relentless reclamation of her lands, the former United States turned into a mishmash of territories and swaths of wild, brutal lands dotted with battle-scarred remnants of civilization. Surrounded by the massive Lolo forest and the treacherous terrain of Yellowstone, Pebble Creek was situated in a natural, narrow valley that created a virtual stronghold in the area that stretched from Idaho through Utah and into northern Arizona. The town served as the Central Territories' nerve center and played a critical role controlling the trade routes that connected the Pacific coast's Northwest Territories to the Rocky Mountain region that spanned into Colorado and the unclaimed areas of New Mexico and Texas. Not to mention, it guarded the straight-shot route to the Northland border.

Just like the Tipsy Shrew, it was all about location.

And speaking of location...

She followed the sounds of a muffled grunt and stifled laughter and turned down a narrow alley tucked between two shadowed buildings. Moonlight spilled over the graffiti-covered brick and inched towards a knot of darkness gathered near the alley's back wall. A rock rolled under her boot and bounced off a discarded bottle, the echo startling in its abruptness.

The knot at the end shifted, broke into three figures, and that fast, she found the distraction she was looking for. The largest figure stepped into the moon's path and waved the other two back to whatever unfortunate soul snagged their attention.

"Whatcha starin' at, bitch?" Shadows fell back to reveal a bulky frame encased in layers of chains and leather. He swaggered towards her, shook drops of blood from his fist, and flexed his fingers. Ink snaked down thick arms and moonlight sparked off the rings that covered his torn knuckles. Unfortunately, the pitiful beard that was doing its best to crawl off his weak chin cancelled out his aura of menace.

She sauntered forward and raked her gaze from the top of his spiked-out hair to his dust-covered boots. She stopped and curled her lip as she recognized him as one of the rats that belonged to a roaming road gang. "Still trying to figure it out. Do I get three guesses?" She clapped her hands with obvious fake excitement. "I know, you're Prick One, and those two behind you, I bet are Prick Two and Three, right?"

He angled his head over his shoulder without taking his eyes off of her and sneered. "Look, boys, seems we have ourselves a real comedian." He dragged out all four syllables and ended it by hurling a wad of spit off to the side. "How 'bout we get three tries to fill your smart mouth with our pricks?" Snickers and ribald suggestions came from the alley's shadows.

Classy.

Fierce satisfaction swept through, and she gave a mental *yippee* for the low intelligence, high bullshit factor at play that lit her nerve endings with anticipation. She folded her arms under her breasts and palmed the hilts of two blades tucked along her ribs. She shook her head, dropped her hands, keeping the blades hidden along the inside of her wrists, and loaded a wealth of sugary sweetness to her voice. "Oh, honey, even if all three of you managed to get them in, which I'm going to guess is way outside your skill level, they'd hardly make a bite." She snapped her teeth in an unmistakable threat.

It took a few seconds for her implication to penetrate the dense air inside his skull, but the moment it finally made landfall blood rushed through his face and his hands curled into fists. Pumped up by a bruised and fragile male ego, he charged.

His impetuous decision caught his two sidekicks off guard Their delayed reactions gave Vex enough time to send both blades spinning through the night. When twin pained yelps sounded, she grinned but didn't get much time to enjoy nailing her marks.

The lead dumbass swung out. She ducked under his arm and managed to sink her fist into his gut. The impact left her hand momentarily numb, but it doubled him over and his knees hit the ground. She followed up with a knee to his face, only to fall short when he nailed her inner thigh with a bruising punch that edged her vision in red.

Motherfucker! Those damn rings hurt.

She returned the favor by doubling her fists and targeting his temple. The impact rang up her arms, but she kept moving, pivoting with a kick that caught him under his pathetic beard. His head snapped back, his body following, and his skull bounced off the pavement. To be sure he stayed down, she slammed a quick double kick into his ribs, the dull thunk of her boot meeting flesh and bone blended with his groans.

There was a blur of movement and a cut off yelp, that spun her around in time to watch one of the two backup dicks stumble back, his hands clutching his stomach. He hit the alley wall and slowly slid down. By the time his ass touched down, it was clear he wouldn't be getting up anytime soon thanks to the hilt of her knife that stuck out of the red ruin of his gut.

She frowned and stepped over the groaning and dazed dumbass at her feet and approached the Gutless Wonder. No way her simple throw resulted in that type of damage. She was within reach when something slammed into her and knocked her off balance. She shot a hand out to brace against the rough brick and avoided a nasty face plant in Gutless Wonder's lap. She did an awkward jig over his outstretched legs and ended up with her back against the wall just in time to watch the last of the trio haul ass as he held his arm awkwardly.

Oh, hell no!

"Hey, dumbass, I want my knife back!" She pushed off the wall and made it to the center of the alley before he hit the entrance and disappeared. "Dammit." Replacing that blade was going to cost her.

"Looking for this?"

The deep voice swept along her spine and coiled around it with a hair-raising grip.

She turned.

A bit of darkness peeled from the wall, slowly straightened from a hunched position, and moved towards her with a stiff gait. As the shadow moved out of the night's hold, it resolved into a man. It appeared that the trio's unfortunate target had found his feet and her knife. He offered it to her hilt first as the moonlight glinted off the polished blade. He waited for her to take it even as he kept his other arm wrapped around his ribs.

Careful to stay out of reach, she stepped closer, then stopped, forcing him to move further into the light so she could see who she was dealing with.

He obliged and took another step forward into the faint moonlight.

Shock locked every muscle and swept her curiosity aside. Despite the obvious signs of violence that decorated his face, the chiseled features framed by midnight hair and a matching dark goatee was disturbingly familiar. "Who the hell are you?"

three

Math stood there beaten to hell and back, while an annoying ring echoed through his skull, and blinked away the blood that seeped into his swollen eye. Once his vision cleared, he studied the woman who stood before him. An enigmatic whisper grew into a maliciously gleeful howl and left him silently cursing his spectacularly bad luck. Out of all the people to hit this reeking alley, it had to be this particular woman.

Just fuckin' great.

His abused muscles screamed as he held out her blade, so he lifted it a few inches, and the small move sent fire licking along his ribs. He stifled his groan and gritted out, "You going to take this? If not, I'm happy to keep it."

That earned him a growl, but she glided closer. "Give me that."

Her hand was a blur as she snatched the weapon out of his hand, and it made him wonder if he had a concussion.

Her gaze roamed over him as she took her time tucking the blade away. Even though the light was for shit, he didn't miss the long, leather-clad legs, or the metal chains that draped her provocative curves as she stood impatiently in front of him.

"Going to give me a name?"

He forced his gaze to her arresting face that was busy frowning at him. A tumble of thin, beaded braids mixed with long, streaked strands of light and dark. She was so close to him, the edge of her lethal vibe nipped at him like impending lightning storm. Knowing full well he was about to poke a snake with a stick, he said, "I'm considering it."

Her dark brows rose over a stunning mix of curious gold and brown. "Might want to decide before you hit the ground, that way I know what name to put on your grave marker, hot shot."

The laugh that tried to escape emerged on a huffed breath, courtesy of his damaged ribs. "Yeah, you may want to hold off on that happy thought."

"Sure about that?"

"It's been a bad week." An understatement of the year. Normally, dealing with three assholes who decided jumping him constituted an entertaining evening, would be a piece of cake. But dealing with them two days after enduring the sadistic tendencies of Greer's men was an altogether different story. He tried to straighten so he could take a deeper breath and the alley slid sideways in a sickening lurch.

It was safe to say his body had hit its limit.

Before he did something embarrassing like collapse, she was there, wrapping one arm around his hips, and tucking her shoulder under his, so the world wouldn't slip out from under his feet. Thankfully, she was tall enough to offset his six-foot-one frame.

"Right. We need to get you some medical help.'

Despite his spinning head, he managed to shake it. Nausea threatened and he swallowed it down. "You can't, I've got eyes looking for me."

A soft snort sounded next to his ear. "Why am I not surprised?" She didn't wait for a response. "Don't worry, hot shot, I'll keep you under the radar."

He managed to turn his head until he could see her profile, surprised to find it so close. "I appreciate it." He barely got the words out around his thick tongue.

Long, thick lashes lifted, her amber gaze met his and hardened. "You fucking pass out on me and I'm leaving your ass to rot, hear?"

"Roger that." He dropped his gaze to his boots and concentrated on moving his feet as she led him out of the alley. It wasn't as easy as it sounded, so he did what he did best—he shoved the pain into a box and stuffed it in a corner.

With his body on autopilot, his sluggish mind churned. It wouldn't be long before Greer's trackers would be on his ass, and not just because of the mercenaries he left in the ditch. He spent the last few weeks making his presence known by ensuring one of her questionable shipments destined for an urban center never made it to its final destination.

In the overall scheme of things, Greer would find its loss no more than a nuisance, but for Math, it represented another volley in a years' long war. At least until he walked into that damn trap and learned of Cam's capture. That changed everything and left Math with limited options.

One of which involved recruiting Fate's Vultures. A tricky proposition, especially since one of the Vultures had no reason to welcome his presence, and the others would not be pleased with the wolves Math brought to their door.

"What kind of eyes you got on you, hot shot?"

Her question dragged him out of his head. "The dangerous kind."

"Not telling me much."

There was a reason for that. "It's better I don't."

She stopped and aimed her amber gaze at him. "Better you do."

Feeling cornered, he reluctantly shared, "Hired guns out of New Seattle."

The arm around his hips tightened, and then relaxed as she resumed their shuffling walk. "That explains the looky-loos at the bar."

"Looky-loos?" he asked as they made their way through the darkened streets.

She didn't answer as she navigated the narrow spaces between buildings with an ease of familiarity and stuck to the heavier shadows.

A door whipped open a few feet ahead and released a burst of rough laughter and conversation on a cloud of smoke and light. Pungent spices drifted on the night air, indicating a smoke shop. None too gently, she shoved him up against the side of the building and plastered her body against his, blocking him from the passers-by.

Her unexpected move left him unprepared for the bombardment of heat and curves. His hands went to her waist and held tight as her hair filled his vision. Her body's warmth sank into his cooled skin and brought a singular point of his anatomy to attention, despite his body's aches and pains. "What the f—"

"Shh!" She hissed as her focus stayed to his left. Despite his hold, she shifted against him, and put her mouth near his ear while her arms curled around his neck. "Try and act interested."

Interested? If he was any more interested, he might hurt himself.

He gritted his teeth and attempted to ignore the faint scent of rain-washed sage that curled around him. He slid one hand down to her hip and adjusted their positions to something less tempting and managed to gain a whisper of space.

Two figures stumbled out of the opened door and slowly made their drunken way down the street.

Tendrils of her hair were caught on his goatee and he inhaled deeply to blow them away. That decision elicited a painful protest from his side and brought him back to his senses.

The hammered duo made it to the end of the street. She uncurled her arms and stepped back. It took him a second longer to let her go.

She stood inches away, her gaze on his and with her patience clearly at an end, she demanded, "Name."

"Math."

A peculiar tension held her still. "Mercy's Math?" At his nod, she turned and stared off down the now deserted street. "Well, damn." Her attention came back to him. "She expecting you?"

"Not unless she's psychic."

That earned a lip twitch, but she wasn't done. "You here for her?"

"No. I need to speak to Reaper."

She folded her arms and narrowed her eyes. "I know he's not expecting you."

He stayed silent since she wasn't asking.

Quiet hummed between them as she studied him. Then she came to some internal decision, dropped her arms, and stepped in close, her arm reclaiming his hips. "Right, let's make tracks, Math."

He slung an arm over her shoulder, held his ribs with the other, and straightened from the wall. As they continued down the street, he allowed her to steer him as he concentrated on staying upright. When they approached a softly lit building, he broke the silence to ask a question he already knew the answer to. "Are you going to return the favor?"

She turned to look up at him. "Favor?"

"Name." He deliberately mimicked her earlier demand.

"Really?" She looked away and shook her head. She led him around the edge of a night-shrouded courtyard and around the side of a multi-story building. She bypassed the faint illumination of the solar lights that lined the curving walkway and stayed with the shadows. "Shouldn't you know it since you're supposed to be a master ninja-spy or some such shit?" She blew out a disbelieving breath and muttered, "Then again, maybe Mercy was just blowing smoke."

Normally her mocking attitude would piss him off, instead he found himself fighting a grin. Not bothering to correct her "master ninja-spy" part, he repeated, "Or some such shit." He could practically feel her eyes roll. "Are you testing my skills, woman?"

"You have skills to test?" she shot back as they shuffled along the narrow walkway.

This time he let his grin escape. "You tell me," he paused, then added, "Vex."

She gave a delicate snort. "As if that was a challenge."

They reached a small, railed stoop that led to a utilitarian door complete with heavy-duty locks and wire mesh that covered the thick, inset window. She shifted her hold to his waist and dug out a set of keys with her free hand. She tilted her head and considered him from under her long lashes. "Can you do stairs?"

He considered the stairs in question. "More than this?"

She nodded.

He braced, shifted out of her hold, and leaned against the railing. "Take it slow, I'll manage."

She took her time studying him, then dipped her chin in acknowledgement. "Hang tight." Then she darted up the stairs, unlocked the door, and propped it open. Then she was back at his side. "Ready?"

Together they made it up the short set of cement stairs,

through the door, and into a narrow hall. Once inside, she reset the locks and then led him down the hall. Light filtered from the end and the faint noise of activity rippled against the well of silence they moved in. She paused next to a door under an old exit sign. Then using her hip, she bumped it open and moved them into a stairwell.

Faced with a mountain of stairs, he couldn't help but ask, "How many?"

"Two floors."

Shit on a stick, this was going to be a bitch. "Guess an elevator is too much to ask for?"

"You're the one who wanted to avoid eyes, my man."

"Right."

Before his dread got a chance to build, she started hauling his tired ass up the stairs. Even though they took it slow, it cost him. By the time they hit the third floor, he was gritting his teeth, a film of clammy sweat clung to his spine, and his head felt like an oversized balloon.

"Stay with me, Math."

He held on to that low voice and focused on putting one foot in front of the other in a jerky shuffle. They hit the next door, and he managed to stay upright as she opened the door and did a quick look-see. Coast clear, they moved into a wider hall, this one well-lit and carpeted. He barely dragged his feet as they shuffled down the hall.

"Here." She propped him against the wall next to a door, got it opened, and disappeared inside. He took advantage of the momentary respite and sucked in a couple of shallow breaths. Light spilled out of the doorway and curled around Vex when she returned. "Come on in, hot shot."

He stumbled inside, his mind fuzzy as he stood there, taking in the room. The light left the interior a study of shadows. Shapes indicated furniture and he aimed for what appeared to be a couch. The sound of the door closing, and locks being thrown chased him.

He managed to conquer a couple more steps before Vex's hand on his arm pulled him to a stop. "Wrong way."

"I need to lie down."

"See that, but not here." She steered him through the dark room and into another one, then hit the lights to reveal a spartan but comfortable space. "This works better."

A standing closet partnered with a set of drawers joined a pair of mismatched chairs. A jumble of leather he recognized as a bike's saddlebags clung to one of them. But what caught and held his attention was the bed sprawled under an intricate metal headboard and situated between two upended wooden crates that doubled as nightstands.

He forced his protesting body to move and aimed for the tempting expanse. Vex stayed at his side, providing a much-needed brace as he sat on the bed's edge. The fuzz in his head started darkening around the edges, and before it could win, a bright flash of light glinting off metal snapped his attention back, but not before Vex set her blade to his shirt.

Over the sound of ripping material, he managed, "What the hell, woman? That's my good shirt."

She knocked his hands away. "Relax." One last slice and his t-shirt, stiff with blood, dirt and whatever else he managed to bring back from the alley, hit the floor.

"Glad I wasn't wearing my jacket." Come to think of it, where was his jacket? Replacing it would be a challenge.

Warm hands cradled his jaw and Vex crouched between his knees. He hobbled his scattered thoughts together and stared into the provocative angles of her face. At any other time her position would present all sorts of intriguing possibilities for him to consider, but now it was all he could do to keep her in focus.

Her lips moved. "Need you to lay back."

That sounded like something he could do. He braced his arm against the mattress and started to recline. Vex went to work on his boots. Her careful movements, slight though they were, left him gritting his teeth. "Leave them, please."

She shot him a dark look complete with a frown. "You're not ruining my sheets. These either come off, or I roll you to the floor." She didn't wait for his decision. Moments later his boots were on the ground, and she was lifting his feet to the bed.

Left with no choice, he carefully shifted from his side to his back. A sharp hiss escaped as he sucked in air, but when he was finally prone, he couldn't stifle his groan of relief. His eyes drifted shut and it took a few seconds for his body to get with the program. His muscles slowly unclenched as his mind slipped into an exhausted half-aware state. Something cool and wet pressed against his swollen eye.

God that felt good.

"Can you hold that?" Vex's voice blended with the hazy awareness and his hand rose to the compress. Her warm skin brushed against his palm as she slid her hand away and let him hold it. "Going to get you cleaned up."

"I need to talk to Reaper." His tongue felt thick, and his words sounded garbled, but she understood.

"Anyone ever tell you patience is a virtue?"

He blinked his other eye open and found her leaning over him. She was close, her hair falling forward, the ends of her braids shifting against his shoulder with a whisper of touch. He got caught in the unusual mix of colors in her eyes. Gold and brown, sprinkled with a hint of green until it melded into an incredible amber.

It took a second for his brain to kick back into gear, and as a man who prided himself on not being taken in by the fairer sex, his hesitation irritated the ever-loving shit out of him. It made his response curt. "I don't know what you've heard, but virtue is not in my skill set. Neither is fucking patience."

Instead of the expected anger, she flashed a mischievous grin, and then tapped the tip of his nose with a finger, throwing him completely off guard. "Be nice."

Before he could figure out what the hell that was all about, she was gone, leaving him staring after her. When she returned, she was armed with another washcloth and a dark bottle. He didn't have the strength to keep the argument going, so he kept his mouth shut, and continued to glare.

She ignored his scowl and with a gentle and efficient touch, she cleaned the blood from his face and worked her way down his chest.

Logically he knew she was simply tending to his injuries. But his body took her attention in a completely different direction, which left him grinding his teeth in an unsettling mix of embarrassment and frustration. Thankfully, it wasn't long before the faint scent of licorice rose as she applied anise oil, a natural antiseptic, to his now cleaned wounds.

Finished, she straightened, half-turned to set the bottle on the nightstand, and then tossed the cloth aside. The solid splat as it hit a hard surface indicated an adjacent bathroom just out of his sightline. When she turned back to him, her hands went to her hips and her gaze swept over his body. "Right, how bad are the ribs?"

He felt a perverse flash of satisfaction at the slight hint of red riding under her cheeks. At least he wasn't the only one affected. "I'll live."

Her jaw flexed at his abrupt tone, but she didn't back off. "Anything else we need to stitch or bind?"

Needing to get this, whatever this was, out of the way so he could get to the real reason he was here, he snapped, "I've survived worse. The sooner you get Reaper, the sooner you get your bed back."

One of her eyebrows lifted. "Did I bitch about you being in my bed?" She dropped her hands from her hips, turned, and walked over to the standing closet. Pulling it open, she dug around inside and yanked out a t-shirt. "Here." She tossed it at him.

Instinctively, he went to catch it before it hit his face, his fist closing on soft material. Pain shot up his ribs and left tiny white starbursts exploding along the edge of his vision.

When he blinked them clear, she was standing at the foot of the bed, exasperation filling her face. "Think you can manage to put that on before you meet with Reaper?"

His attempt to sit up failed and he flopped back with a groan. A loud sigh sounded, then she was there, arm around his shoulders, as she helped him sit up. After a few choice words on his part, and muttered comments about fragile male egos on her part, they got the t-shirt on.

He fought to stay upright. "Now that I'm decent, can I see Reaper?"

"You sure you're up for this?"

He lifted his head with effort and held her gaze. "If there was any other way, I wouldn't be here." Going at this alone would be a spectacular failure, and that wasn't acceptable. Not with Cam's life at risk.

She studied him, judging his intent before turning her gaze beyond him to stare at something only she could see. She worked through whatever was going on in her head and blew out a breath. "Here's the deal. Lay your ass back down and rest. I'll get Reaper."

"I'll go with you." He started to push off from the bed and his body tilted to the side.

She dropped a hand on his shoulder and exerted pressure, not letting up until he relented. "Don't think so." He opened his mouth to protest but she got there first. "Straight up, you couldn't make it out of this room unless you crawled. Even that's doubtful. Besides, based on his reaction the last time he heard your name, you're safer here." Her comment warranted further conversation, but before he could pursue it, she continued. "Plus, tucked away here means the eyes looking for you stay blind."

Her points were valid. Facing Reaper was a test of endurance under normal circumstances. Beaten to hell and back would make it much more challenging. With shit barreling down faster than he could shovel, there was no reason to invite more. His one-word answer was reluctant. "Fine."

"Fine," she repeated, then proceeded to help him lie back down.

She moved around him as he drifted. Something clinked against the headboard, but it wasn't until cool metal snaked around his wrist, that his eyes flew open to find her leaning over him. He ignored his body's protests and snapped his other hand up, wrapping it around her arm, digging in with bruising force. "What the hell?"

She crouched at the side of the bed until they were face-to-face and met his glare with a hard-eyed clarity. She tugged on the chain linking the handcuffs around the metal post of the bed. "I don't want you pawing through my things."

Anger burned through him, but he understood the senti-ment. "What do you think I'm going to do?"

She ignored his punishing grip and shrugged. "Don't know, don't care." Then she placed one arm on the bed and kept her voice low. "Stay out of trouble until I get back."

"Right," he cut out through clenched teeth.

She flashed him a smile, twisted her arm out of his grip, and gave his cheek a soft pat. "Love you too, hot shot." She pushed to her feet, went to the end of the bed, and tugged a blanket out from under his heels. She opened it with a snap of her wrists, laid it over him, and then headed for the door.

"Vex."

At her name, she stilled in the now open door and looked over her shoulder.

When he had her eyes, he said, "The next time you use cuffs on me, you'd better be ready for the consequences."

Her answering grin was full of wicked intentions. "Promises, promises."

Then she was gone, leaving him behind, aching and cursing.

four

Vex left Math tucked in her room and headed back down the main stairs towards Grave Hall's common area. Even at this hour, people would be hanging around, including Reaper. She needed a way to get boss man upstairs without invoking the others' curiosity. God knew the folks of Pebble Creek loved their gossip. One of those facets of being part of a small town, something she was trying to come to terms with.

Traditionally the Vultures preferred life on the road and avoided permanent residences. The only home she had before Pebble Creek was the ramshackle cabin she and her brother left behind in Oregon. Now each Vulture had a two-room suite on the third floor of the Hall. Which worked out great if you had to hide a six-foot-plus bundle of dark-haired trouble in your bed. The image took her mind into areas best left alone.

Caught in her thoughts, she missed the last step of the stairs. The jolt of her misstep sent a twinge of fire up her inner thigh, a reminder of the necessity of a quick side stop before she tackled the common area. No sense limping in looking like she just finished tumbling through a grimy alley. Even if she had.

She shouldered through a double set of swinging doors and stepped into the large industrial kitchen, a leftover from the Hall's previous incarnation. It was perfect for serving the variety of semi-permanent residents, travelers, and locals. It also proved useful when washing blood and grit from your face. She was only a few feet in when she came face-to-face with the Hall's caretaker, Worth.

He looked up from where he was wiping down an over-sized stove and frowned. "What the hell happened to you, girl?"

She breezed by him, her goal the sink sitting under the night-blind window. "Minor disagreement in town."

She nabbed a clean looking cloth, ran it under the faucet, and went to work on her face. In the window's reflection she caught his reflection as he tossed his cleaning cloth aside and grabbed the crutch propped next to him. With an ease from years of practice, he maneuvered on one leg, and stopped at the counter's edge next to her. He propped the crutch, folded his arms over his thick chest, and watched her set aside the cloth to cup her hands under the cool water. She splashed water over her face, washing away the last remnants of the night's misdeeds, and then took the towel he held out to her.

He waited until she was done before starting in. "You need Mandy?"

Mandy was the local doctor and Worth's not-so-hidden crush. It was almost as cute as it was heartbreaking to watch the older couple dance around each other. The odds of Mandy, damaged by a past Vex wouldn't wish on anyone, letting Worth in any closer than he already managed was close to nil.

"Nope, all good." Vex settled her ass against the cabinets

and put her hands on the counter's edge with the towel caught between her palm and the counter. Since Worth wouldn't let her leave until he had his say, she tried to steer their conversational route. "Reaper out front?"

"Yeah, so's Ruin and Simon."

She buried her flinch at Simon's name and focused on her rising excitement of hearing that her twin was finally back after a three-week absence. "Ruin's home?"

Worth eyed her. "How'd you miss that one?"

Her shoulders shifted. "In town. Drinking with Mercy. Dealing with a spot of trouble. Pick one."

He opened his mouth, obviously rethought his words, and finally gave her, "Your brother met up Reaper just after Havoc headed out."

"Nice." An inspired thought popped into her head. "Charity with them?"

Worth shook his head. "She headed right upstairs, said something about a shower."

Hmm, too bad. One of life's little pleasures was tag-teaming Reaper with Charity, Ruin's woman. The results ranged from her fearless leader pulling his alphahole cloak tight, or going all broody, dark, and silent. Either way, it would divert his attention from why Vex now sported her own set of bruises. Not to mention provide her with much needed comic relief. "Guess I'll brave it on my own."

Worth shot her a look and warned, "Watch your step tonight, Vex."

She arched a brow in silent question.

"Reaper was in a nasty mood before your brother returned. Whatever news he carried on his boot heels wasn't good. They sent for Simon and the conversation turned pretty intense." He caught her wince and proving age hadn't damaged his observation skills, he asked, "What's that for?"

She played dumb. "What?"

"Don't 'what' me, girl. Word has it Simon was sportin' a brunette at the market today. You want to tell me what's going on?"

To get Worth off her ass, she elected to go with a half-truth. "Nothing's going on with us."

"Nothing my ass." He groused and then dove in. "You two have had spats in the past, but this here is different. A week ago, couldn't get you away from that boy. Not since the day you and Havoc carried his half-dead ass down from the mountain. Every time you returned from your runs, you two were like a couple of heartsick school kids. Now? You'd think he's carrying the plague."

And this, right here, was one of the many reasons she liked being on the road. No one stuck their noses in your damn business. She dodged Worth's too perceptive gaze and turned away to toss the hand towel aside. She didn't know if it was the booze, the tussle in the alley, or the dark and deadly treasure she brought back tonight, but her emotions bubbled to the surface. "Some things aren't meant to be."

Worth's gentle touch on her shoulder brought her around. He titled his head and his voice softened. "You want to talk about it?"

For fuck's sake! No, she didn't want to talk about it.

She'd rather beat the holy hell out of someone, someone like Simon and possibly the brunette.

Ah, who was she kidding?

Her anger was more personal than that, and the only one to blame was—Vex. Something must have shown on her face because she caught the pity in Worth's gaze. She shoved the messy emotional shit back into the dark corner where it belonged and forced steel into her spine. "Saw a couple city soldiers over at the Tipsy Shrew." It wasn't desperation rushing her voice. Nope. Not at all. "Heard anything?"

Not easily sidetracked, Worth looked as if he would push the Simon thing. Vex offered an unholy pact to whoever was listening to keep the old man off her ass. Thankfully somebody heard, or something in her face convinced him, because he heaved an exasperated sigh before following her lead. "Maybe they're just passing through."

She smiled, and prayed it hid the mess in her head. "Maybe." She pushed off the counter. "Got to talk to Reaper, then I'm heading up to crash." She leaned in and bussed his whiskered cheek. "Good night, old man."

With that, she headed towards the door and was almost free when Worth's low voice pulled her to a stop. "Vex." She looked back and once he had her attention, he continued. "Don't need the details, but I'm here you need an ear."

The gruff, heartfelt offer sank deep, and her throat got tight. *Damn, first Havoc and now Worth.* All these unexpected offers left her shaky. She managed a soft, "Thanks, Worth."

She went through the first set of doors and stopped in the small area tucked between the kitchen and the common area. She took a moment to consider her options.

Approaching Reaper about Math's presence required a delicate finesse. Thanks to Mercy's sharing one night after she and Havoc made it back from Salt Lake, Vex knew Math's skills meant those handcuffs were nothing more than a minor inconvenience. Since he didn't strike her as stupid, just stubborn, she hoped he stayed put and took advantage of her bed. He was going to need his strength.

She hadn't been joking when she told him Reaper's reaction to his name was extreme, so much so Vex found it curious. After Mercy and Havoc returned and shared their adventures, there had been anger, deep and hot, cored with something she couldn't name. Normally the man made ice look warm as his intimidating control extended beyond his temper to all of his emotions. The only time he thawed was if he counted you one of his. Luckily, Vex, Havoc, and Ruin all held that honor.

But after how hot he ran at Math's name, she assumed Math was someone important to Reaper, but uncovering that connection so far eluded her. Well, it had until she saw Math in the flesh. Now she had her suspicions, and if she was right, wouldn't that be a kick in the ass?

A bright burst of laughter snapped her back to the present. She sucked in a bracing breath, pushed through last of the swinging double doors and stepped into the common room unnoticed. She took advantage of her momentary invisibility and scanned her surroundings.

Most of the faces were familiar, even if she couldn't tag them with a name. The laughter centered around the pool table set off to the side. A couple of teens used the dartboard. Her gaze swept over the eclectic mix of tables guarded by chairs scattered through the space. Nothing unusual and no one hit her radar as an unknown. Her attention shifted to the back area used as a library and hit pay dirt.

Guarded by twin bookcases and sprawled in a trio of stuffed reading chairs around a low table sat Reaper, Ruin, and Simon. Together the three men could overwhelm an unsuspecting woman. Reaper's long legs led to a sculpted chest and spread into wide shoulders, topped by a face framed by thick dark hair with matching close-cropped beard, all of it creating a masculine picture of trouble incarnate.

In contrast, the lean frame of her twin, Ruin, barely contained his roguish charm topped with a tangle of gold and copper-streaked brown hair held in check by a bandana.

Then there was Simon. With skin a luscious mahogany paired with startling light grey eyes, the current leader of the Central Territories was missing his typical half grin that drew enough honey to give Vex a sugar high. Since she knew all three males more than most, Vex was spared the heart trauma their combined presence invoked.

Ruin's head came up and locked on to her with the uncanny sixth sense innate to twins. He took her in, head to toe, and years of reading her brother made it easy to catch his flash of worry before it disappeared under a roguish grin. He pushed to his feet, leaped a chair with desultory grace, and moved towards her.

Caught and exposed, she stepped forward, her lips curving as her feet picked up speed, and she met him halfway.

His arms wrapped around her with an aching familiarity. For a brief, shiny moment, everything was right in her world because her brother was here. "Hey sister o' mine, you finished causing trouble?"

"For tonight."

He spun them around until her back was to Reaper and Simon. Then he tucked a finger under her chin, tipped her chin up, and leaned back, taking in the evidence of her nightly exercise. "Might be sporting a shiner tomorrow."

The overhead light aggravated the ache in her head, so she batted his hand away and dropped her chin. "Better than what they're sporting."

Humor lightened his concern. "Need a hand removing evidence?"

"Nah, just a few road rats looking for trouble."

"They came to the right place." He poked a finger into her shoulder and narrowed his familiar amber eyes. "You dragging it back?"

Um, yeah, but admitting that wouldn't get her the outcome she needed so she went with plausible deniability. "Nope."

Because Ruin knew her better than anyone, his skepticism was clear. "Right."

Before he could start in on what would be a tedious interrogation, she asked, "Where's your woman?"

His grin turned slightly goofy. "Upstairs. Getting rid of the road dust, planned on looking for you. Should be back any minute."

Vex's pulse spiked. Ruin and Charity's quarters were just a few doors down from Vex's. If she was lucky, Charity would come directly down after her shower. Otherwise, she would trot downstairs with Math on her heels and Reaper would lose his shit. No way did Vex want to guess where things would go from there.

She crushed her wince before it could escape, and pressed her palm against Ruin's chest, drowning her flash of worry in the comforting beat of his heart against her palm. "Glad you're back."

"Yeah, me too." He gave her one last squeeze then let her go to take a step back. His gaze went behind her and came back. "Why does Simon look like his nuts are in a vice?"

At the implied censor in his question, her hackles rose. "Why are you asking me?"

He didn't miss the combination of her tone and posture and his jaw tightened. "Generally, it means it's you doing the tightening."

She opened her mouth to issue a snappy comeback, but a husky feminine drawl interrupted the downward spiral of their sibling squabble that would make a pair of four-year-olds proud.

"Are you two going to end up on the floor wrestling?" Charity came up on Ruin's side and wrapped an arm around his waist, her bright blue eyes dancing as she watched them. "Because as much as I love you, Ruin, my money's on Vex."

Vex smirked. "Smart and beautiful. What you see in my brother is a mystery." She half-turned and nodded towards Reaper and, unfortunately, Simon. "Shall we?"

Ruin looked to Charity. "You know she fights as dirty as you do."

They moved towards the two men watching them.

"When kicking ass, anything goes," Charity murmured.

"Amen, sister," Vex agreed.

Ruin reclaimed his chair, and Charity perched on the padded arm.

The last grain of sand dropped in Vex's personal hourglass as she joined a glowering Reaper and frowning Simon. She made a point to ignore both thunderclouds and dropped into a chair with a good view of the room and Reaper. "Heya, Reaper." Since she considered the Simon situation a done deal, she kept him on her peripheral and stayed civil. "Si."

His cautious "Vex" collided with Reaper's barked, "What the hell happened to you?"

"Had a little fun in town, nothing to worry about." She shifted her position, hooked a leg over one of the chair's arms and shifted her attention from Reaper to sweep through the busy room. A couple of heads turned their way.

Vex tagged Worth's crush, Doc Mandy sipping her tea and balancing a book on her knee, a couple of women she'd seen around town, their attention on the men (of course), and the trying-not-to-be-obvious teenage gawkers at the dart board. It left her internal alarms quiet and allowed her a moment to relax.

"You sure about that?" Reaper's question proved he and his instincts never missed a thing.

Instead of lying outright, she dodged. "A little concerned about the gun-slinging duo from the city with an unhealthy curiosity hanging at the Shrew." She thought she fumbled the dodge when Reaper's eyes narrowed.

Movement flicked in the corner of her eye as Simon leaned forward. "Say again?"

She twisted her neck to look at him and buried the massive

shit in her head behind an empty screen as she met his dark gaze. "Got two guard types from the city checking out the local scenery."

At her response whatever earlier tension Simon carried, jumped to the next level. His gaze went beyond her to Reaper, his earlier frown gaining depth. "That's not good."

"Maybe, maybe not." Reaper's voice was low. "How curious, Vex?"

She shrugged. "Curious, but not enough to get up from their drinks and draw attention."

"That means they're looking for someone, or something, specific." Charity's observation was worth noting, since her position as 'Hound to Lilith, the Queen of the Rockies', meant her specialty was ferreting out secrets, no matter how deeply hidden.

"Not sure I'm comfortable chancing that," Simon grumbled, one hand swiping over his closely cropped hair.

"Si's right," Ruin said. "Between the shit with the trade routes and rumblings in New Seattle, we can't afford to brush this off."

Next to him, Charity settled back and stretched her arm along the back of Ruin's chair. "How many supply runs have been screwed recently?"

Vex could answer that one. "Too damn many." She swung her leg, then winced as the bruised muscle in her inner thigh twinged. *Dammit, almost forgot about that little souvenir.* Unfortunately, she also caught Reaper's speculative gaze and rushed on. "To anyone watching, a couple of Pebble Creek's shipments have been delayed, not lost." Only because they managed to get the two non-critical, targeted shipments replaced prior to their final delivery point through some judicious wheeling and dealing. "But if it keeps up, our reputation is going to suffer."

"The hell of it is, we're not the only ones being hit,"

Simon added. "Word came through that a couple of shipments out of New Seattle got lost en route."

A speculative light lit Reaper's eyes. "Who was running transport?"

"City militia," Simon answered.

Reaper nodded thoughtfully. "Better them than us."

"Truth." Simon blew out a breath and rubbed a hand over the back of his neck. "If I didn't know better, I'd think we had a guardian angel standing watch."

Vex snorted. "Yeah, one with a bent towards creating chaos." Now that she thought about it, she wondered if the trouble upstairs was connected to that chaos.

"Best kind to have," Charity said. When everyone's attention shifted to her, she shrugged. "If it wasn't for your chaos-loving angel, chances of our shipments being destroyed instead of delayed would be a lot higher. That starts happening, it leaves Simon in a world of hurt."

Even Vex couldn't argue Charity's point.

The Vultures' interest in Pebble Creek only came to fruition after Crane intercepted convoys carrying kids for purposes that made Vex's stomach churn with fury. Crane, Simon's predecessor, had been gutted by Raiders, a tribe of mercenaries who worked to clear the field for the right price. They took their job seriously. To the point they literally nailed Simon to a wall to clear a path to Pebble Creek and its trade routes. After Crane's death and Simon's near-death, the Vultures moved in to help Crane's heir apparent, Simon, solidify his hold on the Central Territories, an endeavor that required a delicate touch.

Since the Vultures considered both Crane and Simon friends, when the last of the blood hit the ground, they made it clear to the unknown puppet and his master that taking control of the trade routes would come at a lethal cost. To ensure their point was driven home, they cut the puppet's strings to his master permanently, but the one behind it all was still out there, pulling other strings.

"Said it before." Simon's voice was low and hard. "Have no intention of letting anyone get their hands on Pebble Creek or the routes."

"Know that, brother." Ruin held his gaze. "Doing our best to make sure you keep hold."

The two shared a silent exchange before Simon broke it. "Appreciate it, but I don't like you or yours—" he nodded to Charity, "—taking unnecessary risks for me."

That nabbed Vex's attention. Her "Unnecessary risks?" coincided with Charity's "Not your call, Simon."

"Whoa!" Ruin held his hands up in a T and tried to stop the impending argument. "Everyone take a breath." He curled his hand over Charity's knee and directed his words to Simon. "I get you're worried, Si, but we promised to have your back until this shit was done. We knew when we opened this can of worms, it would get messy. I appreciate your concern, but Charity's got the skills we need to get to the bottom of this."

Charity leaned over and nudged Ruin's shoulder but kept on topic. "And what we need is proof of whose hand is pulling the strings."

Vex figured it was self-explanatory, seeing how the accepted theory was that Michael, King of the Northwest Territory, wasn't happy with his piece of the west coast and wanted to get his greedy little hands on the entire western half of the U.S. She wasn't the only one following those lines, so was Reaper. Add in the fact that Vex was fairly sure Michael had a personal axe to grind with not just Reaper, but Lilith, as well. All of which left the Vultures firmly in the middle of the two power players.

"Michael's not stupid enough to leave anything to chance," Reaper said. "Including someone getting their hands on proof." Reaper's expression went dark as Charity barely covered a wince and Ruin's jaw went tight. "Do not tell me you fucking think he's not behind this."

Charity raised her hand in a lame attempt to soothe Reaper's formidable temper. "We think he is, but we don't know for sure." When Reaper's expression remained stormy, she continued in a rush, "As much as I hate to rain on your parade, all the mutterings making the rounds in New Seattle indicate it may not be Michael."

"Or not just Michael," Ruin corrected, attempting to redirect Reaper's attention.

It worked because Reaper turned his glare to Ruin.

"Talking with those who have cause to speculate in New Seattle," Ruin said. "It seems Michael may be dealing with some in-house discontent, part of which might explain our continued trouble with the routes."

Oh, for fuck's sake, didn't they have enough to deal with?

Vex's voice was a whip of contempt. "Don't tell me there's more than one dirty hand in the pot?"

Charity gave a small nod. "After Havoc and Mercy's run-in with Greer and listening to the stories swirling through New Seattle's underworld, that's exactly what we're thinking. Which makes getting proof harder than we expected."

Of course, it did, because fate had no intention of letting this be a straightforward power grab, that could be dealt with the judicious placement of a blade or bullet. Nope, fickle Lady Destiny piled the Vultures' plate high with various menu options, including dealing with the evil, demented right-hand of Michael known as Greer. In Salt Lake, the bitch hightailed it out of their reach and damn near blew both Havoc and Mercy, not to mention Math, into a million pieces, in the process.

Impatience edged Simon's voice as he shifted in his seat. "Not sure I give a damn if Michael's completely guilty or just tainted. Either way, I want his nose out of my business." He dropped his voice and added, "Even more, I want our leak terminated."

Simon wasn't the only one feeling the burn of frustration. His sudden promotion and Crane's death were the result of a betrayal within Pebble Creek. Whoever it was continued to pass on information that jeopardized the supply runs. With greedy eyes focused on Pebble Creek, a lost shipment could tear the supply routes out of Simon's hands and leave him scrambling for purchase.

Charity studied Simon with a calculation barely softened by understanding. "What if those soldiers are here looking to contact their informant?"

Sneaky, sneaky woman.

And Vex wasn't the only one to think so. At her implication to use the soldiers' presence to draw out their traitor, Reaper shot Charity a sharp look. Vex braced because Charity's suggestion would force Vex to inform Reaper of their unexpected guest and she wasn't inclined to do so publicly.

Reaper's attention shifted from Charity to Vex. "Havoc and Mercy at the Shrew?"

"I left them there, so I'm thinking so."

Reaper's intent was made clear. "Think you may want to head over and see what's holding them up."

She silently cursed his unspoken order to set Mercy and Havoc on the soldiers' asses because she knew the soldiers weren't there for the rat, and that meant this play had zero chances of success and a high chance of unearthing Math. It was best if she headed of this situation before it edged into dangerous territory.

Flashing what she hoped was her normal smart-assed grin, she pulled her big girl panties up and strove for casual. "Can do but need a minute before I head out."

"Right," Reaper muttered and pushed to his feet.

The others correctly read his move for the dismissal it was.

Vex stood, gave Simon a head tilt (because she didn't need any more tongues wagging about them), and then a small smile and finger wave to Charity and Ruin. As a funeral dirge took up her headspace and her mouth imitated the desert, she led Reaper upstairs.

five

It wasn't a shift in the air, or the rasp of a foot over the rug in the hall. Nor was it an indefinable instinct that something headed his way that snapped Math out of his doze. It was a combination of all of the above.

With a mind to stealth, he stilled the empty cuffs he managed to escape, so they wouldn't rattle against the metal bed frame. Then, keeping his movements as smooth as possible (an accomplishment when every inch ached), he dragged his ass out of Vex's bed. Once upright and out of the bed, he crossed the floor.

The indistinct murmur of voices from the hall gained strength and he made out the low male tone versus an irritatingly familiar female one.

Looked like Vex found Reaper.

Math stopped just shy of the door that connected the two rooms and gathered his composure for the impending confrontation. Even without Vex's earlier warning, he never doubted that was exactly what it would be—a confrontation. Utilizing the light from the bedroom, he shifted until he could see the short entryway and the door. A rattle signaled the latch's release before the door swung open and allowed the light from the hall a path into the apartment's dim interior.

"Please, God, tell me you don't have a body stashed in your room." The deep voice with rough edges belonged to Reaper and roused painful memories.

Vex stepped through, her body blocking the doorway, her head turned to the man on her heels. "Eww, no."

"You act like that's an impossibility, when you and I both know it's more like a certainty if someone pissed you off."

Vex turned at Reaper's dry comment, giving Math a view of her back, her shoulders and spine stiff. "Well, now that you mention it. I may have left a body or two back in town."

There was a pause, then, "Shit, Vex."

"Better there than here. Besides, getting the bloodstains out isn't the challenge, it's getting rid of the smell." On that note, she turned around, and if the small jerk of her head was anything to go by, caught sight of Math. She came to a halt, blocking Reaper's entry. Without looking away from Math, she addressed Reaper. "However, while I was in town, I picked something up for you." She cleared the short hall, stepped to the side with a studied casualness, and gave the man who crowded behind her a clear visual of what waited for him.

Despite the lack of illumination, Reaper had no issues recognizing Math. Reaper's spine snapped straight so fast it was a wonder it didn't audibly break. He loomed in the entryway and let the door swing closed behind him. The soft snick as it closed was overly loud, and the air in the room was so heavy with convoluted emotion it was nearly tangible.

"What the fuck are you doing here?" Reaper's voice dropped into a barely comprehensible growl.

Unwilling to stay in the confines of the narrow space, Math shifted into the front room, aware of Reaper's gaze tracking his every move. The weight of his unspoken assessment raised every hackle Math possessed and abraded against the simmering brew of frustrated fury, diminishing hope, and corroding guilt. It turned his voice harsh and tight as he leaned his hip against a nearby chair. "I was in the neighborhood."

Reaper's stony gaze swept Math from head to toe in a visual inventory before returning to eye level. "I see you didn't waste time making new friends."

The lash of Reaper's disdain triggered a flood of caustic comments that Math managed to lock behind tight lips. Instead of digging the verbal trench deeper, he resorted to a less vocal response with the simple flip of his middle finger.

The admittedly juvenile response had Reaper dragging a hand through his hair as he muttered something foul and pithy under his breath. He turned, paced a few steps, and came back, stopping short of Math's space. "Did you get lost?"

Unwilling to let the larger man play the intimidation card, Math held his position. "Nope, came looking for you." He took a certain amount of pleasure in watching a sliver of shock slide into those dark eyes before Reaper buried it with all the other shit, he kept behind his son of a bitch mask. Not that Math gave a damn, he wasn't here to make friends.

Reaper's upper lip curled, and he folded his arms over his chest. "You found me."

"Lucky fucking me." There was no missing the snide edge to Math's response.

Reaper's jaw locked, but he remained silent.

Math shoved the temptation to keep pushing Reaper's buttons into a dark hole and stayed on point. Not only wasn't he in any shape to take the other man on, it would be a waste of time Math didn't have. *Correction, time Cam didn't have.* "Since I know how much you hate owing others, I'm here to collect."

"Collect?" Reaper muttered before adding, "Are you shitting me?"

The sharp question begged Math to engage, but he

refrained as they stared each other down. The silence stretched and only broke when a low, frustrated growl that sounded suspiciously close to a curse escaped Reaper. Unwilling to retreat from Reaper's obvious temper, Math bit out, "You owe me, asshole."

Reaper rocked back on his heels and blinked. "For what?"

"Saving Havoc's ass."

Reaper snorted. "According to Havoc, the situation turned into a mutual saving of asses." He stepped back, walked over to the couch, and dropped to the cushions. With his legs sprawled out and his arms stretched over the back, he looked over his shoulder at Math. "After which you hauled one of those said asses after Greer."

Reaper's new position indicated a decision against instigating bodily harm and a bit of Math's tension eased. "That I did," Math admitted as edged around the chair that currently served as his leaning post and settled in it.

"If you found her, seems she handed it back to you," Vex offered unhelpfully from her perch on a chair arm. She swung one foot in a lazy glide as she watched them with undisguised curiosity.

Math shrugged. "It's complicated." When he caught Reaper's flash of amusement, he decided to stop dancing around the point. The sooner he got through this, the sooner he could move forward. "She took something of mine." Heat suffused the back of his neck and he rolled his shoulders in a futile attempt to halt its progress. "I made a try for it and failed."

Reaper drew his arms from the back of the couch and folded them over his stomach, his gaze on his boots. "How badly?"

"Don't know yet," Math admitted as the weight of his failure made a comeback.

"What do you know?"

At Vex's question irritation swam through Math's veins. She was good at pissing him off, almost as good as Reaper. "Greer knows she's being hunted, she just doesn't know who is playing hunter."

Reaper nailed Math with a dubious look. "How sure are you about that?"

"Damn sure."

Vex's foot stopped in mid-swing. "Hate to burst your bubble, but if I remember Mercy's version of your showdown in Salt Lake, Greer knows your name."

"My name isn't what's important," he muttered as the conversation slipped into uncomfortable territory.

"Okay," Vex drew the word out with exaggerated patience, "then what is?"

"Who I am."

Her gaze sharpened with speculation, but instead of voicing it, she made a rolling motion with her hand in a clear indication to expand on his abrupt answer.

He braced and dove into the murky conversational waters. "I'm sure Mercy's shared our connection."

Vex's foot started moving again, her eyebrows rose. "You mean the secret ninja assassin club?"

He curled his lip at her flippant response. "Also known as the Strix, yes." He didn't miss the subtle rise of tension in Reaper's pose. "About nine years back, Greer wiped out the entire group."

"On Michael's orders." Reaper's voice was harsh, a world of knowledge adding undeniable weight to his comment.

Math met his flat gaze and drummed his fingers on the chair's armrest. When it came to this old argument, he wasn't the only one suffering from stubborn-induced blindness. Still, the point bore repeating, even if Reaper didn't want to hear it. "Maybe, maybe not. In the end it was Greer leading the death squad and Greer's hand on the trigger."

"Greer doesn't sneeze without Michael's permission," Reaper shot back.

It didn't matter what Reaper believed, Math knew better. After years of questioning the what's and why's that led to that one brutal night of bloody betrayal, he saw a different pattern—one created by a single, manipulative hand. He knew who owed him. "The massacre of the Strix was all Greer. They were never a threat to Michael."

"You can't be sure."

Eyeing the obstinate set of Reaper's jaw, Math's fingers stilled as a familiar mix of resentment and anger stirred. *Some things never change.* "Yeah, I can." He didn't bother to disguise the ice in his voice.

Reaper's eyes narrowed and his laced fingers whitened. "How?"

There were things Math wouldn't share with Reaper. He'd given his word, but he'd pass along what he could. "Because they were about to cost Greer everything, including her position with Michael." That got Reaper's attention, but he didn't interrupt as Math kept going. "She was in deep with the Strix's Directorate, had been for a couple of years."

"A case of you scratch my back, I'll scratch yours?" After getting Math's nod, Reaper laid his head against the back of the couch and closed his eyes. "Got any clue what those deals included?"

"No, it was a need-to-know thing, and I was told I didn't need to know." The Directorate loved their secrets. Looking back now it was easy to call bullshit, but at the time, he trusted them to do what needed to be done. "What I can tell you is that right before she brought in her execution squad, some of the Directorate were looking at her, hard."

"So, she made sure no one was left to do any more looking." Vex's tone made it clear it wasn't a question. "Makes sense."

"Maybe," Reaper said, his doubt evident. He opened his eyes, dropped his feet to the floor, and came up into a sitting position, leaning his elbows on his knees. He leveled a steely gaze at Math. "Be better if we knew what the Strix had on her."

Disgusted with the other man's one-track mind, Math didn't tamp down his derision. "Why? Because you think it's a way to take down Michael?"

"Yeah, I do." Reaper's answer came with a narrowed-eye glare and a darkening flush of temper. "You can claim it was all Greer, but I'm not buying it." The tension that had been creeping out of the room swept back in and curled up in anticipation.

Math shook his head slowly and rubbed a hand over the back of his neck, trying to remember why he was here. "Dammit, Reaper, if you can't shrug off that fucking chip you carry when it comes to him, you'll be staked out in the desert somewhere providing a feast for the scavengers, leaving my ass blowing in the wind. Again."

"If you believe that, then why are you here?" Reaper's question whipped out and drew blood.

Math's grip on his temper slipped. "Because you fucking owe me, and not just for Havoc's ability to breathe."

Reaper got to his feet with a snarl and closed in. "I owe you?"

Frustration and anger dulled the protests of Math's battered body as he launched from his chair to go nose to nose with Reaper. "Yeah, you do."

His abrupt move didn't stop Reaper's mouth or his palms from slamming into Math's chest. "That's fucking rich, coming from you, baby brother."

Math ignored Vex's squeak as Reaper's revelation blew through the thin veil of shared history. Pain from Reaper's hit rocked Math's body, but frayed temper kept him on his feet. "What the hell did you expect?"

Something flashed in Reaper's dark eyes, too fast for Math to read, even if he wanted to. "The way I remember, your debt is far from paid, considering you took what was mine."

Unable to let his verbal attack pass unanswered, Math struck back. "Can't take what willingly walks away."

"You son of a bitch!" Reaper visibly fought the urge to make his point physically and pivoted on his heel to give Math his rigid back.

At the expected response, searing frustration curled through Math in a cold rush and left his voice harder than steel, his contempt clear. "That's right. When the truth hits home, turn away. It's what you do best, isn't it?"

Reaper spun back around, his fist on a direct path with Math's face. It never made contact. Math jerked his head back and whipped his arm up to block the hit. They connected with a dull smack of flesh and bone. For a breathless moment they stood there, caught on the edge of violence, their gazes locked. Math jerked Reaper's wrist back, the move causing a breath-stealing burn along his ribs. With a roar, Reaper spun with the wrist lock and the fight was on.

Although his previous injuries slowed him down, Math was no longer a scrawny teen unable to hold his own against his older brother. With years of fighting dirty under his belt, Math managed to give as good as he got. At first. Then the damage he sustained earlier caught up with him, slowing his reaction time and giving Reaper an edge.

Still, he couldn't stop. Not even when Reaper took him to the floor. Years of resentment and fury, love and betrayal breeched his emotional barriers, and proved irrevocably this wasn't about anything as simple as a disagreement.

six

Vex watched the two idiots roll around on the floor as they destroyed her living room. Since getting between them was beyond stupid, she kept clear of the tangle of battling male limbs. Although pinned, Math managed to nail Reaper with a knee perilously close to his prize package.

Note to self—Math's a dirty fighter.

Obviously familiar with Math's tactics, Reaper twisted to block a follow up and used his heavier build to send them crashing into the couch. Their combined weight shoved it back, knocking cushions askew and toppling a book-filled end table, sending her to-be-read pile to the floor. She winced and shouted, "Watch it!"

Unsurprised when they ignored her warning, she stood clear of the brawl with her hands on her hips and considered her options. Since replacing what little furniture she had would be a massive pain, she needed to separate the two morons and ensure her current furnishings survived. Too bad she liked Reaper enough not to want to inflict permanent damage to gain some peace. They rolled towards her and she skirted out of the way as she continued to the kitchen.

Pained impacts and muffled curses and insults accompanied her search of her cabinets. She sent up a silent thanks that Ruin and Charity weren't in their rooms. The last thing she wanted, or needed, was them getting involved in this mess. With Murphy's Law alive and well, she found what she wanted in the last cabinet. She grabbed the large bowl, shoved it under the faucet, and waited while it filled.

A loud crash had her craning her head over her shoulder to see Math's legs kick her bookshelf as Reaper pinned him in a bastardized version of a half nelson. When the bookcase wobbled and threatened to tumble her collection of bits and pieces picked up along her travels, she yelled, "Hey, watch the shelves!"

With a guttural growl, Math fought to break Reaper's hold and took the fight away from her bookcase. Math's pained grunt left Vex shaking her head at the mystery of testosterone driven egos. It wasn't like it was a fair fight. Not with Math's injuries. Yet the two were determined to pound each other into submission. It was like watching two bulls lock horns.

She turned back to the sink, shut off the faucet, and carefully carried the bowl in her living room. There was one bonus to having tiled floors, it made clean up easy. She timed her attack and when they rolled near, she tipped the bowl.

Water fell in a cold deluge and when it landed, the fight came to an abrupt stop as both men tried to get away. They didn't get far. Curses replaced snarls as they tried to untangle themselves and escape her unconventional interruption. She dodged flailing body parts, but didn't stop until the bowl was empty. She shook out the last few drops for good measure and considered nailing them with the bowl, but with only one bowl and two of them, she couldn't decide who deserved the first hit. Instead, she stood over them, glaring. "You two done?"

"What the hell, Vex?" Reaper lay on his back and wiped his eyes clear, one of which was edged in angry red. No doubt he'd be sporting a beauty of a shiner tomorrow.

He shoved Math's leg from his and rolled to his hands and knees, shaking his head like a dog settling wet fur. Somewhere in the fight, he lost his hair tie and his inky hair now fell around his shoulders in a damp mess. He shifted into a sitting position and pulled at his t-shirt, trying to find a dry patch to wipe his face.

Next to him, Math wasn't much better off. Since he had the misfortune of being on the bottom, he took the brunt of Vex's impromptu shower, as evidenced by the borrowed t-shirt clinging with sodden resolve to his chest. He lifted his head enough to look down as he plucked at the material. Pain and exhaustion painted his face in a myriad of white lines. "Dammit, Reaper, I think you broke one of my ribs."

His complaint earned a nasty grin from Reaper. "You're lucky it wasn't your skull."

With a muffled groan, Math carefully rolled to his side and reached for the overturned couch behind him. "You're a stubborn bastard." The last of his comment disappeared into a muffled groan as he lumbered to his feet, one arm wrapped around his ribs.

Reaper thumbed blood from his split lip. "Pot. Kettle."

Vex eyed Math's weaving form with a smidgeon of concern and decided to wade in. "Okay, boys, enough with the love fest. As fun as it is to trip down memory lane—" and considering the family connection bomb, never had her curiosity wanted to continue the journey more, "—now that you two got that out of your systems, we need to get back on track."

Math took a decided tilt to the left and Vex quickly moved to play support post, curling her arm around his waist. He draped the arm not occupied with keeping his ribs in place over her shoulders, plastering damp cotton and male heat along her side. The sensation seeped through her pores and caused a tiny—a very tiny—shiver, that almost had her dropping the bowl clutched in her other hand. "Reaper, my books." She twitched her head to the side, to indicate the books scattered just outside the spreading puddle of water.

Reaper heaved a put-upon sigh and shoved up from the floor. "Reaper, my books, please," he taunted.

Oh, for f—fragile male egos will be the death of me! "Seriously?"

Reaper shot her a look as he took her books to safety, righted the end table, and dumped the books on top.

Vex guided Math to the chair untouched by the fight, and then settled his frame onto it. Math's thanks came out on a pain-filled hiss.

Now that the brothers had called a temporary truce, Vex turned and headed to the kitchen to dump the bowl. Brothers —a phrase she never thought to associate with Reaper. He'd given the impression of being hatched fully formed and free of emotional entanglements. Which made her wonder, what else lurked in Reaper's past?

The man in question dragged her back to the present, his bad-tempered query indicating her hope of a truce might be a bit premature. "What the hell do you want from me, Math?"

Behind her the tension regained near suffocating levels, and annoyed with both of them, she tossed the bowl on the counter. The clatter of impact echoed through the apartment and she turned to find both men watching her.

Normally having the attention of two men (who, she could safely and silently admit, personified wicked temptation if one was so inclined to dare it) would be a source of amusement, but she had a shitty week, and she was tired. *Really fucking tired, actually.* "I'm not spending all night watching the two of you circle each other like two dogs in a pissing contest. If you want to finish what you started, take it the fuck outside and leave me out of it."

In typical male style, the two idiots looked from her to each other and exchanged grins. For a moment, the resemblance between them was startling, but she shoved it aside to contemplate later, when they weren't snarling in front of her. Tempting as it was to kick them out, she refrained. She grabbed a couple of hand towels and left the kitchen. She threw one to Reaper and found a dry spot on the floor where she could keep an eye on them both. After drying a spot, she sat on the floor, put her back against the couch, and waited.

Math ignored Vex and told Reaper, "Don't want anything from you. I need help, from Fate's Vultures."

A muscle in Reaper's jaw jumped as he swiped at the water on the floor, but he gritted out, "Fine. What do you want from the Vultures?"

Math took his minor victory without gloating. "Greer's holding one of my men at the Hole. I want him back."

Finished with the floor, Reaper sat, his face unreadable. "One of your men? You mean a Strix?"

Math nodded.

"Uh." Reaper rubbed his jaw, calculation burning in his dark eyes. "Going to be hard to find one man in that pit."

Vex refrained from rolling her eyes. *Reaper, the reigning king of understatements.*

The Hole sat in the middle of what used to be the urban center of Boise. Once the towering building would have been a proud nod to man's materialistic accomplishments. Now it served as a home to rats, of both two and four-legged varieties, who scampered through the hidden depths doing business no one spoke of above a whisper.

The place was filled with plenty of hidey-holes and locating one person would be a treasure hunt of epic proportions. Hell, the last time the Vultures cruised through, Vex had to drop at least two determined, yet questionable, bounty hunters on her way to pick up dinner. She left their bodies where they fell because it was faster and safer than sticking around to bury them. Not to mention it also carried the extra benefit of sending an unmistakable message.

Reaper wasn't ready to jump on Math's bandwagon of certainty. "You sure that's where your man—"

"Cam," Math supplied, giving the faceless a name and making it personal.

With a dip of his head, Reaper corrected, "Cam is being held? Seems Greer would have other, better options closer to home."

No doubt she did, but... "It makes sense," Vex cut in, thinking out loud. "Think about it. If she's playing without Michael's permission, it's perfect. The Hole straddles Michael and Simon's territories and is ignored by both for the most part. Hell, even we pay it no mind unless we're forced to." She met Reaper's gaze. "God knows our attention is centered on the routes right now."

When Reaper dipped his chin in agreement, she continued. "Besides, it offers her plenty of privacy to operate under Michael's nose while giving her space to maneuver and maintain deniability. As long as she keeps some distance, it's the ideal solution."

Reaper turned to Math. "Not sure I buy your theory of Greer going solo, but getting Cam out? Yeah, I get that."

She recognized Reaper's backward acceptance and wondered if Math understood. When Math's shoulders lowered she knew the brotherly connection, no matter how tattered, still worked. Despite Reaper's silently implied agreement, Math wisely kept his mouth shut, even when Reaper's gaze sharpened and a smug grin broke out.

Uh-oh, that didn't bode well. She braced.

"Vultures don't do charity gigs. You want our help, you're going to pay to keep the scales balanced." Then he added, "Nothing personal."

Math's answering smile was all teeth. "Yeah, nothing personal." His grin faded, replaced by pitiless calculation. "What do you want?"

Experienced with how Reaper's ruthlessness worked when it came to getting what he wanted, Vex saw the writing on the wall. Especially when it came to utilizing Math's unexpected presence. She silently cursed and wasn't surprised by Reaper's answer.

"You."

"Dammit, Reaper!" Despite Vex's best intentions, the exclamation escaped. Adding Math to the equation was an unwanted complication. "First you want to throw Havoc and Mercy at our visitors, now you want to sacrifice Math?"

Reaper pinned her in place with a familiar look, the one that told her to keep her mouth shut. She folded her arms over her chest and glared back as she pictured slugging the shit out of him. It didn't help.

"You want me to be mole bait for your uninvited guests?" Instead of being offended, Math sounded remarkably calm, almost as if he knew this would be Reaper's play. Correctly reading Reaper's raised brow, he added, "Mercy mentioned you had a situation, when she was trying to convince me to make nice with the Vultures."

"Does everyone know about the mole?' Vex muttered, her temper simmering. "What the hell else did she share?"

Her testy comment got Math's attention. "Just to point out, Mercy worked for me when she shared that tidbit. It's not like I'm known for sharing information."

Yeah, yeah, yeah, whatever. It didn't negate Vex's point. "Check the ego, spy boy, I'm just saying."

Math shot her a frown and then turned back to an amused Reaper. "You've got a plan?"

"Maybe," Reaper said. "Simon's got a shipment coming in, one he can't afford to lose. I want to keep the mole busy chasing his tail so he can't snitch the delivery info. We leak your presence, keep it vague and suggestive, it keeps our unknown rat busy nibbling at your crumbs and blind to the delivery."

Math shifted, his wince there and gone. "And if my presence trips your city visitors up so they fall into your hands for a little information trading, all the better?"

"A definite bonus in my book." Pleased with himself, Reaper rose from the floor, took a moment to stretch and grimaced as his still damp t-shirt stuck to his skin. "Be nice to know if they're here for you or our mole."

Good to know the brothers seemed to share an innate sneakiness. Didn't mean their half-assed plan didn't have holes deep enough to disappear into. "Hold your horses there, boss." Vex scrambled to her feet and faced Reaper. "Those soldier boys go dark, and we may end up with more attention than we want." Say, like when good ol' Michael caught wind the Vultures took out a couple of his men, he'd want payback. If they belonged to Greer? Well, then life would get real interesting. There was no anticipating Greer's reaction. She proved that when she risked blowing her own ass to kingdom come in her attempt to take out Math, Havoc and Mercy. Woman was downright crazy, and everyone knew there was no predicting crazy.

Reaper shot her a raised eyebrow. "Not everything ends six feet under."

"Really? Because when it comes to informants and spies, that's not my experience."

"We'll keep it contained."

Well, that was nicely vague. She let out a disbelieving snort.

He pinned her with a hard look. "I wasn't planning on dragging Math through the streets and shoving him under their nose." He leaned a hip against the couch. "Figured we'd lure them in. Drop a whisper here, drop another there. Say he's hunting a bounty and is willing to split the fee with us. We have Math make an appearance downstairs at breakfast, let the gossips take it from there. Our visitors catch wind and come sniffing. We let them trail Math when he goes after his man, which gets them far enough from Pebble Creek to take them down quietly with no one the wiser."

As much as she didn't want to admit it, it wasn't a bad plan, because the most frustrating part of this mess was trying to figure out which smiling face was lying through their pearly whites. The Vultures agreed that whoever was behind the leak had to be someone close to Simon and knew the inner workings of Pebble Creek, so if a bounty hunter popped up and started asking questions, their mole would be all kinds of curious. There was a slim chance this hare-brained planned would work, but slim was better than none.

From behind her, Math asked, "Don't exactly have to time to waste."

"How's it a waste?" Reaper asked. "You're passing through, tracking your missing man, no one needs to know it's a rescue mission." He shot Math an arch look. "I'm sure you've got a cover to work with."

Math frowned but didn't argue.

"Anyone asks," Reaper continued. "You tell them you're touching base with Mercy, seeing if she heard anything useful. Being the helpful sort, I'm going to offer a few of my connections and Vex's tracking services." A derisive smirk curled his lips. "For a fee, of course."

Math sighed. "Of course."

"Hold up." Vex wasn't finding this at all amusing. "My services? Why me?"

"Because," Reaper said. "You're the one he's spending the night with."

Her spine snapped straight at his implication. "Excuse me?"

Reaper met her glare with a steely resolve. "The split between you and Simon. We're going to use that."

Vex's hands went to her hips, and she narrowed her gaze. "There's nothing to use."

"Isn't there?" he shot back. When she remained stubbornly silent, his lips curved in a hard smile. "You two have been dancing around each other for months while you tried to decide whether or not to let him in. When you got back from Page and started pulling disappearing acts every time he came into the room, your decision was clear. So, when Math waltzes out of your room tomorrow, any lingering questions will be put to bed. Pun intended."

Temper overrode logic and she ground her teeth in mortified fury. "Goddammit, Reaper, my personal life is no—"

"You're a Vulture, Vex, and in this instance, you don't get the luxury of a personal life." His harsh response acted like a face full of ice water.

She swallowed back her snarl and embarrassment knowing Reaper was right and turned away. Silence reigned as she fought and won to hold her tongue. She was a Vulture, and unmasking the mole was more important than the mess masquerading as her personal life. It wasn't as if Simon would care. In fact, he'd probably be relieved. She shoved the bitter thought aside and kicked it into a deep, dark hole. She turned back around and gave Reaper a reluctant nod.

He dipped his chin in approval. "We've got too many balls in the air right now. We need every advantage we can get." He shot a look at Math, who watched them both from under lowered lids. "Got anything to add?"

"Yeah, I need some clothes."

"I'll have some delivered in the morning. Name wise, what are using?"

"Crow."

"Really stretching there, aren't you," Vex muttered and met Math's steel blue gaze filled with faint amusement. She huffed a breath and leaned against wall separating her kitchen from the living room. Uncomfortable with the rapidly changing parameters of this whole farce, she scrambled to regain control. "I'm guessing we want to bury the family connection between you two as well?"

Any lingering amusement in Reaper's face disappeared.

She took his mutinous silence for what it was and shook her head. "Yeah, that's what I thought."

"Have something you want to say?" Reaper's question was laced with ice.

"Got lots, but I'll wait." She just wanted shit settled so she could get a moment to herself to think.

At her answer, he gave her a puzzled frown and slow blink.

Tired and irritated, she didn't have the mental capacity to deal with his reaction. "We put you two in the same room, only a blind man could miss the family resemblance."

"Take it you have an idea on how to change that," Reaper drawled.

"Yeah, a few." Because there were minor changes that could blur the physical similarities enough to throw off the nosey parkers, and the less tangible ones could be easily explained away by their respective positions.

Math dragged a hand through his tangle of black. "I'm not dying my hair."

She moved to the couch and settled a hip on the armrest, folded her arms, and studied him. "You don't need to change the color." Besides considering how dark it was, it was pointless to try. "But we're going to have to cut it back and ditch the beard." Hopefully it would be enough to fuzz the lines of shared blood.

A muscle worked in Math's jaw. "How short?"

She wasn't feeling nice when she smiled. "Short, short."

Thunderclouds gathered in his eyes. "No buzz cut."

She gave him a faux pout and teased, "How about clean and smooth?"

"Not a buzz cut and not bald," he repeated with a nasty look.

"What's wrong, Rapunzel? Afraid to lose your pretty locks?"

He frowned. "Who the hell is Rapunzel?"

"Seriously?" It was her turn to frown. "'Rapunzel, Rapunzel, let down your long hair?'" When he continued to give her a blank look, she sighed. "Haven't you read any fairy tales?"

"Why would I?"

Before she could educate him on the importance of the written word, Reaper cut in and reclaimed their attention. "Enough." He got up and walked over until he stood between them, his gaze on Math. "She's got a point. Best to keep our relationship quiet for now. You let Vex do your makeover."

There was a flash of resentment and something close to pain in Math's eyes before it was smothered. "Are you kidding me?"

Unmoved, Reaper held his brother's gaze for a long, silent moment as layers of unspoken words flowed between the two.

Math finally snapped, "Fine."

Reaper turned away and started for the door. "Vex."

Heeding the unspoken demand, Vex followed him out her front door and into the hall.

Reaper waited until she pulled the door closed before asking, "You up for this?"

His question caught her off guard as moments before he

had all but ordered her to play the role of Math's lover and her response was bitterly honest. "Don't have much choice."

Reaper took a couple steps away, wrapped a hand around the back of his neck, then turned to face her. "If this is going to mess you up, tell me now."

She set her shoulder to the wall, folded her arms, and studied him. "Mess me up?"

"Yeah." He grimaced and a flush of color rode under his cheekbones. "It's getting complicated—you, Simon, and now Math—"

No shit.

She couldn't stop her short, harsh laugh. "That's one word for it." She looked away and grimaced. "Me showing up with Math will give Simon permission to keep doing what he wants without guilt."

"You sure?"

"Yeah, I'm sure." The words hurt coming out. She sucked in a breath, looked up, and made a wry face. "Seems he wants something easy."

Reaper's face darkened. "What?"

Realizing how her comment sounded, she was quick to amend, "Not like that, sheesh Reaper, Simon's not that much of a dick." She forced a cocky smile. "Guess I'm just a bit more work than your average female."

Some unknown emotion softened Reaper's dark gaze as it drifted over her face. "The best things always are."

She managed a jerky shrug at his unexpected reply and wished the pressure behind her eyes would take a hike. "You might be the only one who believes that."

Reaper got close and brushed a startlingly gentle thumb over her cheek. "Don't think I am, babe."

She leaned into his comforting touch for a second, then sucked in a shaky breath and straightened, inching back from his careful concern and the brittle emotional edge she teetered on. "I have a living room to clean up and a man to put to bed if I want any sleep tonight." She gave Reaper her back and put her hand on the knob. "You might want to ice that bruise."

"Right," he rumbled.

She slipped inside her apartment and shut the door.

seven

As the door clicked shut behind Vex and Reaper, Math was crossing the room. He had no intentions on being kept in the dark, especially when it came to his brother's machinations. Years of skulking in the shadows had him moving to the door from the side so he didn't cause a shift in the shadows under the door ledge. The narrow space made it a challenge, but he put his ear close to the door, and Reaper's deeper rumble slowly morphed into, "...you, Simon and now Math—"

Despite the barrier of the door, he caught the bitter edge of hurt in Vex's laugh before she answered, "Seems he wants something easy."

Her comment had Math revising his opinion of Simon's intelligence. *Who the hell wanted easy?* You could pay for that kind of female. Women like Vex, the ones who presented a challenge, not just sexually, but emotionally and intellectually, those were the most intriguing and dangerous types to tangle with.

Once he would've been all about tackling that challenge, but now? With Cam's ass on the line and Greer breathing down his neck, he couldn't afford the distraction. No matter how much the added bonus of tweaking Reaper's shit heightened his lustful curiosity.

The doorknob twisted and he silently cursed his wandering mind. He made it back to his chair in a quiet rush, dropped into his former sprawled position, and closed his eyes just as the door opened.

He forced his spiking pulse to level with a slow exhale as the door closed. Mental and physical exhaustion overwhelmed him as Vex's footsteps came closer, and he considered sleeping right here. Unfortunately, when the tendril of citrus and spice curled around him, he figured Vex had other plans.

Sure enough, a warm palm cradled his face, the sensation sinking through hardened layers like sunlight. "Wakey, wakey, sleeping beauty."

Instead of jerking away, he turned deeper into her touch. "I'm awake." The claim came out jumbled.

"Uh-huh, sure you are."

The warmth of her hand disappeared and left behind a wisp of loss. Then it was back, this time wrapping around his wrist, and tugging him back from the bliss of sleep.

He blinked his eyes open, carefully sat up with a low groan, and let her help him into her bedroom. "I can take the couch."

"You can barely move now," she murmured. "A night on my couch and you won't be able to move at all."

He didn't bother to argue, not with his body aching and his head pounding. Instead, he sat on the bed's edge and went to lie down.

She stopped him. "Not yet, we need to wrap your ribs." She disappeared into the bathroom and came back with the first-aid kit that she set on the nightstand. "Alright, ready?"

He nodded and together they removed his nearly dry t-shirt. She grabbed a roll of medical strength tape, stepped between his knees, and bent forward over his bare torso.

Her hair brushed against his chest, the soft strands causing a different kind of ache. "Here, hold this end for me."

Following her directions, he anchored the tape as she wrapped his ribs with a practiced efficiency. Staring at her bent head, the temptation to bury his hand in the unusual tangle of golds, bronze, and ebony had his hand fisting. He closed his eyes and fought the urge to touch.

Locked in the darkness behind his eyelids, her delicate, intricate scent joined the heat of her touch and burrowed through the cracks of his control. His body ignited with a near electric flash. Curses filled his head, almost pushing aside the dull throbbing headache. He caught her hand, trapping it against his chest and stopping her movements. His eyes opened and clashed with hers. His voice came out rough. "I've got this."

She pulled back, not much, just enough to look at him.

He studied her face in return, noting the pale undertones and the darkening bruise along her cheek. The split on her lip was puffy but closed, but her eyes remained razor sharp. He braced for her snide comment but got a quiet, "Fine" instead.

When she tugged her hand, he slowly let her go. She used his thigh and pushed to her feet, a wince there and gone as she adjusted her weight. She dragged her now free hand through her hair, turned away, and disappeared into the bathroom without a word.

He finished wrapping his ribs. A metallic squeak announced the opening of a medicine cabinet. A rattle of bottles on shelves soon followed. He was tying off the wrap when she reappeared and dropped a couple of pills next to the glass of water on the nightstand.

She caught his gaze and ordered, "Take 'em."

He tucked the end of the tape under and downed the pills.

She went to the makeshift closet as he carefully inched his way down to his back. His ribs protested and his breath escaped through clenched teeth on a long hiss. When he was finally prone, he sucked in a couple of shallow breaths and laid his arm over his eyes to block the glow of the lamp.

"Do me a favor."

He raised his arm enough to see her standing at the foot of the bed, with what he thought was another t-shirt, wadded in her hands. "Does it involve moving? Because if so, the answer's no."

Even with the shadows playing over her face, he caught the twitch of her lips. "Don't die in my bed tonight."

He let his arm fall back into place. "Wasn't planning on it."

"Good."

The air shifted as she came up on his side. He thought he felt something touch his hair, but before he could check there was a soft snick and then the press of the lamp's light disappeared, leaving him in soothing darkness.

"Sleep tight, Rapunzel."

He drifted, listening to the faint sounds of her settling in for the night. The painkillers kicked in as his aching body slowly downgraded to an annoying dull throb. It was enough to have exhaustion send his mind careening in slow, disjointed circles until he dropped into blessed unawareness.

MATH WOKE when he made the mistake of turning to his side. Lesson learned, he shifted to his back and waited for the wave of discomfort to recede. When it withdrew enough to dare another attempt, he slowly sat up. His mouth was dry, so he nabbed the glass of water and drained it. Being upright made it easier to breathe so he managed, with some careful maneuvering, to stuff the pillow behind his back and against the headboard to create a backrest.

He looked to the window, hoping to gauge the time, and found only a shimmer of moonlight squeezing through a narrow opening in the heavy material that obscured the glass. The fading darkness hinted dawn wasn't far away, which meant he managed a few solid hours. He shifted his leg, only to have the muscles seize in protest. To stave off the cramp, he reached down and dug his fingers in deep easing the stiffness.

Now that he was awake, his mind started churning. The earliest he could head out to Boise would be after breakfast. Reaper's deal included tapping his connections which translated into extra eyes and ears on Math's hunt. Chances were high those extras would belong to the Dogs of War, one of the roving bands that trotted through the lawless landscape and was led by an appropriately named bastard known as Dog.

Not a bad choice considering their reputation rivaled that of Fate's Vultures as one of the top in the pile of mercenary trackers. Word was that once given a scent, Dog and his pack of barely sane mutts ran it to the ground. However, to instigate a hunt, you needed to offer the right bone and Math had no doubt Reaper knew exactly which bone to offer.

Thing was, having Dog at his back may not be the wisest move. Mercenary didn't equal back up. When shit hit the fan —and it would—nothing could guarantee Dog and his boys would choose to save Math's skin over theirs.

Cynical though it was Math couldn't forget how deep and how long Greer's poisonous reach. He rubbed a hand over the back of his neck and blew out a long breath. He needed to keep it together because the line between paranoia and skepticism was razor thin.

He shifted to his next hurdle, Vex. Working with her on a purely business level wouldn't be hard. He had first-hand knowledge of how lethal she could be, but he had hoped to get a bit more in the way of back up than one hardheaded woman who threatened to disrupt his entrenched personal boundaries in a very dangerous way.

She bothered him on a level no one touched in a hell of a long time. Actually "bothered" didn't come close to the uncomfortable need she ignited in his body, one he had no idea how to snuff out. Correction, he had ideas, they just weren't all that bright.

How long had it been since he got laid?

He scrubbed a hand over his face and tried to remember. Memory flickered, then sputtered out. Obviously it had been too damn long. He briefly considered searching out an available female that wasn't Vex, but something told him that would not end well. For now, he'd suck it up and keep an iron hold on his libido. He owed Cam at least that much.

Maybe he could convince Havoc and Mercy to join in? God knows having them around might offset Vex's presence. It wouldn't be hard to get Mercy to agree, not only was she a Strix, but she knew Cam and would be all about getting him back. The problem was Havoc. His loyalty was to Reaper, which meant if Reaper said no, there'd be no Havoc, and if Havoc didn't sign on, chances were damn good Mercy would stay behind with her man.

Relationships complicated everything, especially the sticky-ass line of love versus loyalty.

Math grimaced because he knew he wouldn't ask Mercy to choose, especially since last time he'd done so, she followed her heart. Besides, it seemed every time that line got drawn, Math ended up on the short end of the stick. Vex's stark expression when Reaper went after her about Simon hit Math and made him wonder if he wasn't alone in that opinion.

And why the hell did that matter?

It didn't. It couldn't. His priority was to get Cam back,

and to do that he had to pay his dues to Reaper. Not speculate on the illogical battle between love and loyalty or how hard his body got whenever Vex was around.

Since sleep wasn't in the cards, he decided to brave a shower. Sweat, dust, and other less pleasant things coated his skin in a grimy film. He eyed the partially opened door and struggled to his feet, listening for any sounds from the woman in the other room. When the quiet held thick and steady, he shuffled over to the rickety closet to rifle through the drawers. He hoped Reaper would come through with new clothes because depending on Vex's charity left him with limited options.

He unearthed a well-worn pair of sweats when the first sound drifted from the front room. He stilled, ears straining. The barely there whimper would have gone unnoticed if he hadn't been near the door. As it was, he waited for a repeat, and when it stayed quiet, shook his head, and turned towards the bathroom. He had only gone a few steps when the sound came again.

Even knowing it was none of his business, he couldn't help but turn back and open the door fully. He stood in the doorway and barely made out the murky outline of Vex, sitting on the couch, her feet to the floor, and her head bent, visibly shuddering. Seeing her like that got to him and before he could think twice, he called carefully, "Vex."

Her head jerked up, but she didn't turn his way. "Go away."

A cautionary voice urged him to heed her edgy order, but he had his share of similar nights and understood going at it alone wasn't always the answer. "Nope."

His refusal got her attention, and she turned her head towards him.

He leaned his weight against the doorjamb and flashed her an arrogant grin because any other approach wouldn't be welcomed. "Figured since you're up and I'm jonesing for a shower, we might as well get this hair thing over with. Two birds, one stone."

Her huff of amusement held a sharp edge. "Sure you trust me near you with a blade?"

"You going to hurt me?"

She rose and stretched, the movement pulling the oversized t-shirt up her bare thighs and revealing her long legs. "Not unless you make me."

He slapped back a wicked impulse to a lot more than that and somehow managed to keep his voice casual as he shot back, "Then no problem." Deciding he'd danced close enough to the fire for now, he turned away and headed for the bathroom. He didn't take an easy breath until her footsteps sounded behind him.

Once inside the narrow confines of the bathroom, he tossed the sweats over the shower rod, and sat on the only available seat, the toilet's lid.

Vex came in and crouched in front of the sink, rummaging in the cabinet. "How's the ribs?"

"I'll live."

She turned, armed with scissors and a towel. "Put this around your shoulders." She tossed him the latter, rose, and went back to dig in the medicine cabinet.

He caught the towel, wincing when it pulled against his bound ribs. "Why bother?" He went to set the towel aside. "I'm taking a shower after."

Comb in hand, she turned back to him. "If you don't use it, you'll be itching like you've rolled around in poison ivy."

"Think I can handle it."

She shrugged and settled back against the sink. "Your choice, but no don't blame me if you move at the wrong time to itch and—" she widened her eyes comically and covered her mouth with the hand holding the comb, "—oops."

He snorted and carefully shook out the towel.

A hint of laughter lingered in her murmured, "Good choice."

He held the towel around his shoulders and waited as she stepped in front of him. When she tapped his knee with the comb, he obliged and widened his legs, giving her room.

She handed him the scissors. "Hold this." She waited until he took them before running the comb through his hair, curiously gentle as she worked out the tangles.

He closed his eyes and enjoyed the sensation.

All too soon, she said, "Okay, ready?"

His lifted his lashes only to find his visual field filled with unrestrained curves. The thin t-shirt she wore didn't do much to hide her generous tits or the betraying fact her nipples were erect. His hand on the towel tightened as a heavy breath escaped. He gritted his teeth as those alluring points stiffened. His mouth watered and the urge to reach out rode him hard.

No touching, idiot!

He clenched the towel in one hand and gripped the metal scissors tight in the other that rested on his thigh. *Oh hell, this was a bad idea. A really bad idea.*

"Math?"

He jerked his gaze up to find her holding out a hand.

Awareness colored her face and darkened those unusual amber eyes, but her voice was steady when she repeated, "Scissors?"

Shit! Right. Focus, man.

He handed them over, then as Vex got to work, closed his eyes in a desperate attempt to ignore what was in front of him. The snipping of the scissors filled the quiet, pausing now and then as she drew the comb through, followed by her fingers. A few times she adjusted her stance and soft heat would press against him, leaving him choking back hungry groans.

Finally, just before his body threatened to hit a breaking point, she stepped back, her voice husky. "There, done."

He wadded up the towel, dumped it on the floor, and rose on unsteady legs. He used the movement to covertly adjust himself, releasing some of the pressure on his aching dick. When he caught sight of the pile of dark hair that littered the floor, he couldn't stop his free hand from going to his shorn skull in a quick check. Hair met his touch, but it still took courage to look into the mirror. He blinked.

"You still need to get rid of the beard, then you'll be set." She stood behind him, her head coming up just behind his shoulder as she studied his hair with a critical eye. "I think it came out damn good."

"Not bad." He ran his hand through strands shorter than he was used to, but still long enough not to leave him resembling a shorn sheep. Even with this simple change, he could see the difference. The shorter cut made his face looked leaner. He tugged on his beard, then using the mirror, looked at her. "You got a razor I can use on this?"

She handed the scissors over his shoulder and when he took them, she dropped her hands to his waist. The feel of her palms against his skin sent a line of goosebumps over his spine. He submitted to her nudge to get out of the way and stepped to the side.

She shifted to his front, crouched, and once again dug through the cabinet. Her position triggered a wildfire of lust through his veins, but before it could burn his control to ash she muttered, "There you are, you little bastard." She rose and held out an old electric razor. "You can use this. Not sure how long it will last, but it may get through most of it."

He took it.

"Once you get through the main layer, I've got a straight razor in the cabinet. Help yourself." She went to leave, only to nail her knee on the still open cabinet door. She cursed and stumbled into his chest.

He curled his arm around her waist to hold her steady even as his sore ribs protested. With an armful of warm flesh and alluring curves, his body buckled under the rising tide of desire. His held her close and buried his face in the wild mess of her hair to muffle his groan, that was equal parts need and pain.

Her hands went to his wrists and held on as his hips ground against her ass. She shuddered and pressed back, her head falling back to his shoulder.

The air surrounding them grew thick with anticipation and fuzzed his brain. It was the only explanation for what happened next. He pressed his lips to the silky skin where her neck met shoulder, ran his tongue along the tendon, and took her taste deep.

The grip on his wrist tightened as she squirmed against him. "Math." His name was shaky even as she angled her head, granting him better access.

Not about to miss an opportunity he took it, running a series of open-mouthed kisses along her neck. He pressed a soft kiss behind her ear, and she arched back. The movement scraped across his ribs and a mind-clearing shaft of pain had him lifting his head on a hissed breath through gritted teeth.

Vex stilled and before he could say anything, she broke his hold and disappeared through the bathroom door, leaving him aching and cursing.

eight

What the hell are you thinking?

Vex all but ran from the bathroom and headed for the safety of the kitchen. Short of leaving, it was the farthest she could go to escape the temptation behind her. She braced her hands on the counter and stared unseeingly at her most precious possession, her refurbished coffee maker.

She needed to get tangled up in Math like she needed a hole in her head. The merciless reminder couldn't cool the lingering lust ignited by his simple touch. As tempted as she was to go back and finish what he started, she didn't dare. Just because he could make her body sit up and beg didn't mean shit.

Completely off-kilter and in need of something to keep her shaking hands busy, she shoved the empty carafe into place, dumped ground coffee into the basket filter, and hit the button. The local tinker had magic hands and managed to salvage her battered caffeine dispenser until it was almost as good as new, and now it worked diligently to dispense her necessary caffeine hit. The sound of the shower being turned on sapped some of her tension.

Now that she wouldn't be heard, she released a groan, turned, and slid down the cabinet until her ass met cool tile. With her feet flat against the floor, she braced her elbows on her knees, and dropped her head into her hands. Her fingers clutched at her hair and tugged, the tiny bites chasing away the last hazy remnants of lust.

All right, it was just a momentary lapse, nothing to worry about. Put any male and female in tight quarters and sparks would fly, right? Right. She thumped her head back against the cabinet and muttered, "Lame, Vex, really fucking lame."

Okay fine, so she wouldn't mind spending a few sweaty hours tumbling Math, it didn't mean she had to act on it. Hell, in a few hours they'd be riding out with problems on their ass as they went to rescue someone who might not even be breathing. Sex should be the last thing on her mind. Hell, it shouldn't even be on her radar. Hadn't she just bitched and moaned about Simon being a dick and sworn off men altogether? Add in the tiny fact that Math was Reaper's *fucking brother*, and that was more than enough to cool her rabid hormones.

Besides, for all the grief she gave Reaper, he owned her loyalty and respect, and hooking up with his baby brother? She shuddered.

Years ago, after their old man never returned from a hunting trip, she and Ruin ended up in the urban jungle of Portland's streets, running with a gang and living on the edge of feral. It worked for them until the leader of their little band of cutthroats decided Vex and Marnie, the only two females in the group, were better used as bait for older, more vicious predators. Brutal wisps of memories crowded close and she shut them down with hard-earned practice.

Vex kept her twin in the dark until things hit a critical point, and only after it tipped into spilt blood, had she clued him in because for Ruin, it didn't matter if older was a matter of minutes, he took his position as the eldest seriously. A truth the head cutthroat learned quick, which meant the sneaky bastard hadn't wasted any time exploring his options on eliminating his newly earned problems and sent the twins after the bikes of two known mercenaries.

Even now, years later, Vex could recall the quick rush of adrenaline and arrogance as she and Ruin pit their quick minds and quicker fingers against the challenge that was Reaper and Havoc. Luckily for the twins, Reaper and Havoc gave them another choice—go down with the gang or make amends. With a mind to saving their asses, the twins chose to make amends. And not a day went by that Vex didn't count her blessings.

So yeah, repaying Reaper by exchanging what equaled a genital handshake with his estranged brother was asking for trouble. Contrary to popular belief, Vex wasn't keen on deliberately pissing Reaper off. Pushing him towards the edge? Sure, but not straight over it. No woman in her right mind would tempt that kind of hell.

The image of a half-naked Math woke an evil little voice. *"Might be worth it."*

The shower shut off, yanking her out of her chaotic thoughts and up to her feet. Since the coffee was done, she made up her cup, took her first sip, and wandered back to the couch. She was halfway to her destination when knuckles hit her front door. She paused and glared at the door.

Who the hell thought dawn meant visiting hours?

Not inclined to find out and certain they would leave if she ignored them, she turned away, aimed her ass to her couch, settled in, and took another sip of her coffee, closing her eyes as the caffeine hit her system.

The knock sounded again.

What the hell?

She stared at the door. Reaper said his piece last night, so he was out. It was too early to be Havoc, and Mercy wouldn't let a lock or tact keep her out. And after days on the road, she doubted if Ruin or Charity were even up.

The third knock was sharp with impatience.

She heaved a huge, irritated sigh, got to her feet, and moved to answer the summons. She took another sip and left the mug on the kitchen counter. She interrupted the fourth round of knocks by yanking open the door. Her mood dropped faster than Simon's raised hand.

Oh, for fuck's sake.

"Hey, Vex." He stood there, one hand braced on the door-frame, the other slowly falling to his side, while an awkward mix of emotions washed over his face.

Hearing her name in his voice caused a confused ache in her chest and twisted her gut. Then she remembered the brunette and irritation replaced all those inconvenient emotions and she barely resisted the urge to slam the door shut. Instead, she tightened her hand on the inside knob where he couldn't see and struggled to keep her voice even. "Simon."

"Mind if I come in?" He dropped his hand from the frame and shifted forward as if her answer was a foregone conclusion.

"Yep." She didn't move and satisfaction surged when he blinked and jerked his head back, obviously not expecting that answer. "What's up?"

He studied her, but she knew he'd see what she wanted—casual indifference. No way in hell would he ever know how much his decision to walk away stung.

He offered her a small smile. "I need to talk to you a minute."

Unmoved by his tried-and-true charm, she said, "Talk."

"Come on, Vex." When she remained silent and unbending, his face hardened. He muttered a curse and added, "Not out here for Christ's sake."

She kept her grip on the door, leaned out, and craned her neck to see around the doorjamb, then deliberately did the same in the other direction. When she resettled in the opening, she set her shoulder to the edge of the doorframe and blocked the entry with her other arm. "Think we're as private as we need to be, and not to be a bitch—" *okay totally being a bitch here,* "—but rather not have you in my rooms."

"Always the hard ass, aren't you?" Temper added a nasty edge to his voice, and it scraped over the raw spots she'd be damned he'd ever see.

She locked her emotions under a glacier built by years of practice and ice coated her voice. "Yeah, Simon, I am."

Simon flinched and blew out a breath. "Dammit." He dropped his head and rubbed a hand at the base of his skull. When he raised his head, his temper was replaced by regret. "Look, I didn't come here to argue, I just wanted to see if you were okay."

God knew it would be so easy to curl her lip and blow his ass off, and not just because of the play Reaper instigated, and she was tempted, so tempted. But the shared years of friendship that preceded their misguided attempt to make it something more, had her reeling back her bitchier tendencies. With a deep breath, she forced the tension back and defrosted the chill. "I'm fine, Si. Nothing I haven't had before, and trust me, I'm pretty sure it'll happen again."

Since they both knew that was a given, he tried a different tact. "The ones who gave you that," he brushed the bruise under her eye, "are they going to be looking for a rematch?"

She pulled away from his touch and shook her head. "Don't worry, nothing's coming back to your doorstep."

He fisted his hand and dropped it to his side. "I'm not

worried about stumbling over a mess," he muttered, then shuffled his feet as if he wasn't sure if he wanted to stay or go.

A frustrated hurt and an angry kind of sadness bloomed because just days earlier he made it crystal clear he was done with her and now she wanted to ask why the hell he was here, but pride wouldn't let her. "Then what are you worried about?"

"Ran into Reaper last night." He settled in against the opposite side of the frame. "He said something about a bounty hunter hitting town, someone Mercy knows, looking for help."

Reaper hadn't wasted time planting his story about Math. She made a noncommittal hum and waited.

"Said you were heading out with him this morning. That true?"

"Yeah." When he frowned and looked away, she added, "What?"

He met her gaze. "You sure this guy is on the up and up?"

She snorted. "Tell me you didn't ask Reaper that."

He shook his head. "Do I look stupid?"

Don't answer that. "Then why are you asking me?"

He folded his arms over his chest. "Something about the timing—this bounty hunter hitting town at the same time as the soldier boys from the city, the godsdamn traitor—it makes my gut ache."

It should because he was being lied to and she felt bad about that, just not enough to disobey Reaper. In the long run it came down to keeping Simon safe. If the worst happened, and Michael or Greer found out the Vultures hooked up with Math, they would bear the brunt of it, not Simon, and not Pebble Creek. The Vultures swore to protect both, and that's exactly what they were doing.

She let impatience creep into her voice. "It's a tracking job with a decent payout, nothing more. Could the timing be better? Sure, but then we don't always get what we want, do we?" She didn't need Simon's flinch to regret her question. She hadn't meant it that way, but she wasn't going take it back. "Look, Simon, it's the butt crack of dawn. I didn't sleep worth shit last night, so if there's nothing else, how about you—"

The door was pulled out of her hand and threw her off balance. A half-dressed, clean-shaven Math stood in its place, his attention aimed at Simon. "There a problem here?"

Obviously, Math was of a mind to add credence to Reaper's story because he wrapped an arm around Vex's waist and drew her back until they were pressed together, presenting the picture of intimacy.

The air went electric as Simon's face flashed from shocked, to hurt, to pissed, and then straight into a blank slate in a matter of seconds. He split a look between the two of them and it didn't take a genius to read his mind.

"Who the hell are you?" The question shot from Simon like a bullet.

Freakin' hell, it was too early to deal with this crap.

"Crow." The rumble of Math's voice vibrated along her spine, and she dug her nails into his arm that was curled around her waist in a silent warning he ignored. He rubbed his chin over the top of her head. "And you?"

"Simon." He dropped his gaze to Vex, then lifted it back to Math. "Bounty hunter?" Math must have nodded because Simon looked back to Vex, a muscle twitching near his temple. "Right." He stepped back and shot Vex a dark look. "Sorry for the early wake-up call." He turned on his heel and stalked away, anger trailing in his wake.

Before she could decide if she should follow, Math walked her back inside and closed the door. She jerked out of his hold, spun around, and slammed her hands against his chest. He winced but didn't budge and her jumbled emotions found a convenient target. "Dammit to hell, Math."

He studied her, his face unreadable, before he shook his head, turned, and wandered into the kitchen. "From here on out, in public, it's Crow, Vex. Need to get used to it."

"What the fuck ever." She didn't dare follow him, instead she went to the living room where she had room to pace. Better to keep moving because if she stopped, she might be tempted to work her frustrations out by beating on the annoying man currently making himself at home in her kitchen.

"I'm guessing Reaper's already spreading the tale of my presence?"

His purposely casual question brought her to a halt. "You'd guess right." She shot a venom-filled look at his bare back and absently wondered where the binding for his ribs disappeared to. "You didn't have to do that."

"Yeah, I did." The muscles under his olive skin shifted and flexed as he doctored his coffee. He turned, cup cradled between his hands, and took a considering sip, watching her over the rim. "Don't get pissed at me, woman. This is Reaper's game, not mine, I'm just playing my assigned part."

She ignored the painful pinch in her chest. With no snappy comeback for his valid point, she returned to pacing in front of her couch.

"Thought you said he didn't want you."

Her nails curled into her palms, and she throttled her frustrated shriek. "He doesn't."

"You sure about that?"

His question brought her up short and she stopped to glare at him. "Yeah, I'm sure."

No way in hell was she discussing another failed relationship attempt, especially with Math. According to Mercy, emotions weren't his forte. Math lost his shit when Mercy chose Havoc, but then he was all about the Strix and his vengeance. Determined to escape this minefield of a conversation, she switched gears. "Reaper works quick. If he already planted his story with Simon, chances are he already reached out to Ruin and Havoc with the details. We need to have our shared story straight before we get downstairs."

He raised an eyebrow. "You know the people here better than me. What are they going to swallow?"

She ran a hand through her hair. "They'll believe whatever we give them."

"So, what do you want to give them?"

She stood there and tried get her brain into gear, only to have it stall. "Give me a minute."

She resumed her pacing, only this time it was a bit slower. Her route was interrupted when her mug, recently refilled, appeared under her nose. She blinked and found Math in front of her. She wrapped her hands around the warm stoneware and tried to ignore the fascinating lines exposed by his clean-shaven face. "Thanks."

He wandered over to the chair and she dropped back on the couch. She nabbed the blanket, drew her legs up, and flipped it over her lap. She sipped and thought. Finally, she shared. "We stick as close to the truth as we can. After leaving Havoc and Mercy at the Shrew, I ran into a couple of wannabes. You crossed paths with me on your way to Reaper and joined the fun."

"Ok, then why not show up at your side last night?"

"Because you took a couple of nasty hits and weren't up for a public meet."

He studied her, his thoughts well hidden, but finally dipped his chin. "That could work."

"It's going to have to work." Done with the conversation, she set her coffee down and rose. "I'm hitting the shower." She got to the bedroom door and threw over her shoulder. "If anyone comes knocking, play nice." She didn't wait for his answer before escaping to the bathroom.

VEX CAME out of her room and found Ruin on her couch, a steaming mug balanced on his stomach, his legs sprawled and crossed at the ankles. "Morning, sunshine."

"What the hell are you doing here so early?" She stepped over his legs, dropped her boots to the floor, tossed her custom silver hand armor in her brother's lap, and sat down.

He lifted the mug towards Math who rose from his chair. "Dropping off clothes, so our boy here isn't running around naked."

"Aren't you just the helpful sort?"

"That's me, all kinds of helpful." He brought the cup to his mouth, which didn't do a thing to hide his grin. "Reaper got word to Dog, found out Bane's in Boise already."

She leaned over and started tugging her boots on. "And?"

"And he'll keep his ears open and fill you in when you two hit town."

Well, that was something. Hopefully, Bane would have the intel they needed.

"Vex," Math called.

She lifted her head.

"You done?" He titled his head towards the bedroom.

"Have at it." She watched him disappear into the bedroom and only when the door closed did she turn back to her boots.

Ruin gave her hair a teasing tug and without looking up, she slapped his hand away. "What?" When another, harder tug followed, she finally looked up to find her twin watching her. "What?"

"Talk to me."

She blew out a breath, stomped her heel against the floor, and knocked the thick-soled boot into place. "About?"

"Vex." He packed a wealth of warning into her name.

She shot him a look, and when he nailed her with his relentless glare, she braced her arms on her knees and hunched her shoulders. "Dammit, Ruin." It came out perilously close to a whine. "Don't start, okay?"

"Nope, not okay. I want answers." There was a note in his voice, one she knew meant he was about to dig in until he got what he wanted.

She took her time putting her other boot on before she sank back and matched his pose. "Ask your stupid questions."

He took up her ungracious offer and he got right to it. "What's going on?"

Not really in the mood to deal with any of it, she sulked and muttered, "Figured Reaper explained it, considering you brought clothes and all."

"Not talking about Math—"

"Crow," she corrected snottily, as she nabbed her glove from Ruin's lap and slid it on, flexing her fingers until the sharpened tips fell into place.

"What the fuck ever." He waved his mug between them, his impatience loud and clear. "Talking about you and Simon."

One of the biggest pains about being twins was that your sibling had no qualms about nosing around your private life. Granted, she didn't mind poking at him and Charity, but having it turned around on her sucked big time. "There is no me and Simon."

"And why is that?"

The undeniably sarcastic edge to his question flipped her defenses to red alert and released her inner bitch factor. "I don't know, since you seem to have all the answers, why don't you tell me?"

Instead of swiping back, he held her furious gaze. "That what you want?"

Between his serious tone and somber gaze her pulse tripped, and her stomach pitched. She folded her arms, and reached for a snarky, but honest answer. "No, what I want is for you to drop it, but I'm guessing that's not gonna happen."

He heaved a not so silent sigh, sat up, and set his cup on the floor. "Vex, girl, you know I love you."

She braced.

He shifted until he faced her and kept one leg on the couch. "But you don't make things easy."

Right, because this was all her fault? Self-righteous anger flared over the spark of guilt and left her voice sharp. "Is that what I'm supposed to do, Ruin? Make it easy? Did you when you met Charity?"

His face hardened as her hit found its mark. "That's not the same."

Unwilling to back down, she unfolded her arms and drilled a finger into his chest, shoving her point home. "You're right, it's not, because she didn't give up on you."

He caught her hand and pulled it away, a frown replacing his irritation. "Give up? Is that what you think Si did?"

Instead of restating the obvious, she tugged her hand free and contented herself with arching a brow.

He rubbed his palm over his chest. "It's a two-way street, you know."

Because she wanted this conversation done, when he said nothing more, she followed his prompt. "What's a two-way street?"

"Loving someone."

At that she couldn't help it, she rolled her eyes and couldn't quite stifle her sneer. "Just because you lucked out and got your happy ending, doesn't mean that's the end game for all of us."

"When are you going to stop punishing yourself, Vex?" Impatience and frustration finally won out, and Ruin didn't hold back, striking at her heart as his ruthless honesty tore through her protective layers with a skill only blood held. "You think I don't see it? It was me who failed you and Marnie, yet you keep believing it's you that has to pay the price. I spent years trying to convince you otherwise, but you refused to listen. After our last visit to Portland when you disappeared for three days, I thought you managed to finally lay shit to rest so I didn't push it. Instead, you came back dragging night-mares and doing your damnedest to reinforce that wall you keep between you and everyone else. Then Si gets taken, and a crack appears. I'm thinking, 'Fucking finally, she'll wake up.' Instead, here you are, ensuring that peace is the last thing you find."

Ruin's aim was devastatingly accurate and shattered her protective illusions, leaving behind nothing but the ugly truth, a truth she didn't want to see because it just fucking hurt. "He walked away from me, Ruin." Just like everyone eventually did.

He cupped her face in his hands, his touch careful, but he didn't relent. "Did you try to stop him?"

Her gaze slipped away before she could check it.

He caught the telling move and his voice softened. "Yeah, see, babe, that right there says it all." He drew her close and pressed a soft kiss to her forehead, something he used to do when they were younger. Then he let her go and sat back, one of his hands covering the fist in her lap. "You won't share what's dogging you and I won't make you, though God knows I want to." He squeezed until she lifted her gaze. "But Vex, you want a happy ending, you have to make a change. Take a risk, show them you're willing to fight for them too. No one wants to keep banging their head against a door if you aren't even willing to unlock it."

"He gave up, Ruin." Stupid, stupid tears pressed against her eyes, and her throat was thick. "Said I was too much work."

Ruin winced, even as his gaze darkened in sympathy. With a sigh, he shifted until they were shoulder to shoulder on the couch. "Then, as much as I hate to say it, maybe Si's not it for you."

Hearing her brother voice the painful realization she held in her heart, soothed the worst of the lingering ache. It still stung, but the bite of it lessened. She dropped her head to his shoulder and swallowed against the lump in her throat. "Yeah, that's kind of what I figured."

They sat there for a long moment before he finally broke the quiet. "Promise me something."

"Maybe."

"Don't use this as another reason to punish yourself."

She lifted her head and went to push away. "Ruin—"

He stopped her by simply laying a hand on her knee. "Ease up, babe, you think Marnie wanted you to go through this life miserable?"

She raised her head and met his gaze, unable to escape the knowledge and love staring back. There was only one answer she could give. "No."

Something in his face relaxed, revealing a glimpse into the love he held for her. "Then find a way to forgive yourself before you lose whatever chance you have at finding your own slice of happiness, yeah?"

Somehow, someway, this time, his request managed to get in and set up shop. He was right, she knew it, but damn if his request wasn't scary as shit. So, she gave him the best she could. "I'll try." Unable to leave things heavy and serious, she added, "But only because you're a pain in my ass."

He flashed her a cocky grin. "It's my job, and one I take great pride in." He stood up and stretched.

She rose and was unsurprised to find herself wrapped in his arms. "Love you, Ruin."

"Love you too, troublemaker." He let her go and turned to leave. "I need to go drag a certain hot blonde out of bed, so we can get this show on the road."

She followed him to the door. "I don't need the kinky details of your life, brother of mine. Especially not before breakfast."

He chuckled and pulled opened the door. In the hall, he turned. "You going to Mandy's before you head out?"

She leaned against the doorjamb. "Yeah, want to check in on Katie." The last of the girls Simon and Crane managed to save from the Raiders, but not before Katie endured a brutal rape that left her in a coma for weeks. "Her parents are due today. Want to make sure she's steady before she leaves."

Grim understanding lurked in his eyes. "You've been good for her."

The quiet pride in his voice settled over her with an uncomfortable weight. "She's a survivor."

Something dark came and went before he chucked her chin. "Takes one to know one."

nine

After an interesting morning of half-truths and sideways glances, Math stashed the last of the supplies into one of the two saddlebags on the back of the bike Reaper arranged. Vex stood off to the side, talking with the burly-chested Boden, Simon's second-in-command, about patrol assignments.

So far, the bounty hunter story was holding strong, and while they weren't obvious about it, the Vultures had kept Math's presence low-key. There had been no sign of the city guards, but he didn't think that would last much longer. With their bikes packed, he was ready to hit the road with Vex.

He walked over to where she and Boden were talking, catching the tail end of the conversation. Vex's gaze flicked to him before returning to Boden. "Charity said she'd be happy to cover my shift, but Simon might need her to run guard on the next delivery."

"With Ruin back, he can take your position, leaving Charity to help out here." Boden's attention shifted to the pack of kids that raced through the main square. This time in the morning the place was chaotic as deliveries arrived, traders set up their booths for the day, and people bustled about their business. When the kids barreled closer, Boden snagged the collar of the one in the lead. "Jess, what did I tell you about racing through here, boy?"

The mopped headed pre-teen tried to pull off sheepish as he dangled from Boden's fist. "Sorry. We're late for class."

"Be later if you knock over someone's display. Slow it down." After getting an enthusiastic nod, he freed the boy and turned back to Vex. "You heading to Mandy's?"

"Yep, making a quick stop before we head out." She gazed out over the square. "Any idea when Katie's parents are due?"

"Last I heard, should be arriving around noon." Someone called Boden's name and he raised a hand in acknowledgement. He turned to Math. "You following your bounty west?"

Not at all surprised by how fast the community grapevine worked, Math stuck to the vague details Reaper set loose. "Signs indicate he may be looking to get lost in an urban center. Be nice to get in front of him before that."

"That might be a bit of a challenge, even with Vex helping you," Boden warned.

"Are you doubting my skills, old man?" Vex drawled.

Boden shook his head with a rueful grin, but his eye stayed serious. "You be careful, girl. I'm tired of patching up my friends." The older man offered Math his hand. "Good hunting."

Math took it. "Thanks."

He and Vex watched Boden walk away before Vex shifted towards the bikes. "Know you're anxious to get moving, but this will only take a few. We can ride instead of walk."

"Not a problem." He fell into step beside her. "You mind if I ask why we're stopping to see Pebble Creek's doc?"

"Not a secret," she answered, but there was a curious tension to her shoulders. She shot him a sidelong glance. "Mercy tell you about the kids the Raiders took?"

"The ones Simon and Crane managed to intercept? Yeah, fucking twisted shit." Unfortunately, the vile business of kidnapping and selling kids was far too lucrative and happened all too frequently. "Heard Istaqa's son was one of them."

"Yeah, ever met him?"

Math shook his head.

"Good kid." Vex stopped by the bikes and turned to him. "Katie was the oldest of the girls in the group."

He noted the shadows of anger lurking behind her set jaw and felt a pit open in his stomach, but he didn't interrupt.

Vex's gaze drifted over his shoulder and focused on something only she could see. "She protected the younger kids from the Raiders." Her throat bobbed as she visibly swallowed, but her gaze came back to him, fury a flame in the amber depths. "But it cost her."

He didn't need the details because his mind could fill in the blanks. A young female at the mercy of the animalistic Raiders? It was a miracle she survived.

So, when Vex asked, "Mind waiting outside when we get to Mandy's?"

He didn't hesitate. "Not at all."

Her stiff shoulders visibly loosened. "Thanks."

Together they mounted their bikes, kicked them to life, and headed out.

She led the way through town into a tucked away neighborhood dotted with old growth trees and turbine blades that captured the wind to power the neat homes below. Flat roof gardens showcased the rural attitude of utilizing natural resources in stark contrast to the cities that still relied on the more expensive fossil fuels.

Vex turned into a ranch style home guarded by a well-tended yard and shut down her engine. The door opened before the rumbles of their bikes faded to be replaced by the relaxed quiet. An older woman with dark hair and glasses stepped out on to the porch, then waited at the top of the steps.

Math recognized her from breakfast at the dining room at Grave's Hall. She'd been sharing a table with a man Reaper called Worth. Vex got off her bike and made her way up the steps. Math waited with the bikes.

"Hey, Mandy."

"Hey, Vex."

"Wanted to swing by before I headed out, see if Katie was up for a visit."

The older woman shifted to the side and gave Vex a straight shot to the house. "I think it'll do her a world of good. She's been a bit anxious waiting for her parents."

Vex stopped at the doorway. "I promise not to stay long."

Mandy patted her shoulder. "Take your time, you know she likes being with you."

Vex didn't answer but ducked inside.

Mandy wandered down the steps. "Morning."

"Morning." Math studied the doctor as she drew close.

When she reached the other side of Vex's bike, she tilted her head. "Saw you this morning at the dining hall. Crow, right?"

"Yes, ma'am." He offered her a friendly grin.

Her nose scrunched. "Just Mandy, ma'am makes me sound old."

"Apologies, Mandy. Though not sure that's a worry for you."

Her return smile eased the lines around her eyes, but even her soft chuckle couldn't erase the stress she carried. She turned her face up to the sun and closed her eyes behind the wire frame glasses. "Beautiful morning."

"That it is."

They shared a quiet moment before she dropped her head

and opened her eyes. "Looks like you and Vex are heading out. Taking her some place interesting?"

He tucked his hands in the back pockets of his jeans and rocked on his heels. "Depends on your definition of interesting." When she quirked an eyebrow, he elaborated. "I've been tracking a bounty west, but the sucker's been a bit slippery. Heard Mercy was hanging here lately and figured since I was in the area might as well stop in for a visit, see if she was interested in helping."

"I'm guessing she turned you down?"

He managed to pull off a passable 'aw shucks' expression. "Might've been able to convince her to join me but seems I can't compete with the bruiser she hooked up with."

Mandy waved to a couple walking down the sidewalk and waited to continue their conversation until they were out of earshot. She hitched a hip against Vex's bike. "So, how'd you end up with Vex instead?"

"Not quite sure." He managed a bemused frown. "I think I caught Reaper in a charitable frame of mind."

"Uh-huh." A wealth of disbelief hung in her response. "More likely he's hoping you'll keep her out of trouble."

His grin widened. "Reaper may have mentioned that when he sprung the news on Vex."

An easy silence settled between them, and Math watched the humor fade from Mandy's face only to be replaced by a pensive frown. For some reason he thought the look held more naturalness than her earlier amusement. Seeing it, he found himself asking, "Mandy, you okay?"

Her gaze jumped to his as if she'd forgotten he was there. A hint of red seeped along her cheeks as she waved a hand absently. "Sorry, my mind wandered." She straightened from the bike and brushed a hand over her hip. "Actually, I was wondering. You mentioned you were heading west. Any chance you'll be stopping in New Seattle?"

He cocked his head, curiosity perked. "Maybe, but I'm kind of hoping we'll get ahead of him before he hits the urban areas, especially New Seattle. Damn hard to track people there. Too many places to hide."

She worried her bottom lip. "We hit a snag with one of our medical shipments. I was hoping Vex might be able to pick a few items up and bring them back."

Just then Vex pushed out the front door and drew both of their attention. Math clocked her strained smile. He wasn't the only one.

Mandy studied the younger woman. "You okay?"

"Will be." Vex dragged the hand not covered in silver through her hair and blew out a long breath. "Sometimes I wish—"

"Don't." Mandy's admonishment was sharp, but the next came out gentler. "You can't change what happened. Focusing on it does neither of you any good."

Math didn't need to be a student of human nature to hear the weight of a story in the doc's warning and he wondered what the older woman survived to earn such knowledge.

Mandy patted Vex. "The road ahead won't be easy, but Katie won't be alone. She has you, and she has her family. That's more than most ever get, right?"

"Right." Vex agreed.

"Okay then." Mandy stepped back and her tone took on a brisk note. "I was just telling Crow, if you two happen to make it to New Seattle, there were a couple of items I could use."

"Yeah, that last shipment was short." Vex settled on her bike. "Give me a list and if we make it that far, I'd be happy to make time."

Mandy pulled a folded sheet from her pocket. Vex tucked it away and they exchanged goodbyes. Mandy went back up the steps as Vex kicked her bike into gear. In minutes, Math was following her out of the neighborhood.

She pulled over just before they were due to hit the main road, braced her feet, shut her bike down, and leaned over the handlebars.

He came to a stop next to her enjoying the picture she made. Long legs clad in denim, her curves tucked into the fitted t-shirt, and her wild hair banded carelessly back, one of the thin, beaded braids trailing her profile.

She turned to him. "Need to ensure we gather our shadows, so going to head down the main street."

"Works for me." Their passage would hopefully garner enough curiosity to snag their city visitors.

She nodded absently. "When's the last time you swung by the Hole?"

Mimicking her pose, he picked through his memory. "Passed through about six, maybe seven months ago. You?"

"Closer to five for me." The silver-tipped hand drummed absently on her bike's grip.

He didn't find it difficult to follow her thoughts. Not only did they need privacy for their impending one-on-one, but it would be best if he and Vex could choose the spot where their meeting would occur. Utilizing home field advantage, as one old Strix used to say. Problem was, Boise didn't have the most stable community. The deeper you went, the more slippery it got, until you hit the stagnant depths of the Hole itself. "Shit shifts like the tides there. Do you have a spot we can use as anchor?"

He let her think, enjoying the way the morning sunlight sneaked through the leafy covering and glinted off the streaks of gold woven among the blacks and sables. After about a minute, she spoke. "Got a couple ideas but can't make a decision until we talk to Bane. Still, I think our first stop should be Gus."

"Gus?"

She gave him a grin. "Yeah, crusty old mechanic with a big mouth, magic hands."

He leaned to the side and took in her bike. "Not seeing anything wrong with your ride."

"Not yet." She tugged her bandana up over her nose and settled a pair of protective lenses in place.

He shook his head and pulled his bandana up. He admired deviousness and this woman had it in spades which only enhanced her physical draw and drove him to distraction.

Their bikes roared to life, their pipes unmistakable as they cruised through the center of Pebble Creek. Heads turned, exactly as they wanted. By the time they hit the public gates, the back of his neck itched and the spot between his shoulder blades stung. Anticipation simmered, and even the annoying aches from his ribs and bruises couldn't dim his delight.

Come and get me, assholes.

ten

It took three hours for Vex and Math to hit the outskirts of Boise. Since they weren't trying to shake their shadows or keep their approach on the down low, they followed the rusted-out tracks of an old rail line to the first signs of life. At their last pit stop, Vex upgraded her fuel line with a tiny hole. Just enough to ensure a recognizable stutter by the time they hit town.

They passed a couple of questionable outposts and ignored the eyes tracking their passage and taking their measure. The residents were clearly familiar with the concept that curiosity killed since they scrambled further into the shadows, even as they marked the arrival of outsiders.

Vex turned off and threaded her way through the rusting hulks of ancient big rigs and cracked concrete that threatened to shred the bikes' tires. They drove through the crumbling arch of a partially collapsed building that opened into a cavernous garage.

Stripped down car frames crouched on pitted lifts under thick chains that dangled from exposed beams. In the metallic web, an old engine block hung like some weird insect. Shelves lined the walls, piled high with unidentifiable parts, and battered tool chests of every size littered the floor. Based upon the jumbled mess of vehicles—two and four-wheeled—in various states of repair, Gus's place wasn't hurting for business.

They rolled to a stop just inside, the deafening racket of their bikes filling the space. Even after they shut them down, Math's ears still rang. As Vex dropped her stand and swung a leg over her bike, Math stayed seated, but pulled his bandana down. The competing scents of oil, metallic dust, and corn-based fuel clogged his nostrils. He kept his eye on Vex.

She shoved her glasses up into her wind-tangled hair and tucked her bandana under her chin. "Yo, Gus! You home?"

Somewhere in the hidden depths a door bounced off a frame, followed by a bellowed, "Throttle your thrusters, I'm coming."

"Throttle your thrusters?" Math repeated, quirking a brow.

Vex came to stand next to him and settled her ass just behind him against the seat's edge. "Gus is a fan of old space movies."

"Ahh." Math's amusement deepened when the man in question rolled into view. Rolled being the operative word.

Skin tanned to a leathery finish covered thick arms as they propelled a clearly modified wheelchair across the garage. The way the barrel-chested man navigated the maze of tools and parts revealed a skill honed by familiarity. Instead of hair, a scrawl of black and blue ink covered his skull, but the eyes in the craggy face were sharp. They swept over Math in a quick threat assessment. Careful speculation carved deep grooves across his forehead. When it switched over to Vex, Gus's eyes narrowed. "Ah hell, Vex, what are you doing here?"

She didn't move from her position. "You still fix bikes, right?"

Grime-coated hands braked the wheels just in front of the bikes as he did a quick evaluation. "Don't see any bullet holes, nothing's on fire." He scowled at her. "So gonna ask again, why are you here, woman?"

Vex pushed off of Math's bike and strolled closer to Gus. "Pretty sure I nicked my fuel line."

Gus's jaw jutted. "Easy enough fix."

She shrugged and circled behind the mechanic, so she could brace her arms on the back of the wheelchair, and leaned in. Gus did a piss poor job of hiding his panic as she hooked her chin on his shoulder. "Figured I'd let you patch up my baby while I wandered into town and took care of a little business."

His throat bobbed, betraying his nerves, but his voice came out rock steady. "Always happy to have a paying customer, but I got other jobs ahead of you."

Vex straightened, then did a slow revolution that took in the cluttered garage. She made a soft hum while Gus craned his neck to keep her in sight. When she finished, she leaned in, and ran one sharp tip over his other ear. "Funny, I don't see anyone else with a pulse waiting around."

"Dammit, woman!" The mechanic jerked his head away and shoved his chair towards Math, before executing a tight turn so he could face the threat behind him. A move Math found hilariously stupid since it sandwiched him between the two biggest threats in the garage. "You know you can't just roll in here and cut in line without someone getting pissy with me."

Vex waved away his concerns as she walked forward. "Don't worry, I don't need it until tomorrow." She stopped next to the chair and shifted her gaze to Math. "Me and my friend—" her underlying implication of how close that friendship was came through loud and clear, "—will keep ourselves busy in the meantime." She gave the top of Gus's head a warning pat before moving towards Math once more. "What'll it cost to squeeze me in?"

Gus adjusted his chair and watched her like he would a venomous snake. Whatever worries he had about helping disappeared under a hint of craftiness that slithered along the lines and folds of his face. "You wanna trade?"

With her back to the cantankerous mechanic, Math watched her roll her eyes and couldn't miss her exasperated amusement, but her tone didn't shift in the slightest. She kept coming towards Math as he straddled his bike and left him well and truly caught when she seriously invaded his personal space. "Depends."

Over her shoulder, Math caught Gus's gaze zeroing in on Vex's ass even as she ran that lethally tipped hand down Math's chest and trailed it along the edge of his jeans. The teasing touch garnered an expected response, but he forced his body back in line even as instinct and lust had him curling an arm around her waist and tugging her close.

The move jerked Gus's attention off her ass and brought his eyes up until they clashed with Math's.

Gus's face turned pasty and his "On?" sounded like it was stuck in his throat.

When Vex dug her metal nails in a silent warning, Math looked down to the woman who filled his arms.

Vex's gaze was hot with challenge and irritation, yet her voice was close to a purr when she turned and forced his hands to her hips as she faced Gus. "Your price."

Gus dragged a hand over his skull, before angling his chair over near a set of shelves. He started rummaging around while he answered. "Got a delivery for Trip, a custom job, y'know." He pulled something Math couldn't make out into his lap, before wheeling back over. "The kind of job I don't need a bunch of noses stickin' into. Lately, the Snooper Troopers have been poking about more than normal. Rather not cross their paths, but I need to get this to Trip. Easier if you could swing in and drop it off."

Math knew the name. Trip was the nastiest of the bunch in the Hole, which translated into him being in charge.

Vex folded her arms and cocked a hip, her voice taking on a chill. "What the hell are city soldiers doing here?"

Gus shrugged. "Don't know, don't want to know. All I know is they've been making themselves a pain in various asses lately and shit's getting hairy."

Vex's voice hardened. "You want me to hit the Hole, make a drop off to a man whose sanity is highly in question, all while dodging soldiers? How the fuck is that easy, Gus?"

"Easier than me trying to get around on this," he wheedled. "Look, Vex, you're a fuckin' Vulture, fly in, drop it off, fly back out. Easy. Just like fixing your damn bike."

Since Math couldn't see her face, he figured she must be giving Gus enough to make him believe she was teetering on his offer, because the mechanic whined, "You do this for me, I'll have your bike ready by morning and I'll make sure no one touches your shit."

Vex leaned back against Math and titled her head back so he could see her face. "What do you think?"

In keeping with his strong and silent role, he took his time studying Gus, noting a thin layer of sweat on his forehead, and then dropped his attention to the box sitting in Gus's lap. Math shifted his gaze to Vex, slid an arched brow up, and lifted his chin in silent question.

"Yeah, I'm wondering too." Vex turned back to Gus. "What's in the box? I don't want to end up tangled up in someone else's mess."

Gus patted the package. "Scavenged boom-blocks, no timers, so you just hand it over and you're golden."

Boom-blocks, or recovered explosives, were highly sought after. If the powers that be knew you were holding some, they'd get twitchy. If someone like Trip wanted it, odds were high it wasn't for anything virtuous.

Sticking to her role, Vex turned back to Math. "Well?"

Math let Gus sweat it out before finally, with obvious reluctance, dipping his chin in agreement, and dropping his arm so she could move.

Vex sauntered out of his arms and over to Gus. She bent and snagged the box. "Deal. As long as he doesn't blow us up."

She straightened, tossed the box to Math, who caught it, and tucked it away in his saddlebags. When he turned back around, she was at her bike, pulling off her saddlebags. She hefted them to her shoulder and aimed a vicious and bright smile at Gus. "Don't worry, Gus, if I can't pick up my bike, my friend here will be sure to swing by to settle the bill."

Not missing her implication, Gus's throat worked, but nothing came out. Instead, his wide eyes tracked Vex as she climbed on behind Math.

He grinned and kicked his bike into gear. The roar of pipes filled the cavernous garage like thunder as he turned the bike. He felt Vex twist behind him, probably to give a snarky wave to Gus. He hit the throttle and shot out of the dubious safety of Gus's garage and straight into trouble.

eleven

Perched behind Math, Vex directed him by touch since the bike's engine made talking a bitch. They drove through the streets and worked their way closer to the Boise River, that divided the town into two distinct sections, civilized and not-so-civilized zones. Sitting dead center in the uncivilized section was the Hole.

Vex kept an eye on the other travelers as they moved through the more acceptable section. She wasn't overly worried about those on foot, but a couple of motorized transports, heavy on the wear and tear, had her concerned. It was hard to tell if their operators were mercenary or city hired as she and Math zoomed by. Thankfully, both vehicles lumbered off in the opposite direction, leaving Math and her behind.

Vex settled deeper against Math's back as his shortened hair blew across her face and brought a hint of dust, heat, and male mixed with the familiar scent of her shampoo. The tension in her shoulders eased as she enjoyed the shift of muscles as he handled the bike, the absent brush of his jaw against her hair as he watched their route, and the disturbing sense of contentment that sung in her veins.

As much as she wanted to claim it was the simple pleasure of being on the road—the wild speed and freedom of the ride—honesty made her admit that generally riding bitch turned her cranky. This time it was different and all because of the man in front of her.

She deliberately steered her mind away from that particularly thorny path and kept her attention on the passing scenery as they swept past the crumbling white clock tower and twisted through the ruined maze of tree-lined streets. Every time she cruised through an old, abandoned city, it sent a shiver of discomfort down her spine.

The aftermath of the Collapse, especially in the more populated areas, left behind bones etched with horror stories. After seventy plus years, signs of life violently interrupted by the city born riots were still in evidence, even though the memory of it remained only with the old-timers.

Faded red numbers and letters from a cryptic code no longer understood decorated abandoned buildings. The endless pits of empty window frames stared down at those who dared to pass in their shadows like ghostly watchers. Mother Nature reclaimed what was hers with green arms that curled around the carefully planned communities but couldn't hide the burned-out husks and abandoned shells of cars parked neatly in weed-choked driveways.

A few homes had been rescued and repurposed into modern dwellings, but those signs of life only added to the uneasy shroud that fell over the neighborhood. It wasn't until they got closer to the busy, reconstructed city center, that she was able to shake the weirdness off.

Her stomach rumbled and she figured it was time to hit one of the nearby roadhouses. Not only could she and Math fuel up but it would give their shadows time to catch up. Of course, it also meant that their arrival would be noted and shared, and she wasn't sure if that was a good or bad thing.

Initially, her plan was a tried-and-true tactic of poking around until they uncovered hints on where Cam might be held. However, Gus's trade made for a better approach, especially when having to deal with the head psycho of the Hole, Trip. Not only did it serve as cover for a direct approach, but it was also a faster route to collect information, and faster was always better.

Ahead, one of the few remaining bridges loomed and a set of round towers sat to the right of it. Various transportation options clustered at its base and small groups of operators and owners hung around smoking and talking. Remembering Math's ribs, she shifted her hold from his waist to squeeze his thigh. He angled his head, and she jutted her chin in the direction of the bridge. Math aimed the bike toward the bridge, and they parked under the weight of watching eyes.

Vex swung off first and stretched, the scent of smoked meat making her stomach rumble. Next to her, Math dismounted and a couple of female traders that were making their way down the steps, slowed to watch his show. One of them made a *"meow"* sound and Vex hid her flash of amusement under a *"he's mine"* glare.

Guess she was on hussy patrol, otherwise Math might not make it out unmolested. She took her new role to heart and braced her metal-tipped hand on his stomach as she turned into him, her voice low. "Don't leave those behind or they won't be here when we get back."

At her proprietary touch amusement and something she didn't understand dance in his eyes, but he grabbed his bags and simply murmured, "Gotcha."

She nabbed her saddlebags and together they strode by the hungry women and headed up the faded red stairs. From behind the protection of her tinted lenses, she scanned the lot and clocked the lanky teen with impressively wide-chested mutt at his side that was perched on the low wall that butted against the stairs. Tagging him as the self-appointed lot guard, she dug into a pocket for some credits, but Math beat her to it. He tossed the flash of silver at the kid, who managed to snap it out of thin air.

Vex ignored the kid's personal space and got right in his face. She waited until his cocky ass smile faded, and then issued her warning. "Anyone touches, your ass pays the price."

Her threat earned a lame attempt at a sneer. "Payment gets you an hour." The last part of his response cracked on a revealing octave.

"They touch the bike, I touch you." She ignored the wall of nausea-inducing body odor and traced a silver-tipped finger along his cheek until it pressed under his chin. She exerted pressure until his face tipped to hers. "Promise only one of us will enjoy that. Yeah?"

A bead of sweat slid over pitted, pale skin and disappeared into an even weaker attempt at a beard, but he managed a jerky nod before cautiously pulling back. Satisfied her message was delivered and received, she went back to Math, and they headed inside.

They stepped through the doors and into a wall of voices, music, and activity. The lighting was for shit, but that was expected. The low haze of smoke—a mix of tobacco and cannabis—competed with the scent of fried food, grilling meat, and sweat.

She and Math wound their way through the maze of tables and chairs and headed towards the bar that stretched out under what she swore looked like stained glass. On the floor, disgusting puddles tugged at her boots. Bodies, on stools and on foot, lined the bar. Vex had no desire to rub shoulders with the unclean masses, so she tugged on Math's belt loop and brought him to a stop.

When she had his attention, she leaned in and put her

mouth near his ear so he could hear her. "Why don't you grab us something edible and cold, while I claim a table."

Someone jostled them and he wrapped an arm around her waist. He pulled out of the stumbling path of one of the patrons and dragged her close. "Any preference on the food?"

She twisted her neck to check out what the various plates held and wrinkled her nose. "Something that resembles what it came from would be good."

His lips twitched. "No promises." He looked over her head, scanned the room, and then tilted his head to the left. "Table over there is about to open."

She followed his gaze to a group that was leaving a table just shy of center. "Got it." When he didn't let her go, she turned back. "What?"

He dipped his head and stole a kiss. The simple brush of his lips lit a flame, but before it could gain strength, he pulled back. "Got to keep those tongues wagging."

Even though the reminder did shit all to snuff out the heat that curled through her, she got a little of her own back when she brushed her hand down his chest and then lower, to cup the impressive package caught between them. With a delicate squeeze, she held the dark temptation of his gaze and smiled. "They'll wag, all right." She rose on her toes, gave his lush lower lip a small punishment, slipped his saddlebags off his shoulder, and set her palm against his chest in a small shove. "Go get us food, hot shot."

She turned away and claimed the vacant but none too clean table. She dropped the bags in one chair, gathered the empties, and dumped them in a bucket carried by a passing waiter—or what passed for one in this place.

Once she settled into a seat, she did a slow scan of the room. Avid eyes slid away, but she was satisfied that their entrance had been duly noted. She kept a half-eye on the crowd, but eventually found herself watching Math. More specifically his ass as he leaned against the bar and spoke to the harried man behind it.

It wasn't a bad thing that he got her engine revving. Maybe it was just a case of frustrated libido considering it had been months since she'd indulged in sex.

Yeah, she and Simon had played around, but sadly, he had been in no shape to follow things to a happy conclusion. Those fucking Raiders had all but crucified him and his recovery had been a long, slow, and painful process. Then, after her run to Page with Havoc, she and Simon never found their footing. Mainly because when push came to shove, she hadn't been able to follow through. Even now, with the possibility of her and Simon nothing but dust, she couldn't pinpoint why she hesitated. But she had, and now... well, now her hormones were clamoring for attention. From Math.

She knew the attraction was mutual because it was hard to miss the evidence her touch evoked. But while scratching that itch with him would be fun and memorable, instinct warned it might not be in her best interests. If she could keep it all about the physical, she'd be golden. The question was, could she?

She drummed her fingers on the table, the metallic tips leaving nicks on the battered surface. There was no doubt the whole Simon incident had left some serious cracks in her confidence as a female. Having someone like Math widened those fractures would guarantee lasting scars. Scars were survivable, she had enough on her heart to prove that. So, what was a few more? She didn't doubt it would be worth the ride, and it wasn't like she was the happily ever after type. Happy right fucking now worked.

A shadow fell over the table and broke through her whirling speculation with a silky combination of warm honey and charm. "Well, well, well, if isn't the wicked bitch of the west."

She grinned at the male currently making himself at home in a chair he plucked from another table and kept her legs sprawled and crossed at the ankles as he set his bottle down. "Well, hell, if it isn't the bane of my existence."

"Har-de-fucking-har-har, woman." He rocked his chair back until the front legs left the floor, and linked his hands behind his head, revealing intricate ink crawling over his arms. "You can do better than that."

Maybe, but she loved giving Bane shit, and as one of the Dogs of War, he could take it. "What brings you to Paradise, Bane?"

"Paradise?"

She waved an arm to indicate their surroundings.

He snorted. "Same as you, I'd bet." He craned his cropped blond head around as Math's heavier tread drew close, then followed his progress as he settled into the chair opposite Vex. "Business."

Vex checked for and came up empty on the three other men that normally trotted alongside Bane, then she raised a brow. "Where are the strays?"

She took the plate and bottle Math offered and slid them closer. She picked up one of the deep-fried potato wedges, dipped it into the puddle of ketchup, and took a bite. Salt and starch hit her stomach, which rumbled in appreciation.

Bane dropped his chair with a dull thud and reached over to steal one of her fries. She smacked his hand, but he only grinned. "The boys are out and about, doing their thing." He chewed and shifted his attention to Math. "Know you."

"Do you?" Math looked completely unconcerned as he took a healthy bite of his sandwich.

Vex picked up her bottle and threw back some brew, prepared to enjoy the show as Math handled Bane.

"You've cleaned up some—" Bane circled the last bit of his fry over his face in clarification, "—but yeah, you were the spook who hooked up with Havoc back in Salt Lake." He plopped the last bit of potato in his mouth, everything but his gaze the picture of casual. "Last seen, your ass was tracking that demented bitch north. Didn't get far, did ya?"

Math took his time chewing and swallowing before he answered. "Far enough."

"Think so?" Bane's smile was full of teeth. "Hate to burst your bubble there, spooky, but I'm gonna have to disagree with you there."

Math held Bane's flinty gaze as he took another bite, chewed, then nabbed his bottle and tipped it to his lips. His unspoken taunt came through loud and clear.

As the two males went into a stare down, Vex decided to soothe Bane's ruffled fur before things got messy. "Why is that? You know something we don't?"

Bane reclaimed his drink and then stole another fry from her plate, this time coating it in ketchup. "Why I'm here, right?" He set his elbow on the table and waved the fry back and forth before taking a bite. "I know lots of things, babe."

Vex shifted in her seat and matched his pose—elbow to the table, but set her chin on her palm, and studied him. "Like?"

He grinned and tapped her nose. "Like the recent increase in the observant and curious types which makes doing business around here a mite tricky." He lifted his bottle and took a drink.

"Sucks to be you then," she murmured. It was one thing for Gus to mention the uptick in new faces, but for Bane to confirm? That was cause for concern. On one hand it added weight to Math's belief that Cam was being held nearby. On the other, it made life difficult for her and Math. They needed more information. "How tricky?"

Bane set his drink aside and popped another fry as speculation lit a spark in his dark gaze. It was a reminder that if Vex didn't want him sniffing in her business she best watch her step. "As in, you can't turn around here without tripping over one of them or their snitches."

"Could see how that might crimp a deal," Vex agreed.

He grimaced and shook his head, his disgust evident. "A pain in the ass is what it is."

"Any chance they happen to be hanging in one area over another?" Math asked.

To his credit, Bane thought his answer over. "Couldn't say for sure but know someone who would."

Vex snorted and grabbed her drink. "Let me guess—Trip?" When Bane simply grinned, she shook her head. "Yeah, we were planning on dropping in for a visit." She raised the bottle to her mouth and washed down the salt and potatoes. When she was done, she saw concern had replaced Bane's earlier amusement. "What?"

"You two going in," he warned, "not smart."

She agreed, but their options were limited. Next to her Math shifted in his chair, probably getting ready to shoot off some smart-assed comment. Since that was her area of exper-tise, she didn't take her gaze off of Bane but flicked a finger in Math's direction in a "shut-it" order. "I'm aware, but I don't have much choice." She sat back and balanced her bottle on her stomach. "Got something he's waiting for."

"Might want to rethink that, darling." When she didn't respond the speculation in his gaze whooshed into a flame of knowledge. Bottle in hand, it was his turn to sit back. "What? Is Gus tricking out your ride?"

Sniff, sniff.

She hid her wince as Bane locked on to the scent, but figured it was better to brazen it out. "Nah, just doing a solid in return for a repair."

"Right." A world of disbelief existed in his response. He

took a moment to suck back another drink and study the two of them before he heaved a sigh. "You need an escort?"

The poorly hidden mix of resignation and anticipation made her laugh. She kicked his boot. "What do you think?"

He flashed a grin filled with devilish intent. "I think you'd walk up to death and pull on his whiskers if you could."

"And you wouldn't?"

"Nope, I'm more likely to kick his balls and get the hell out of reach."

The image of Bane beating feet from the grim reaper made her grin widened. "Good luck with that. Heard he has a long ass reach."

He tapped his bottle against hers. "True that."

A loud curse followed by the harsh scrape of chair legs over concrete cut through the wash of the crowd and drew their attention to an argument blooming on the far edge of the room. When the curses morphed into nothing more interesting than a drunken shoving match, Vex returned to the conversation. "So, you boys on delivery or escort service?"

Bane followed her lead, but not far. "Neither now."

"So, you're just, what?" She arched a brow. "Hanging around town?"

He adopted a hangdog expression. "Hey now, the road gets lonely. Here is as good a place as any to spend some credits." When Vex snorted with obvious disbelief, he shrugged, but his voice lost its teasing drawl and shifted straight into business mode. "We just finished escort duty for a family needing an armed guard on their trip from Salt Lake. The man of the house is a bit worried about his overabundance of daughters, what with the recent unrest on the routes. While we were in town, a little bird mentioned trouble to Dog, trouble with a bounty." He slid a pointed look in Math's direction and turned back to her. It was enough to leave Vex's stomach in knots. Bane lifted his bottle. "And you know Dog…"

"He decided to go sniffing." Vex was aware that if Dog thought trouble was drifting through, he'd be all over it, looking for the most profitable angle. In this instance, maybe using Reaper's inquiry to jump ahead of Math to collect the supposed bounty. She tried not to curse because if they had to dodge the Dogs of War while hunting down Cam, they were beyond screwed.

"Yep." Bane took a drink.

"Catch any interesting scents?" Math's quiet question held an underlying hum of menace.

All pretense of indifference went up in a puff of smoke and the air at the table went electric. The tension wrapped along Vex's muscles tightened as the two men danced on the razor edge of violence.

Bane's eyes narrowed, but Vex was grateful to note, his relaxed position didn't change, and he moved out along that edge. "You looking for one in particular?"

Math kept his balance with startling ease. "Might be."

Bane made a move. "Maybe one that belongs to that crazy bitch?"

"You find that one—" Math parried, "—I'll be more than happy to join the hunt, but thinking you'll come up empty there."

"Maybe, but you never can tell who or what pops up around here." The two men held each other's gaze and Vex had no idea what silent manly conversation took place, but the testosterone-choked atmosphere lightened. "However, I'm happy to share your interest with Dog."

"You do that."

Bane dipped his chin in acknowledgement.

Right, now that the boys were done comparing dicks, Vex

toed Bane's chair and reclaimed his attention. "You going to answer my question now?"

Bane dropped back into his easy-going role and drawled, "Depends."

With exaggerated patience Vex said, "Anything stinking more than usual around here?"

She grabbed what looked like a chicken leg and then nudged her plate in his direction when he went after another fry. He pulled it closer. "Other than the infestation of snoopers, not yet."

More resigned than surprised by his answer, she nibbled on her chicken. It would've been nice to have a starting point so she and Math could bypass the guaranteed messy interaction with Trip and go straight for retrieval. Plus, the thought of putting the boom-blocks into Trip's sketchy hands made her uneasy. Of course, they still had to get rid of the shadows tagging their tracks.

Hmm, what if... her mind spun with possible options that covered both the explosives and soldiers. Her thoughts derailed when someone in the crowd tagged Bane's attention.

He jerked his chin in recognition and got to his feet. "Gotta bounce." He rapped his knuckles against the table. "You two sticking around?"

Vex grimaced. "Just long enough to make Gus's delivery. Hoping to head out in the morning." Which was probably wishful thinking, but it could happen.

"Right then. We hear anything before then, we'll let you know." He lifted his fist to her.

She tapped her knuckles to his. "Appreciate it."

With nothing more than a nod to Math, Bane moved off and disappeared into the crowd.

Since their upcoming evening was jam-packed with exciting events like trudging into the pit of slime that was the Hole and hooking up with a lunatic with violent tendencies, Vex decided to tuck in and finish her meal. There was no telling when they'd get the luxury of enjoying the next one. Next to her, Math did the same, and companionable silence fell between them.

When their plates were empty, Math spoke. "Guess it was too much to hope for."

It was easy for her to follow his thoughts since his priority was finding Cam. "Yeah," she agreed. "But we're not done yet."

"Dealing with Trip..." Math shook his head and absently drummed his fingers on the table. "Vex, you and I both know that's a slippery ass slide."

Yep, right into hell, but... "Got any other ideas?" Because no matter how she turned it, she came up empty. The noticeable presence of soldiers meant they were on the right track, but the Hole covered a shit ton of ground, ground that was littered with hidey-holes. The only way to get close to the right one, was to deal with the one person who knew the area better than anyone else—Trip.

Math curled his hand into a fist and stared over the crowd. Finally, he grimaced. "Fuck if I can think of one."

She got his frustration. Boy, did she get it. "Right, so we deal with the devil and hope we don't get fucked." It wasn't much comfort, but it was all she had to give. *And wasn't that a kick in the ass? This need to comfort the man next to her?*

His gaze drifted over her face, his thoughts hidden. "You don't have to do this."

What the hell game was he playing now? She leaned forward, arms folded on the table, and didn't bother to hide the ice-coated steel in her voice. "Promised Reaper."

His lips twitched, but whatever he found humorous didn't touch his eyes. "And you don't break promises."

"Right." There was something in his tone she couldn't decipher, and with her temper pricked by his implication that she'd even consider walking away, she was in no mood to worry about it. "We head in, make enough noise to catch Trip's attention—"

"And our shadows."

"And our shadows," she agreed. "Once we have a location on Cam, we pick our spot and grab our stalkers. Hopefully they'll be talkative so we can go pick up your guy and get him back to Pebble Creek." And yes, there were a hundred different snags in the scenario, but if they wanted to save Math's man, this was what they had to work with.

Math's response was grim. "We're going to get fucked."

Yeah, odds were they would, but that was how the game was played. Impatiently, she snapped, "Fine, let's just be sure we can walk away when we're done." She pressed her palms to the table, ready to leave.

His hand shot out and wrapped around her wrist, stopping her. His gaze burned into hers. "With Cam."

Unable to deny the fierce demand, she promised, "With Cam."

twelve

An edgy impatience rode Math as he led the way out of the lung-clogging haze of the eatery and back into the relatively fresh air outside. He stopped at the top of the steps, dropped his tinted lenses to help cut back the sear of afternoon sunlight, and rolled his shoulders. Vex swept past and headed to the street rat keeping an eye on their bike. He left her to it and tried to pinpoint what the hell was wrong with him.

His infamous control was tenuous at best and there was a cloud of doom dogging his heels. Neither boded well when they were preparing to drop into the devil's den. Vex's earlier claim that he might be on friendly terms with death held merit, but he had no intentions of turning it into a permanent partnership.

He picked apart the emotional morass. First up, frustration. Being forced to wait until things lined up so he could go after Cam was chaffing Math's ass. As a Strix, offense was his preferred approach method, not defense. Worry lay under that. He hadn't lied to Vex when he said they were fucked when it came to dealing with Trip.

Previous, painful experience had carved the hard-earned knowledge that if there was a way for Trip to profit from multiple parties, he'd be all over it. In this situation? Fucking prime pickings for Trip, especially since Math was dragging a bounty and soldiers along his trail. Which meant when he and Vex finally copped a face-to-face with the psychopath, they would have to watch their backs.

There was nothing wrong with risking his neck, just another day in the life. But dangling Vex's out there, too? *Fuck that.* Bile crawled up Math's throat and it had nothing to do with imagining Reaper's reaction should something happen to her.

"Fucking white knight syndrome will get you killed, brother."

Cam's warning from years earlier whispered in Math's ear, and harsh though it was, as he watched the infuriatingly sexy and equally lethal woman deal with the kid, the truth of it perversely steadied him. Yeah, she could handle herself. A fact proven multiple times over, from how she found him in the ally, to how she dealt with Reaper, all the way though her latest interaction with Bane.

Math gritted his teeth as he ran face first into the realization that he was fucking jealous of her easy relationship with the mercenary. How the hell she managed to get to him, so deep and so fast, was anyone's guess, but Math couldn't deny the attraction between them. It would be stupid to try considering the lame ass excuses they used to touch and tease. But it wasn't just sexual, because if it was, watching her and that bastard, Bane, wouldn't have scraped him raw.

It was obvious to him that Vex was oblivious to Bane's underlying motives, but Math hadn't missed the purely male interest in the other man's gaze as he watched Vex. It had taken too much self-control not to plant his fist into Bane's smirking face. Repeatedly.

Someone bumped his shoulder, and riding the mean edge of his temper, he turned his head, his lips curling back on a snarl, only to have Vex's voice cut through his dark thoughts and slipping temper.

"Hey, hotshot, we riding?"

Turning, he was hit with the image of her—long legs, curves, witchy face under a tangle of ebony-streaked sable. Lust took front and center, offering a carnal image of the kind of ride he'd prefer. He throttled a groan as his dick got enthusiastically on board. He shook his head like a hound shedding water, knocked the image out of focus, and started down the stairs. "Yeah."

She waited for him by the bike, the street rat nothing but a memory. When Math got close, he could feel her studying him, even though her gaze was hidden behind the dark lenses. "You good?"

Not even close. "Yeah," he lied. "We got a plan, or are we just going to dive in and hope we don't get sucked under?"

Her lips twitched. "Figure our soldier boys aren't too far behind us. So, getting across, not an issue." She looked to the river, and he followed her gaze. "Getting through that..." From where they stood, the tops of the trees guarded both sides and spread out like an emerald canopy, while the forest underneath marked the line between those with mercy and those without. "Not getting ambushed, that'll be tricky."

"Tricky, but doable," he agreed.

"You know," calculation colored her voice as she continued, "there is a possible upside to going in there."

"And what would that be?"

She lowered her voice, keeping their conversation as private as possible considering their surroundings. "Our shadows are city dwellers. We disappear inside that, and they go to follow, means we can circle around and let them forge the path."

He thought of the soldiers tramping through the dense vegetation with the finesse of a bull in a china shop and vicious satisfaction filled him. "We let them trigger the traps."

"Exactly." She shot him a fierce grin, sharing his anticipation of turning the tables on their trackers. "Then, when they're all tangled up, we happen in to offer our help."

He arched a brow. "For a price."

"Of course. Nothing in life is free, right?"

He gave a hum of appreciation for her idea as it meant they wouldn't have to worry about the logistics of setting a trap, just take advantage of what was already in place. But... "What about those already in place, you know, just waiting for some idiot to come traipsing through?"

She tilted her head. "If we play it right, the city's idiots will trot in all cocky. We take care of them where we have enough privacy to ask our questions and get rid of the evidence."

He analyzed her plan. Boise sat on the edge of the Lolo Forest, a sprawling wilderness that reconfigured Idaho and surrounded the current reincarnation of the city. The river ran through town, and once upon a time the nearby greenbelt might have been a well-tended ribbon, but now it was nothing so tame. Over the years the vegetation reclaimed the ground, swallowing pieces of the city along the way until only the forest remained. Thanks to a zoo that didn't survive the Collapse, there were stories of non-native wildlife living within the wild tangle. Trip's people used both the landscape and wildlife to lethally discourage unwanted visitors to the Hole. It made for a simple and effective checkpoint.

Finally, he conceded. "Risky, but it could work."

"Gee, don't sound so surprised." She bumped his shoulder. "I can come up with good ideas every now and then."

Her humor slid over his unsettled emotions, dulling the sharp edge, and he shared her grin. "I'll give you this one."

She rolled her eyes. "Mighty generous of you."

He chuckled at her dry comment and ran a hand through his hair, startled when he encountered the shorter strands. *Damn, that would take some getting used to.* "We'll have to stash the bike and bags on this side of the river, then make the rest of the trip on foot."

"Yeah, no way to sneak up with an engine in full throttle." She worried her bottom lip. "Got an idea." She angled her chin in the direction of the river. "There's a path, mostly hidden, that runs alongside. It leads to the old steel bar bridge. Last time I used it, there was a shack tucked off the path. If it's still standing, we can stash the bike there."

"Means we'll have to double back to the bridge, which might get us unwanted attention."

She rolled her shoulders. "True, but using the main bridge keeps the truly curious eyes focused on us."

It could work. By using the most direct route it would guarantee the soldiers would follow, which in turn would get Trip's people's attention. "Once we're out of sight, we can circle around, come at them from behind."

"Got ourselves a plan then."

He threw his leg over the bike, kicked it to life, and waited as she climbed on behind him. He walked the bike back, turned it around, and headed back along the main road. He followed Vex's directions to the turn off, then wound along the path at the greenbelt's edges. Other than a couple of travelers heading in the opposite direction, they appeared to be the only ones on it.

They rode along the river for a handful of minutes before Vex squeezed his waist, pointed out a barely discernible turnoff among the thick tree-trunks, and put her lips next to his ear. "Stop here."

He slowed and pulled in.

Vex hopped off and slipped away before he shut the bike

down. The engine was ticking into silence when she returned. "This way."

He got off and walked the bike into the foliage. When he spotted the still standing weathered boards of an old shed, he gave a low whistle of appreciation. Looked like their luck was holding strong. Together they managed to get the bike inside. They took a few minutes to pull a variety of knives and supplies from their bags, and then tucked them into pockets and other hiding spots. He adjusted the harness that held the set of razor-sharp blades along his back.

"Ready?" Vex tucked Gus's package into one oversized pocket in a battered leather vest she pulled on.

He shoved the last short blade into the side of his boot, dropped his foot, and did a quick body twist to check for ease of movement. "Yep."

They left the bike and bags in the shed and then shifted the surrounding vegetation to once again conceal the structure. Not wanting to advertise their presence, they took the time to blur their passage as they made their way back to the narrow path. Ten minutes later they were back at the main bridge and had rejoined the spotty crowds.

They didn't rush, but instead paused at various stalls to examine the offerings and indulge in casual conversation, knowing their pursuers lurked among the crowd. They steadily made their way further across and closer to the forest, their passage earning numerous turned heads. Not unusual since most travelers preferred the safer side of the river.

They ran across a tinker busy fixing a broken axle on his wagon while his horse stood with a cocked foreleg and his tail making desultory attempts at keeping the flies at bay. He looked up as they approached, squinting against the afternoon light. "Afternoon."

"Afternoon," Math returned. "Need some help there?"

The tinker straightened and pressed his hands into the small of his back as he bowed his spine. "Nah, just about done." He gave them a once-over, not missing the weapons tucked here and there. "You heading in there?" He tilted his head towards the greenbelt. When Math nodded, the tinker grimaced. "Might want to rethink that, even with that hardware."

"Appreciate the advice," Vex said. "But not much choice, got a job to do. You know how it is."

"Yeah, I hear ya." He rubbed a hand over his narrow chin and shook his head solemnly. "Best take care and hope the pay's worth it, because dead men don't spend much money."

Math couldn't help but snort at the wry pearl of wisdom. "Hoping to avoid that outcome but appreciate the head's up." With that, he and Vex left the last of humanity behind and headed into lush depths of the greenbelt.

thirteen

Once under the verdant protection of the forest, the temperature noticeably dropped, and Math was grateful this was happening in mid-afternoon versus evening. By the time darkness hit, hopefully they'd be somewhere relatively safe in the Hole, preferably with Cam.

If wishes were horses, beggars would ride. It was a saying his mother had been fond of sharing and it fit now.

He followed Vex along the nearly imperceptible path, and conscious of how voices carried, they shifted to hand signals to communicate. They kept their eyes peeled for traps and stepped carefully, tension shadowing their slow progress. Math estimated they were about a half mile in when he noted the fresh scars on a tree trunk to their left. He reached out and snagged the back of Vex's vest, bringing her to a halt.

She froze as he stepped up to her side and pointed out the marks. Only one animal created marks that uniform. A careful scan and a timely breeze revealed the thin wire stretched across the path ahead at both ankle and neck level. With the odds high that unfriendly eyes were currently trained on them, Math pulled one of his blades free, while Vex did the same.

Cunning, devious bastards.

One at a time, they stepped between the tripwires and left the trap undisturbed. Once safely on the other side, Math dismantled the neck level wire. If their shadows hit this, they'd lose their heads, which meant no one would answer his questions. After Vex freed the other end, Math coiled it, and with no room in his already stuffed pockets, tossed the bundle of thin wire deeper into the undergrowth.

He rejoined Vex in the middle of the path, and as the hair on the back of his neck stood on end, he pulled his second blade free. Shadows shifted in the dense vegetation ahead and held their attention. Even as Math focused on the figure strolling towards them, there was a whisper of movement up and behind him to the right.

Looks like the greeter's partners stuck to the branches above. Smart.

Light and shadows shifted as a beefy male covered in layers of browns and greens stepped forward and deliberately blocked their way. Thick arms decorated in colorful ink were folded over a broad chest. Those same designs crawled over his skull and disappeared into an impressive mohawk. Under a series of metal rings dark eyes glinted with feral anticipation, and thin lips curled into a sneer. "You lost?"

"Nope," Vex shot back, one hand on a cocked hip, the other occupied as she wove her blade through her fingers with a skilled deliberateness. "Know exactly where we're going."

Mohawk boy jerked his gaze from Vex's mesmerizing dance of metal and flesh to her face, his sneer tightening. "That right?" He turned to Math, his gaze tagging the blades, then returning to eye level. "Nice slicers." His unvoiced threat dripped with avarice.

Unimpressed, Math adjusted his hold and bared his teeth in mock friendliness. "They do the job."

Mohawk matched Math's hostile grin. "I bet they do."

Overhead leaves rustled and quivered as Mohawk's partners inched into place, but neither Math nor Vex looked away from the immediate threat. Mohawk dropped his arms and moved forward another foot or so, shrinking the distance but not enough for Math to risk attacking.

Still playing the distraction game, their new friend kept up the not so witty conversation. "Where'd you pick 'em up?"

As much as Math wanted to lunge, he wouldn't leave Vex to face an unknown number of fighters, all with the higher ground advantage, alone. But Mohawk wasn't the only one who could play the distraction game.

"Custom made, out of New Seattle." Math shifted forward, twisting his wrist to demonstrate the blade's lethal beauty, and drew Mohawk's attention away from the other lethal beauty at Math's back. "Why? Interested?"

The blunted angles of Mohawk's face tightened as greed and calculation took control. "Actually, yeah. But don't get into town much."

There was a collection of snickers that gave Math a possible count of at least three more in the trees. *Two to one odds, doable.*

Mohawk shifted his stance as an ugly hunger filled his face, his hands curling and uncurling at his sides. "To save me some time, why doncha hand one over?"

Love to, asshole, just need you to come a little bit closer.

Determined to turn his wish into a reality, Math coated his voice with arrogant contempt. "Now why would I want to do that?"

Like a whip to a horse, Mohawk's shoulders snapped tight, and his muscles quivered with a need to lunge. Then he settled, barely. "You want through and I'm hankerin' for a new blade. Even trade in my books."

Math silently cursed Vex as she shifted from behind him and came up to his side, deliberately drawing Mohawk's attention. "Funny, seems to me you're getting the better end of the deal." She tapped the tip of her blade against her chin, then pointed it at Mohawk. "Now, say you offer to carry us in, on your back, like the jackass you are."

Math tensed as anger swept over Mohawk's ugly mug.

Vex's mocking grin didn't even flicker. "That's a trade we might consider."

Instead of the expected explosion of fury and spit, Mohawk rocked to his toes. Math barely clocked the flash as a knife dropped into Mohawk's fist before he leapt. Math went to intercept Mohawk leaving Vex to deal with the incoming attack from above.

Behind them, the rush of air sounded, and the shift of light revealed three more fighters as they dropped from the trees to play. Grounded, Vex and Math didn't wait for their attackers to touch down, instead they rushed in, taking advantage of the overly dramatic entrance.

Math closed in with Mohawk and a distant part of his brain noted they were evenly matched in height despite their weight difference. However, it didn't stop Mohawk from closing in with bruising force. Metal flashed, then shrieked with ear-splitting pitch as edge met edge, neither man giving ground. For a moment they stood there, teeth bared, locked in a violent embrace. The standoff couldn't last, and knowing that, Math shifted his weight and tipped the balance.

Mohawk stumbled forward as Math hit the ground in a roll. He didn't stay down long but used the momentum of his fall to roll to his feet with a fighter's grace. Mohawk darted in, his reach such it had Math jerking back and pivoting so not to get his gut laid wide open. Math blocked Mohawk's slice with one blade and brought his second into play. Mohawk skillfully executed a complicated move and managed to avoid the worst of Math's wicked swipe with his second blade.

Math deflected a gut shot, then a quick-silver throat strike.

Stings of minor injuries bloomed as they continued to circle in search of an opportune opening. As their blades clashed and blurred, the iron scent of fresh blood rode the air.

A sixth sense, honed by years of fighting multiple opponents and covering his own ass, had Math ploughing his fist into Mohawk's face, even as he swung out with his other hand, shifting to a reverse hold on his blade. Math's fist landed on Mohawk's nose with an audible crack, but Math continued his spin, his blade leading, until he faced the idiot trying to stab him in the back. The same idiot now clutching his midsection and trying to keep his guts in place, as he dropped to his knees with an agonized wail.

Grunts, curses, and the occasional yell came from behind Math, reassuring him that Vex was keeping her targets busy. For how much longer was anyone's guess, but Math had bigger problems. Mohawk charged and with a flick of a wrist, Math flipped his blade until he was holding the sharp end and sent it sailing through the air. It flew true and sank into Mohawk's shoulder with enough force to break his momentum. Math didn't waste the momentary distraction and went in low, using the lethal X pattern that was as natural as breathing to him. A ruby red trail bloomed in his wake.

Mohawk backhanded Math with a heavy fist, demonstrating he earned his skills on the street. Math stumbled back as white stars exploded over his vision and his ears rang. Luckily, he still blocked the incoming punch by locking Mohawk's arm and wrenching it back. A bellow was followed the sickening sound of bone breaking. But it wasn't enough to stop a fist from sinking into Math's side. Pain lit every nerve ending and reignited the misery of Math's earlier injuries. His mind shifted into a cruel clarity driven by survival.

Time to end this shit.

Math gritted his teeth, shifted his stance and set a foot behind his foe's legs. With an explosion of strength, he twisted, using his weight against Mohawk, and forced the other off balance, until he stumbled back. Between the unexpected move and blood loss, Mohawk's reaction time lagged. Math's blade flashed, flesh parted, and blood flowed. In a matter of moments, Mohawk's corpse lay at Math's feet.

A shift in the light or air, brought Math's head up. "Oh shit!" Without taking his gaze from what headed towards them, he raised his voice, "Vex, incoming!"

"A little busy here, hot shot!" He looked back to see Vex dodge a swipe from the whipcord scarecrow determined to slash her to pieces.

"Drop him, dammit!" He turned back to see the figures pouring from the surrounding foliage. He turned back to Vex, jumped over the still groaning (albeit weakly) backstabber, and with a brutal jab to the base of a skull, sent one of Vex's opponents back to the ground in a boneless heap. "We need to move!"

He checked their company's approach again and suddenly found himself eating dirt when a weight slammed into his back, the impact sending his blade skittering across the forest's floor. Something tangled in his hair and pulled, forcing his head back. Flattening his hands against the ground, Math's muscles tensed to move only to freeze at the cool kiss of metal against his throat.

"I wouldn't, pretty boy." The sibilant threat coiled around his ear and sent chills down his wrenched neck.

His muscles quivered with the need to move, but since he wasn't keen on acquiring a ruby necklace, Math stilled and gritted his teeth.

A nasty chuckle sounded. "Smart." The fingers in his hair tightened and pulled, forcing Math's neck back further. The edge of the blade pressed closer, opening a stinging line in warning. "Call your bitch off."

From his prone position, Math was forced to watch as five

men surrounded the clearing. A couple leveled crossbows at what Math figured was Vex since the dangerous points were aimed at a target behind him. The undeniable threat triggered a bitter, metallic taste. He ignored the flash of fear for Vex and embraced the icy fury at being caught in such a position. *Motherfucking son of a bitch!* Outnumbered and outgunned, he went along. For now.

"Ease up," he squeezed out. The pressure eased, not enough to consider making a move, but enough he could talk without cutting his own throat. "Vex!" When the sounds of a struggle continued unabated behind him, he throttled back a frustrated growl and snapped, "Vex!"

A pain-filled yip sounded, then an endless moment later came a clearly furious and feminine snarl. "What?"

"You done?" *Okay, not what the ass threatening to fillet him meant, but...*

A very put-upon sigh was followed by a whimper, both echoing through the strangely tense quiet. "Maybe. You okay?"

Depended on your definition of okay.

Before he could answer, a man separated from the others and sank to crouch in front of Math. He didn't say a word as he used the tip of his bowie knife to tilt Math's chin back even further. From his forced angle, Math took in the shit brown hair that hung in a tangle of knots and braids around a narrow face pitted with scars. Brown eyes stared into his with a depth of coldness Math recognized—from one killer to another. The unspoken message came through loud and clear.

With no choice, Math held the merciless stare and finally answered her. "As long as your boy keeps breathing. So, be gentle, yeah?"

fourteen

With her back to a thick tree trunk, Vex tightened her grip on the stiff scarecrow she held and wished his long limbs offered more substance as a shield, say like the moron laid out by Math, but beggars couldn't be choosers. She used her hold and her knife to shift her human shield's position so if one of the jumpy jennies tried something they would have to go through him first.

And there were plenty of nervous nellies standing around, but the ones that worried her were the roly-poly gnome perched on Math's back, his long blade held at Math's throat, and the ugly bastard with a viciously thick knife crouched in Math's face. Based on the size of their weapons, it was safe to assume they were compensating for size in other areas.

As tempting as it was to share her snarky insight or tighten her metal-tipped hand on the vulnerable throat in her grip, she refrained because the uneven odds equaled messy. Despite her racing pulse, she kept her voice cool and casual. "So long as they don't damage your pretty face, hot shot, I'll be as careful as a whore in church."

Somewhere close the dull thud of a fist sinking into soft

flesh cut off a snicker, but the ugly fucker in charge turned his head slowly and flicked a glance to the man in her arms. Not for a second did she think he missed her knife poised at the unfortunate fool's kidney or the lethal claws at his throat.

He turned his soulless gaze to hers, and she took the hit without a flinch, despite the chill settling heavy in her gut. "There's more where that came from, so why shouldn't I have mine slice and dice yours?"

A tremor shook the man she held as his soft whimper escaped. She couldn't blame him, boss man's voice was creepy, like slimy cobwebs. *Definitely one badass mofo.* Almost Reaper-esque. But almost didn't count, and despite the frantic warnings of common sense that begged her to shut the hell up, she couldn't do it. "You do that, and guaran-fucking-teed mine will come in and leave nothing but ashes and bones in their wake."

Ugly turned his knife from Math's chin and pointed it at her. "Even if that's true, you'd still be dead."

She peeked around her human shield and made sure her manic grin couldn't be missed. "But I'll be laughing my ass off in hell when Reaper sends you boys down to join me." Her grin went vicious. "Last I heard, Reaper's patience with Trip was just about done. Can't say I blame him." When the gnome jerked Math's head again, she lost her grin and pinned the little shit with a hard stare, her voice arctic. "Do that again and I'll put your boy down, and make sure you're right on his heels."

Ugly flicked his hand, and Gnome loosened his hold.

Vex acknowledged the move with a chin lift. "Now, I'll be happy to return your boy for mine. And just for the record, we didn't start this."

Without taking his attention from her, Ugly rose to his feet and pointedly looked at the bodies on the ground. "Didn't you?"

"Can't blame us because your boys lack simple manners. Anyone ever tell them it's impolite to take things that don't belong to them?" She didn't wait for a response, not that she expected one. "Besides, people tend to be a little possessive about their things. Some of us more than others." Her gaze touched briefly on the dead between them. "And, well, I'm not so good with sharing."

"Is that so?" It was hard to tell with that face, but it might have been amusement that pierced his emotionless mask before it settled back into place. "You'll have to excuse their rudeness, we don't get much company. And the company we get is normally by invitation only." He cocked his head and a dangerous light lit in his dark gaze. "Don't remember sending an invite to Fate's Vultures."

Okay so, maybe the normal fear associated with the Vultures didn't apply here, but that didn't mean she couldn't brazen her way through this cluster. "You didn't, but I got a delivery for Trip from Gus. Figured that was invitation enough." She paused. "Or am I wrong?"

"Depends." He tucked his bowie into its battered sheath strapped to his thigh and the tension in the clearing dropped a notch. "Delivery boy is a bit below the Vultures' norm."

Despite her position—and the ache in her side pressuring her to change it up quick—she managed a creditable shrug. "Usually, but my bike needed Gus's touch and a walk in the woods seemed like an even trade." She used her blade to motion at Ugly's band of thugs and their current standoff. "Kind of rethinking that now."

"Understandable." He held her gaze and scratched at his chest. "What kind of delivery?"

Since this was Trip's man, she didn't bother to lie. "The kind that goes boom."

Ugly's misfits exchanged knowing glances and a whisper of excitement broke out. It was quickly silenced when Ugly shot them a single look. Order restored, he signaled the gnome, who released Math and sprung back with surprising grace.

Math took his time regaining his feet and reclaiming his blades, before wiping a hand over the thin trail of blood on his neck.

"Your turn."

With Math armed and, on his feet, Vex gave Ugly his point, but she put her lips to Scarecrow's ear and warned, "Don't be stupid."

She peeled her fingers from his throat and with a not so nice shove sent him stumbling forward. The tangle of arms and legs stumbled over to a bigger man armed with a crossbow and once at his side, turned and shot her a shaky sneer.

Instead of snapping her teeth in response, she eyed the steely-eyed archer. "Be careful where you point that thing."

He didn't react until Ugly simply said, "Win", and then the crossbow dropped.

With the threat of imminent impalement delayed and looking unconcerned about being outnumbered, Math walked over and did a quick head to toe exam. "You good?"

She returned the favor and noted the smears of blood decorating his skin and clothes. Nothing serious, just the expected results from a knife fight. "Yeah, you?"

"I'll live."

"Good to know," she muttered as the men around them began to move, sticking to the shadows and gathering their injured and dead.

Ugly, Gnome and Win huddled in an intense conversation, and Math shifted to Vex's side. "Think we're about to get an escort."

"Sure looks like it." Vex played her blade through her fingers and kept her voice low. "Screws our plans for our shadows."

"Maybe not," Math murmured back. "If these guys are busy with us, makes it easier for them to slip through."

Maybe, but if Trip's men decided to eliminate the soldiers first, maybe not. Deciding to put a little faith in Math's optimism, she looked on the bright side. If the soldiers made it through to the Hole, she and Math might get their chance for that talk. Even better, once their Q&A session concluded the Hole was the perfect spot for disposing of whatever remained. Hell, if Lady Luck was feeling generous, she and Math could pin the soldiers' disappearance on Trip and redirect the resulting heat.

As Ugly took point and Gnome motioned for her and Math to follow, Vex smiled.

By the time Ugly led Vex and Math through the streets guarded by shattered buildings afternoon had slipped into evening. Vex didn't need the skittering sense of unease to know they were being watched. Maybe it should have concerned her but drumming up the energy to worry was too much work. If experience taught her anything, it was that worrying was a fucking waste of time. Shit happened, and there wasn't much you could do but roll with it.

Right now, though, her roll was a bit slow. On the hike in it hit her that it this was turning out to be a very long day. At this particular moment, she concentrated on putting one foot in front of the other instead of humiliating herself by tripping over her feet and kissing dirt. It didn't help that her adrenaline levels took a nosedive replaced by the various aches and pains clamoring for attention.

Suck it up, buttercup!

The pitiless reminder sounded suspiciously like Reaper,

but it worked, slapping her out of her funk and refocusing her attention on her surroundings. Thankfully Ugly and friends hadn't trussed her or Math up or taken all their weapons. Not that they needed to because it would be stupid to try taking on their motley escorts. Not only would they be skewered before they could blink, but the crew resembled metallic porcupines thanks to the armory they sported. In fact, she had her eye on a particularly intriguing blade Scarecrow kept playing with, in between giving her the hairy eyeball.

They wound their way along the river as it snuck into the Hole, seeping around heaps of rusted, overturned cars, and pooling into nooks and crannies. It made navigation a watery game of hopscotch. Buildings rose into the purpling sky like skeletal fingers while a vegetative scarf wrapped around the crumbling edges. She craned her neck to catch the glint of sunlight high above from the few remaining windows gamely holding on.

Math stumbled into her with a curse, his foot sliding off some half-submerged object. She kept him upright by wrapping her arm around his waist and getting her shoulder under his. She shifted her hold to ease the pressure on his ribs, the white lines around his mouth visual reminders that his previous injuries had little time to heal.

"How bad?" she asked softly, trying to keep the question between them. Not an easy feat with the eerie silence that earmarked abandoned places.

Instead of the expected denial, he gave her the truth. "Bad, but I've survived worse." He glanced at Ugly's back. "I'm surprised he didn't just gut us and take the damn boomer." Math adjusted his arm, so it was less like he was leaning on her and more like holding her.

She adjusted her gait and hold to mimic his and wondered if he knew he was stroking her arm, but since she liked it— maybe too much—she chose to ignore it. "Whether he wants to admit it or not, he's not stupid enough to go up against the Vultures. What I said earlier about Reaper salting the earth, wasn't bullshit."

Wry humor eased a bit of the strain on his face. "Yeah, age hasn't mellowed Reaper's need to exact retribution."

His unexpected opening begged her to barge in and root around for more information on his relationship with Reaper, but before she could their unwanted guide stopped and raised his hand in a silent signal for everyone else to do the same.

Math dropped his arm and his stance switched from exhausted to primed. He withdrew one of his blades and held it with a deceptive casualness as his head did a careful swivel of their surroundings, his focus high. Vex put space between them so she had room and did the same but kept her attention closer to the ground.

A movement in the dim recesses had her warning Math with a soft clicking sound. His angled his head her way and together they watched as figures emerged from the ruins and took up positions around the group. Vex recognized the approach from her days running the streets of Portland. One of the many street gangs that called the Hole home was about to introduce themselves. Hopefully they were on friendly terms with Trip otherwise... "I've got four on this side."

"Five on mine," Math replied.

Welp, they were well and truly surrounded.

A rush of air preceded a loud crash as a whipcord figure landed in a crouch on a rusted-out car roof. As it meant to, the dramatic entrance of who Vex suspected was the leader, caught everyone's attention.

She, on the other hand, would have laughed her ass off if that corroded metal roof disintegrated under leaper boy's feet. Ignorant of her thoughts, he worked his entrance, slowly straightening, before skipping down the car until his booted heels hit the street. Two of his group fell in behind him as he swaggered up to Ugly.

He stopped just out of arm's reach. "What's going, Ori?"

Between the flashy entrance and the cocky attitude, Vex clocked him as a kid, likely mid to late teens, but it was hard to tell because the mix of paint and dirt obscured his face and his frame was draped in a jumble of mismatched clothes. Not that age made him less of a threat.

"Heading in." Ugly, aka Ori, widened his stance, folded his arms over his chest, and matched attitude with ice. "Why the interference, Bon?"

The kid asked a question of his own instead of answering. "Going straight to Trip?"

Ori nodded.

Bon's smirk grew feral, and he motioned to one of his crew. "Got something he might want."

A mix of grunts, curses, and dull *thunks* preceded the appearance of two of Bon's crew dragging a third, bound and gagged, between them. They dumped him at Ori's feet. As soon as the two stepped back, their whimpering gift tried to scramble back. He didn't get far because Bon dropped to a crouch behind him, grabbed a handful of stringy black hair and yanked the captive's head back. Bruised and bloody features came into view and Vex gave them credit for creativity when she clocked the ball gag stuffed in his mouth.

Bon kept his eye on Ori but said, "Say hello."

The eye not swollen shut pinwheeled and the sounds behind the gag picked up as Ori got closer and dropped to his heels, taking him to eye level. "Who's this?"

"This is Milt." Bon used his grip on Milt's hair to pull his head back a little more and Milt's high-pitched whine escaped around his gag. "Milt sold Lily to our tourist."

Vex froze as something ugly raised its head at Bon's answer. *Sold? Did he say sold?* When Math slid her a puzzled glance, she shoved her reaction away and forced her fists to unclench and her shoulders to loosen. *Wrong time, wrong fucking place.*

"Is that right?" While Ori's expression didn't change, there was an unsettling menace to his question.

"Yep," Bon popped the last syllable. "Milt here has been a bad, bad boy." Bon yanked his hand free of Milt's hair, and pushed up, brushing his hands over his thighs.

Milt's head lifted and when his gaze hit Ori's, he froze, like a mouse in front of a very hungry, very large cat.

Ori held the sniveling male's attention and let the tension stretch. Finally, he straightened, and motioned to his men who came and dragged Milt off to the side. He turned to Bon who was now back with his crew. "You get anything from him?"

Feet braced, arms crossed over his chest, Bon shrugged. "Fucking useless excuses." He shot another ugly look to Milt. "If Trip didn't want him, he'd be nothing but a smear in an alley."

Ori grunted, then scanned the watching faces before ending on Bon. "Anything else I should know?"

Bon nodded as he rocked to his toes and back. "Got more nosy bitches sniffing around."

Ori cocked his head. "Where?"

"Here." Bon waved an arm, indicating the direction Vex's group came from, and then started to walk backwards. "There." Another sweep of an arm followed, this time in the other direction. "Every-fucking-where. Don't like Trip puttin' a ban on our play." He sauntered over to Vex and Math. "Don't like being reined in, Ori." He danced closer. "Too many snoopers means they're looking for something." With an unexpected abruptness he stepped between Vex and Math and threw his arms over their shoulders with a manic cheer. His fingers dug into Vex's upper arm as he squeezed. "Or someone, see?" His attention returned to Ori. "Since we can't play, me and mine are in need of a little flash for our pockets. How about we ease your burden?"

Vex briefly considered what moves were necessary should Ori decide to hand them over to the kid who wanted to score a finder's fee.

"Appreciated, but no." Ori's response was hard and flat.

"Could try changing your mind," Bon wheedled.

"How about we change yours?" Vex turned into the kid until they were face-to-face and caught him off guard. Ignoring the stench of body odor, she stepped close and wrapped her arms around his neck in a mocking affectionate move. When the clawed tips of her fingers dug into the back of his neck his eyes widened, and his body went poker straight. She tapped the flat side of her blade against his skull and ensured she had his undivided attention. "I can be very persuasive."

With a cocky grin, Bon proved street smart didn't equal intelligent, by letting Math go to drop his hands straight to Vex's ass. "Could be fun."

Math used his hand to move her head back enough so when his palm knocked against Bon's skull, she didn't end up getting a head-butt. She appreciated the sentiment since she didn't need to add a bloody nose to her growing collection of bodily damages.

Math's head slap was followed by his low growled warning, "Could be fatal, kid."

Bon pulled back and left some hair behind in her metal tips as his lips curled into a fairly decent snarl. When he spun to face Math, there was a flash of metal in his fist. Not keen on letting the kid gut Math, Vex shot out a hand and wrapped it around his wrist.

Undaunted, Math leaned closer, his expression hard enough to rival granite. "You don't seem stupid."

Bon hissed, jerked his arm from Vex's hold and slipped out

from between Vex and Math. In typical teen fashion he spat, "Asshole."

Vex shifted until Math stood behind her and with a condescending smirk, held the teen's furious gaze. "Run along and find someone else to tag, kid."

Bon hurled a wad of spit in her direction then spun around and stalked away, motioning his crew to follow. Vex and Math watched, as did Ori and his crew, while Bon and his followers faded into the murky shadows.

"Bon."

At Ori's use of his name, the teen turned back. "What?"

"No playing." Ori's unspoken threat vibrated along the distance between the killer and street rat, like tickling a spider's web.

The order earned a flip of a middle finger before Bon clambered up and over the metallic husk of the car and slipped away. A heartbeat, two, passed before Ori said, "Let's go."

He didn't wait for a response, simply turned on his heel and led the way.

Vex sighed and followed the abrupt order because it wasn't like she had much choice. She slipped her knife back into its sheath with a sigh, resettled her vest, and began the trek through the cracked asphalt. She skirted around a tree growing from a manhole and realized Math wasn't following. She stopped and turned back to see him staring off to where Bon had disappeared. He wasn't the only one not moving. One of Ori's men stood silently to the side, his attention on Math and his hand playing with the weapon at his waist.

"Hey, Crow!" she called, and when Math turned, she asked, "You coming?"

Math's shoulders moved as if throwing off a weight, but walked towards her, tucking his knife away. Behind him another of Ori's men slipped out of the ruins and joined the first one, and together they trailed in Math's wake.

She waited until Math reached her before she resumed walking. With a mind to privacy, she kept her voice low. "If you don't want Ori and company honing in on your intentions, don't telegraph them."

Math frowned and shot her a look. "I wasn't intending anything, just wondering about a few things."

She snorted. 'Right.' She couldn't blame him for wanting to follow Bon, but making that move now? Beyond dumb. Better to pump Trip for information, get the psycho's blessing to tromp through his demented little kingdom, and maybe narrow down their search areas. That last item being a necessity because a fatalistic voice insisted Cam was running out of time. *If he hadn't already.* She barely caught her flinch at the thought and snuck a glance at Math's grim expression. Yeah, she wasn't the only one worried.

His expression pinched at her and created an uncomfortable moment as she tried to find some way to offer comfort. Thing was, she remembered what it was like when the Raiders had Simon, the mix of fury, fear, and under it all a gut loosening dread of not moving fast enough. She wasn't sure she had anything to offer Math that would offset the weight of guilt and frustration she knew he was dealing with, so she gave him what she could. "We deal with Trip first. Then we tear through his territory."

Math's answer was a soft grunt as they picked their way through the narrowing trail and kept space between them and their escorts. The rest of the journey passed in silence but Vex memorized the path in case they returned this way.

A hint of smoke and the faint wash of music provided the first signs of life and broke the eerie quiet. Ori led them down a tree-choked street littered with broken red bricks. It wasn't long before the street widened into a circular area surrounded by a mix of single and multi-storied buildings. The structures blocked the fading sunlight, but a series of barrel fires lined both sides of the street and kept the leading edge of darkness at bay.

Light, both natural and generated, glowed from empty window frames or slipped around makeshift barriers. As they passed by shadowed openings harsh laughter rose and fell, carrying a desperate cruelty. A mix of creative propositions and slurs followed in their wake. All of it came together in a familiar chorus, one that resonated on numerous streets in various cities. Born from the ugly pits of poverty and chaos native to the urban centers, the lyrics reflected a shit ton of shattered hopes and twisted lives.

When a grubby hand snatched at her back and latched on to her vest, Vex pivoted and locked her arm on the offender's with vicious speed. A calculated twist and a wrenching turn had the handy bystander on their knees and her knife at their throat. "No touching."

The face that stared back was young in years, but old in experience. A scar, thick and twisted, carved from temple to the snarling mouth. The eye it bisected was a milky white, but the other was a muddy mix of brown and greens. "Fuckin' let me go, bitch!" Long matted hair and the oversized clothes made it difficult to tell gender, but there was a feminine whine in the demand.

Leaving the shifting watchers to Math, Vex tightened her hold, and her prey arched her spine to ease the pressure. Vex adjusted her blade's position so the girl wouldn't slit her own throat. "Don't move." When she was certain she had the girl's attention she said, "Promise to keep your hands to yourself and I'll consider not slitting your throat."

"If I don't?"

Before Vex could answer, a thick hand grabbed the matted mess and dragged the girl out of her grip. The girl's ear-piercing screech cut off abruptly as Ori held her on her toes and stared into her fear-slackened face. He didn't say a word but lifted his gaze and aimed it at the shuffling figures now edging back.

The din of noise fell into a well of silence. He tossed the girl aside and sent her stumbling into the waiting group. They kept her from sprawling on the ground, but as soon as she gained her balance, she was gone, taking her tribe with her. Mutters followed, punctuated by a curse or three, before cresting into the familiar din as activities resumed.

Ori ignored Vex and Math and gave his men a series of silent hand orders that had them closing ranks, keeping Math and Vex surrounded. He set off, his pace unhurried but determined, and left the others to follow.

"Well, that was fun," Vex muttered under her breath.

"Takes skill," Math said, his voice low, his gaze on Ori.

Confused by his out of the blue remark, Vex shot him a quizzical look. "What?"

He lifted his chin in Ori's direction. "To threaten without saying a word."

Vex rolled her shoulders and tried to shake off the subtle tension that resulted from being surrounded by the not-so-friendly. "I don't know about skill, but it's definitely fun."

"You would know."

His cool sarcasm left her grinning. "And you don't?"

His lip twitch spoke louder than words.

fifteen

The Hole hadn't changed much since Math's last visit. Granted, his business had taken him into the darker twists and turns tucked between the buildings and below street level where an entire world of greed, sex, and every other vice you could think of, thrived. Now, with Vex at his side, he was escorted straight into the heart of Trip's domain.

They approached a building that dwarfed the rest and stretched eighteen stories above the mangled streets. Math craned his neck to take it in and wondered how it managed to survive intact. The bottom third of the outside walls wore a pitted finish, created by weather and violence. The floors above still held their reflective surface, with an occasional gap bridged by wood or metal. A random pattern of light danced behind the glass, the brightest collection coming from the sixth floor. Whatever its history, it now housed Trip's loyal—and not so loyal—followers.

Across the street on the flat roof of a two-story building, armed guards held their positions. Vex's muttered, "Figures" told Math he wasn't the only one taking notice of Trip's security. He gave them credit, on the surface it appeared impressive. Thing was, he already clocked a couple of holes he could slip through without earning a bolt in the ass.

Ori led them past graffiti-laced metal sheets that lined the ground floor where door-sized windows once hung. They came to a wide opening guarded by a tall woman armed with a crossbow and a burly male kitted out with various firearms and partnered with, what looked like, a wolf-hybrid.

The woman stepped forward taking the lead. "Ori."

"Tam."

"Heading up?"

"Yeah."

Tam scanned the group, her gaze pausing on Vex and Math and lingering a little longer on the limp form that hung between two of their escorts. She turned to Ori and arched an eyebrow. "See you've managed to find some trouble."

Ori's mouth twitched, once, before he shrugged his shoulders. "Or it found me."

"Uh-huh." Tam sighed, shook her head, stepped back, and waved them through. "Make sure you don't leave a mess."

"This one's all Trip's," Ori replied, then turned his head and lifted his chin to the group behind him before striding inside.

Math stayed at Vex's back as she followed Ori and Gnome through the guarded entrance, and the rest of their escort disappeared into the night. A sudden burst of activity from behind him had him turning to witness a reluctant Milt's fruitless struggle. The men on either side remained unmoved as the noises behind Milt's gag gained strength. Considering Trip's uncertain temperament, Math understood the idiot's misgivings. Given a choice, Math would skip getting permission to hunt in Trip's territory. Unfortunately, Vex was right. They didn't have time to waste, so Math would have to suck it up.

The wide-open main floor was currently filled with clusters of people in the midst of various transactions. Tables were filled with jaded card sharks and their oblivious marks. Others lounged in chairs and on battered sofas, their glassy eyes and dumbass smiles adorned smoke wreathed faces, while the undeniable sweet smell of marijuana hung in the air, carrying a bitter bite.

Then there were the strung-out junkies looking to score, and the boastful grins of those who knew what price the market would bear for hard to obtain products. Credits flashed as they shifted from hand to hand. A tangle of wires siphoning juice powered a pit filled with electronic games the controls manned by a group of kids. Shouts, shoves, and trash talk competed with the buzzes and bells.

Business was booming in the Hole.

He kept pace with Vex, not missing the attention they earned, mainly thanks to Milt's pitiful moans, but as soon as that attention snagged on Ori, it would slither away. Shouts rained from above and he tilted his head back to look up through the open-air center to spot a shoving match underway on the second floor.

Next to him, Vex said, "That's not going to end well."

Together they watched the show as the two men continued to punch and push. Her point held validity considering there was nothing—no railing, no wall—to stop either of the idiots from tumbling off the edge.

"No, it isn't." He put a hand to the small of her back and nudged her a little faster. He had no intentions of being the ones who broke their fall.

Gnome's gaze held a glint of malicious humor as he turned back and caught Math's movement, but the squat little man didn't say a word. They made it through the bottom floor without being hit by falling bodies and walked up the frozen metal staircase to the second level.

Similar scenes from the floor below played out around

them as Ori wound his way through without pausing. The two combatants stumbled across their path in a flailing tangle of body parts, grunts, and curses. An abrupt course correction left Math with no choice but to twist sharply out of the way. He sucked in a breath as torquing his torso reignited the blaze in his ribs. He gritted his teeth and regained his pace.

Ori turned to the left and stopped next to another guarded set of smooth metal doors and relief washed over Math that no more stairs appeared to be in their future. The doors slid open with a few dull *thunks* and a dying ding.

Ori and Gnome positioned on either side. Gnome's grin was all teeth as he mockingly waved Vex inside. "After you."

Vex swept by and patted Gnome's head. Math stayed on her heels and hid his grin. Gnome growled but once Math and Vex were inside tucked in the corners, he and Ori took front position. Ori hit a button, the number worn away from use, and the doors clanked shut.

Math held his breath and braced against the walls as the elevator car lurched its way up like a drunken pinball. He met Ori's gaze in the wavy metallic surface. "Something wrong with the stairs?"

Gnome turned his head. "What's wrong? Scared?"

Math adjusted his weight at another jerky shift of the car, dropped his gaze, and gave him a nasty smile. "Nope, just concerned I'll puke all over you."

Gnome snarled and rocked forward on his toes, only to be brought up short with Ori's low, "Jack."

With one last snarl, Gnome, or Jack, turned back to mimic Ori's stance.

The elevator groaned to a halt, and there was a long moment filled with enough pops and snaps to question how many more trips it had before it became the express to hell for some unfortunate rider. Finally, the doors opened and neither Math nor Vex wasted time exiting the death trap. They stepped out onto a floor much different than the ones below. Behind them the elevator began grinding its way back down to pick up Milt and his escorts.

Ori and Jack led them through an open archway and into a room that carried hints of opulence it once housed. Weather, time, and circumstances blurred the previous grandeur, but glimpses of it peeked through.

Two of the walls were covered in a double row of windows and they melted into a ceiling decorated with weather-worn paintings tucked inside ramshackle trim work stained by smoke. The remaining walls were covered with various store signs cobbled from ransacked buildings and were intermixed with framed artwork. It was strangely compelling art collection.

Some enterprising soul managed to add in eye patches and mustaches on some of the larger portrait paintings. One particular piece dominated by a dour looking man full of disapproval, included a scrawled warning of 'Sees all, knows all'.

Mismatched rugs and furniture, probably dragged in from the same buildings as the artwork, covered the floors. Couches and chairs clustered around a working fire pit, the flames adding a surreal lighting effect to the cavernous ceiling and blind windows. Solar lights dotted the floor as well, pooling their illumination over tables cluttered with unidentifiable items.

Stretched out across chairs, couches, and floor was a multitude of bodies, with heads tipped back, eyes staring with hallucinogenic wonder into the stained ceiling, and blissed-out smiles they represented no threat. The threat came from those shifting out of the light and into the shadows, as they maneuvered to circle the incoming group, including the three figures that shifted from casual to full alert in a mere blink before stealthily moving into position at the opposite end of the room.

Math ignored the dying bell of the elevator arriving and tracked the shadows guarding the perimeter. A pair of gutsy females—one brunette, the other blonde—their courage obviously boosted by whatever they'd inhaled or swallowed approached and Vex slowed to a stop. With admirable coordination the female duo surrounded Math and Vex.

The glassy-eyed blonde played with Vex's braids. "You two looking for some wild?"

Not about to be outdone, the brunette left an impression by trapping Math's arm between her impressive tits. Considering her eyes were unfocused, he wondered if it was more for balance than flirting. Her breath was rancid as she leaned in. "We promise not to disappoint."

Over the brunette's head, Vex flashed him a mischievous smile, then turned to the blitzed blonde, cupped the woman's chin, and used the metal tips of her glove to trace the painted lips. "Darlin', I don't think you're quite up to our kind of wild."

The blonde pouted, but before she could respond, a thick arm wrapped around her waist and pulled her back. "Mind the rules, Amy girl."

The blonde turned in the man's hold until he had no choice but to maintain his grip or find her in a puddle at his feet, her interest in Vex forgotten. "Aww, baby, I know how you like to play."

With practiced ease, the man adjusted his hold and reached out to collect the brunette. "How 'bout this time, we keep it to you, me, and Lynn, 'kay?"

The blonde tipped her head back and it was a wonder she didn't fall backwards. "Sure, baby."

"Can do, stud." The brunette snuggled closer and laid her head on his shoulder, her eyes drifting to half-mast.

The man turned his armful of buzzed females away and led gave Vex a leer that he shared with Math. "If you're feeling wild, find us later."

Math arched a brow but didn't answer since the only kind of wild he was interested in was the woman currently blowing the stumbling trio a kiss.

"When you're done hooking up, you might want to catch up." The warning was Jack's as he waited a few feet away, a sneer on his face, hands on his hips.

"Jealous?" Vex shot back as they caught up with Ori.

They crossed the last bit of distance to the one who waited at the end as swirling chatter filled the overly large room. But as they got closer the din slowly died, creating a wave of silence that was broken by Milt's muffled protests and the high-pitched, nervous giggles of their watchers, who were quickly shushed.

The weight of attention made Math edgy as he was used to drifting on the edges and sticking to the shadows. Especially when he clocked specific individuals who were paying a little too much attention, like the dark-haired man edging along the far wall and staring at Vex as he stalked their progress. There were too many damn threats in the confined space.

Ori slowed to a stop before a makeshift throne padded in black with ornately carved back and arms. Perched on a collection of wooden crates arranged to create a trio of steps under a faded blue flag sporting a yellow seal and the still readable words STATE OF IDAHO, it held Trip and a slender female curled in his lap, her head resting against his shoulder, her face shadowed by his hold.

The only feature Math could make out was her rainbow-colored hair. In stark contrast, Trip's long brown dreadlocks were pulled back from a rough-hewn face inked with an intricate design that did little to disguise the precise scars that marred his visage. Those scars continued down his thick arms, indicating Trip had spent some time at the mercy of someone's knife.

The facial tattoo connected with a neatly trimmed goatee and matching soul patch. Light glinted off his pierced lower as he held a bottle of brew in one hand and gestured with the other as he talked to a person sprawled on a nearby couch. To complete the image of self-indulgence, Trip had one leg thrown over the chair's arm while the other bounced in a restless beat. He broke off his conversation and watched them approach.

Off to the throne's side was a metal kennel with a person huddled inside. The smell indicated whoever it was, had been there for some time. The tatters that passed for clothes did jack shit to conceal the bruises and blood testifying to prolonged torture.

Unfortunate fuck.

Trip waited until the group stood below him before swinging his leg from the chair's arm and nudging the slender, but by no means fragile, woman from his lap. She slid to the side of the chair, the move revealing the purple and yellow bruising that ran from her temple to chin, indicating someone had a vicious backhand. Not Trip, though, because there was too much arrogance in that jutting chin and fierce gaze, an arrogance that wouldn't be tolerated by whoever thought raising his fist to her was acceptable.

Trip leaned forward in his seat, braced his elbows on his knees, and shot them a crazy-assed grin. Math's worry they caught him after he had indulged in the drugs being passed around was shot to hell when those mismatched eyes hit his. The only thing in those crystal-clear depths was speculation. Trip's gaze slid to Ori. "Well, well, well." He lifted his drink, threw some back, then wiped his chin with the back of his hand. "I see you brought me visitors!"

Ori's response was blunt. "Found them in the Green mixing it up with Tribble's crew."

"The Green?" Trip pushed to his feet, stretched, and aimed his gaze to Vex. Recognition tightened his smile and hardened his gaze. He waved a hand and Ori and Jack stepped aside, giving Trip a clear path to Vex. He took his time coming down the three steps. "What is a Vulture doing in my Green?"

Math didn't like Trip's vibe and since Vex had no sense of self-preservation, he braced.

Sure enough, she answered, "Giving your boys a lesson in manners."

Her response put a hitch in Trip's step, and he paused on the last step and blinked. "Who the hell needs manners?"

Vex opened her mouth but didn't get a chance to answer because as soon as Trip's foot hit the floor, a furious shriek erupted from behind him. He barely caught Rainbow as she rushed by him, snagging her around the waist with one arm.

Undeterred, Rainbow's attention was focused on the quivering form of Milt half hidden behind Vex and Math as she clawed at Trip's restraining arm. "You mother fucking son of a traitorous bitch!"

"What the fuck, Lily?" Trip barely kept her contained but did a hell of a job salvaging his bottle of brew.

The enraged female might be slender, but she was deter-mined. "That's the fucker, Trip." She kept trying to pry his arm from her waist, her lips peeled back as she glared at the cringing Milt. "That's the piece of shit who sold me to the tourist."

As the scene played out Math didn't miss Vex's quickly masked flinch or the way her lips tightened, and her eyes narrowed. There was something there, something he needed to get at later, much later.

Trip's lazy humor fled, replaced by a hard-eyed calculation. "That so?" He eyed Milt and tucked his chin on Lily's shoulder. "Not to worry, sweets, we'll make sure he apologizes." He whispered something more in her ear, and whatever he said knocked her death glare down to feral satisfaction.

She calmed and patted Trip's arm. "Okay, babe. I can wait for that." She shot a vicious grin at Milt. "This will be so much fun." She pressed a quick kiss to Trip's inked cheek, then skipped out of his hold and joined the man sprawled on the couch.

Trip turned to Ori. "Where'd you find him?"

"Hand delivered, courtesy of Bon." Ori shot Milt a disgusted look. "His name is Milt."

"Milt, uh?" Trip took another drink from his bottle, strode past Math, and crouched in front of a clearly terrified Milt. "Milt, buddy, you have some explaining to do." He tapped his bottle against Milt's glistening forehead. "Once I finish with our guests, you, me, and Lily are going to have a chat." He straightened and ordered the two handlers, "Take him to the conference room. Sit on his ass until we arrive."

Milt was whisked away, leaving Vex and Math to take his place. Trip turned, his bottle hanging from his fingers as he sauntered over to Vex. He stopped, lifted his hand, and managed to point his index finger, wiggling it inches from her face. "Where's the rest of your gang?"

Vex lifted her chin, tilted her head, and folded her arms over her chest. Her lip curl was echoed in her derisive tone. "Hello to you too, Trip."

The calculation that slipped into Trip's gaze made Math antsy. So did the way he stayed on topic. "Where's Reaper?"

"Not here." Proving she hadn't missed a thing, she informed him, "You may as well know, before you start playing your games, Reaper knows I'm here."

Math's fingers curled into a fist when an ugly smile broke over Trip's face before he murmured, "Is that so?"

The urge to wipe out Trip's smirk was riding Math hard,

even knowing Vex wouldn't appreciate it, but he checked it. Barely.

Interestingly it was Ori who cut through the rising tension. "She's bringing you shit from Gus."

Trip rocked back on his heels, his gaze going from Vex to Ori and back, his disbelief clear in his disgusted tone. "Are you kidding me? Since when do Vultures run errands for pissant mechanics?"

A muscle flex along Trip's jaw and his fingers whitened on the dark glass of his bottle. Math shifted closer to Vex until mere inches separated them. Vex's spine stiffened, and she shot him a narrow-eyed glare over her shoulder. He ignored her displeasure, justifying his knee-jerk reaction as preparing for when things took a disastrous turn, say like Trip losing his temper and swinging out with that damn bottle. Reactions like that were expected when Vex's smart mouth engaged.

Unfortunately, his movement also caught Trip's attention and those mismatched eyes came to him, narrowed, then returned to Vex.

She snagged the bottle out of his hand, brought it to her mouth and tipped it back. She grimaced as she lowered it. "You need better brew, Trip." She handed it back. "That tastes like shit."

"Fuck you, Vex." Trip snatched it back, finished it off, and then threw the empty bottle at the far wall, where it shattered on impact. Based upon the existing stains, it wasn't the first one. "This a solo venture?"

She jerked a thumb over her shoulder in Math's direction. "Do I look alone?"

Trip gave Math a once over. "Doesn't look like a Vulture."

"That's because he's not."

"Then who the hell is he?" Trip spun away, paced, and muttered. "Fucking overrun with tourists. What the hell do they think? That they can drop in uninvited and waltz around messing with my shit?" He wrapped a hand around his neck and pivoted to eye Vex and Math. He stalked back, closing in on Math, and jutted out his chin, belligerence all but dripping from his pores. "Who the fuck are you?"

Math kept his voice empty and reigned in his urge to knock the overly dramatic ass down a peg or three. "Crow."

Trip started to circle them with a slow, deliberate pace, and Math followed Vex's example, holding still as he clocked Trip's progress. "Crow? Don't recognize that name." Trip spun out to address the room, arms wide. "Anyone know a Crow?" When the catcalls and jeers died down, he returned to his circling and leaned over Math's shoulder. "Why don't you tell us about yourself, Crow?" Trip sneered his name.

Vex pivoted to face Trip, which kept Math in the middle. "Go ahead and piss me off, Trip," she warned in a low, vicious whip, "And I'll take Gus's gift for myself." A cruel smile curved her lips. "Maybe," she all but purred, "I'll do some renovating around here." She waved an arm to encompass the room. "Shake things up, knock out a few walls. Could do the place a world of good."

Trip snarled and stomped back around, Vex turning to keep him in sight. The itch along Math's spine eased as Trip went from his back to his front. With his hands curling and uncurling at his sides, Trip paced in front of his throne and then stopped. "You didn't come here to run errands."

"Nope."

"I've got enough unwelcome visitors lately. Don't need more piling on shit." Trip's jaw worked and he pinned Math with a furious stare. "What are you doing in my territory, Crow?"

It hit Math that the bounty story might prove too tempting for Trip and backfire, but then he considered Trip's rant about uninvited tourists. That, he could work with. It was a slim, but possible, chance that Trip's current frustration would work in their favor. So, he tweaked his answer. "Tracking a hunt based out of the city, hoping to get ahead of the rats who think they can nab my cheese."

Trip's gaze narrowed. "And what? You tracked your rats here?"

Math held his gaze. "Yeah."

Trip looked to Vex. "Let me guess, you're looking for help in return for handing over my property?"

"Help is appreciated, not expected. Which is why we'd like your permission to poke around a few holes, see what slithers out." She shrugged. "Sounds like you have an infestation, maybe we help thin out the numbers." When Trip didn't say anything, she added, "Can't hurt, right?"

"Oh, it sure as hell can." Trip paced away, one hand rubbing his neck, the other propped on his hip. When he turned back, angry annoyance masked a hint of unease. "You poke around and tick off the tourists, who do you think the blowback is going to hit? You?" He shook his head and waved his arms. "I let you chase your rats and when you start thinning the herd, they'll come back at me." He jerked his thumb at his chest. "Me, not you. They're always looking for a reason to screw with us and this gives them a bright, shiny opening." He stopped directly in front of Vex and leaned in. "I'd be better off letting you indulge in your redecoration by boomer."

Vex held her ground and her mouth, so Math stepped in. "If we could promise no blowback, would you change your mind?"

That snared Trip's attention and he angled his head so he could study Math. "Can you?"

Math shared a look with Vex, both of them clearly recalling the conversation with Reaper that started this whole deal. If they agreed to keep Trip free of the city guards' wrath, it would put Greer's attention solidly on the Vultures.

Initially Math was more than willing to pay that price for Cam's return, but that was when this scenario was nothing more than speculation. Now that it was fast becoming a reality, his certainty was rocked with doubts. He held Vex's gaze and let her see the shift in his internal landscape. Trip's question wasn't Math's to answer because it wasn't just his ass on the line. Not anymore.

Vex's gaze stayed locked on Math's and when grim acceptance darkened it, he knew she was following the same train of thought. So, she was the one to answer. "Yeah, Trip, we can."

Not completely oblivious to the undercurrents, Trip took his time considering their offer before finally waving a hand in acceptance. "Fine, go do your poking, but—" he pinned them with a sharp glare, "—don't expect any of us to ride to your rescue." He held out his hand and curled his fingers up in a 'give me' motion. "Hand over my boomer."

"Fair enough." Vex reached into her vest and pulled out Gus's box. She extended it and when Trip went to take it, pulled it out of reach. "Got one more request."

Trip snarled and rolled his eyes. "What a fucking surprise." His hands went to his hips and his chin jutted out. "What?"

Apparently amused at Trip's snippy response, Vex flashed a mocking grin. "Like you, not a fan of riling up the rats. To that end, we'll go in during the dead hours. Got a set of eyes we can borrow so we get in quick and quiet?"

Trip held up a hand and counted down with his fingers. "You want a place to hole up and a guide?" He canted his head, looked from his fingers and then back to Vex. "That's two requests.'

"So it is." Unruffled, Vex wiggled the boomer back and forth. "Deal?"

Trip snatched the boomer from her hand with blurring speed. "Deal."

sixteen

*W*hat the hell did I just do? Equal parts panic and impotent frustration cruised through Vex and left her faintly nauseous with the beginnings of a headache as she stood next to a night shrouded window, the top half protected by a thick sheet of metal.

The decision to put the Vultures squarely in Greer's crosshairs wasn't hers to make, it was Reaper's. She couldn't even blame Math for offering it as an option considering Reaper put it on the table in the first place. Still, even that couldn't ease the weight of responsibility should things turn to shit. The only bonus in this cluster? She and Math could hunt for the missing Strix unhindered, but until Trip was ready to let them walk, she was stuck here twiddling her thumbs with the attractive pain in the ass behind her.

"We could twiddle something else," whispered the hormonal hussy in her head. Heat bloomed under her skin.

Math interrupted her private musings before the visuals went full-blown. "You've got yourself an admirer, Vex."

She turned away from the sketchy entertainment of the streets below and shot Math a frown. "What?"

"In Trip's throne room." His dark eyes watched her, his expression impenetrable. "There was a guy when we first walked in, couldn't keep his eyes off you."

She wracked her brain trying to remember but since she'd been more concerned about keeping Math from doing something crazy, say like taking out Trip, she didn't clock the curious. "Didn't notice."

Math's response was a non-committal grunt.

Now that he had her attention, it was difficult to ignore the dangerous hunger he invoked. As if he knew just what kind of havoc he created, the sexy bastard was stretched out across a thick pallet of blankets piled in the corner, his arms behind his head, and his lashes at half-mast, practically issuing an invitation to come play.

There was no doubt he knew the temptation he presented, which was why she stayed near the window and kept her eyes on the street below, brooding instead of taking him up on his invite. Occasionally she snuck a peek, drinking in his long legs and broad shoulders poorly concealed by his t-shirt, which only fed her inner hussy's hunger. That silly wench was all about tracing those intriguing dips and valleys with her tongue.

"Vex?"

Distracted by a tangle of erotic images, she blinked. "Yeah?"

Under the soft glow of the solar lamp, the steel blue of Math's eyes held her with an uncomfortable intensity. "You okay?"

"Just tired." *And horny.* Not that she shared that last bit. Together it made for a very bad combination. She scrubbed her hands over her face in an effort to wipe her mind clear, blaming her thoughts on the adrenaline letdown. She searched for their lost conversation, one that didn't involve naked playtime. *What had he said? Something about somebody watching her*. In a desperate bid to escape his siren song, she teased, "Afraid I'll leave you for something better?"

"Babe, ain't nothing better than this."

His confidence made her inner sex kitten purr. "Cocky."

"True." He gave her a wicked grin and his gaze flared with unmistakable heat. "On both counts."

Vixen Vex perked right the hell up because it was clear he wanted to play as much as she did. She pushed off the wall and crossed the small space, taking in his battered appearance.

His once clean-shaven skin now sported a dusky shadow of stubble, which added a dangerous cast to his already lethal looks. *God had it just been this morning when she helped with his makeover?* It felt longer. She curled her fingers to hold back the urge to reach out and brush her hand over the rasp and soak in the heat of him. Her gaze snagged on the thin red line circling his throat from Jack's knife. Hell, even the cuts and bruises couldn't detract from his overall nefarious vibe. A vibe that was honey to her bee.

A romp with Math would be fun, but the aftermath, no pun intended, was uncertain. Based on her past, she figured the odds leaned toward disastrous. They'd known each other all of two days, and in those two days he managed to get into a fight, what? "Three times?"

"Three times what?"

She stopped at his side and her gaze jumped to his at his question. "What?"

"Three times what?" he repeated.

She shook her head, only then realizing she'd spoken out loud. She turned away and rubbed at an ache setting up shop behind her shoulder. "Sorry... thinking out loud."

He sat up, caught her wrist, and tugged until she turned back to him. He studied her face so intently she worried he could see what was simmering beneath. "Three times what?"

Feeling unaccountably foolish, she grimaced. "Fights."

When he continued to wait for more details, she blew out a breath. "In the two days since we've met, you've managed to get into three brawls."

Now it was his turn to look baffled. "Has it only been two days? Damn, seems longer."

The wry note in his voice as he echoed her thoughts made her laugh, but it faded as she something deeper than interest rose in the steel blue depths of his eyes. Mesmerized, she couldn't look away as his thumb brushed absently against the sprinting pulse in her wrist. "First time I've heard that."

Wary of his undecipherable expression and caught by the incandescent lure of his gaze, her voice was quiet. "Heard what?"

"You laugh like that. Looks good on you." Before she could fall further down that rabbit hole, his voice lost the soft and went back to a familiar tease. "Need I remind you, I wasn't the one who started the fights?"

"I'll give you two." She pulled against his hold, not much, just enough to get him to let go as she played along for now. "The punks in the alley, yes. Trip's welcoming committee, also yes. Reaper? Not so much, my friend."

Math's grin turned full blown as he resumed his earlier reclining position, tucked his hands behind his head, and crossed his ankles. "I'd like to point out, you were a willing participant in two of the three."

"There is that," she murmured doing her best to ignore the urge to stroke and touch. To keep her hands from betraying her, she shoved them on her hips. "But the rolling around in my pad with Reaper?"

"Don't tell me you and Ruin never get into it."

"Well, yeah, but..." She and her twin knew exactly what buttons to push to get a reaction. Most siblings did. But Math and Reaper were different, and not just because of the disturbing depth of their underlying anger. "Seems like what's between you two isn't going to be solved with a couple of shoving matches."

Math's grin faded until all that remained was a weighty consideration. He studied her for what felt like forever, his thoughts tucked behind a blank wall while tension crept higher with each passing second. Finally, he came to some internal tipping point and broke the quiet. "You offering family relationship advice, Vex?"

She took his question seriously because during this morning's ride, bits and pieces of Math and Reaper's confrontation dogged her, bringing a shit ton of questions She knew stepping into that mess was unwise, but she ignored the warning bells and did it anyway. "Not sure I'm good on the advice front." Mainly because her only reference was her relationship with Ruin, and lately even that felt off. She was completely out of her depth and treading the emotional currents like a mad woman, but it didn't stop her from saying, "But I can offer an ear."

Another long moment spun from a mix of unnamed emotions stretched between them before Math sighed and patted a spot next to him on the pallet. "Sit before you fall down."

She eyed the makeshift bed with serious concern. Granted, beds were scarce at the Hole, and as Trip's "guests", they rated such a luxury, along with the privacy of a locking door, but still, a woman had her standards... "How are you not afraid of what's nesting in there?"

He cocked an eyebrow. "Better than sleeping on dirt and rocks."

Conceding his point, she sank down, her body stiff with nerves and a healthy dose of 'what-the-fuck-are-you-doing-Vex'. Her ass hadn't yet settled when he curled up, snagged her waist, earning her undignified squeak, and drew her down alongside him. She laid there, blinking up at the water-stained ceiling as her thoughts scrambled for purchase. Heat his body seeped into locked muscles and replaced them with taffy. With no idea how to start this whole advice thing, she left the opening gambit to him.

The arm around her shoulders tightened and brought her closer as if offering a protective harbor. "Relax, Vex. I won't bite."

I might. She silenced her wanton though by biting her lower lip, because this was so not the right time. Hell, the right time might never hit at this rate. She blew out a soft breath, draped an arm over his waist, laid her head on his shoulder, rested her cheek against his chest, and curled into him. She was so close she couldn't escape the luscious scent of warm male with a hint of spice.

"How long have you been riding with Reaper?" Math's voice was a comforting rumble under her ear.

She managed a shrug. "Close to ten years now."

He played with the ends of one of her braids and ran a thumb over the beads, his knuckles brushing the upper slope of her breast. "You met in Portland?"

She forced her attention to stay on their conversation. "Yeah, Ruin and I ran the streets with a crew. Had been for... I don't know... four, maybe closer to five years." An echo of Ruin's accusation about being closed off whispered in her head and she knew if she wanted to get from Math, she'd have to give. "We grew up in the Dalles—a valley outside of Portland—in a cabin in the mountains. It was far enough off the beaten path we didn't worry about getting on anyone's radar. Our dad bailed after Mom died. Left to go hunting, never came back. Ruin thinks something ate him, I think he just kept walking. Either way, we stayed at the cabin until the provisions ran out. We decided to try our luck in the city. Typical kid stuff."

"Yeah, I get that." His hand left her hair and started stroking her spine in a slow, absent motion.

She brought her hand up from his waist and rested her palm against his heart. She lifted her head and set her chin on the back of her hand so she could see his face. "You and Reaper grew up together?"

"For a bit." A muscle in his jaw flexed and a flash of vulnerability was there and gone. "Reaper and I share a mom, different sperm donors. For a while it was the three of us, then when I was about twelve—probably closer to thirteen—Mom got sick."

Vex's heart winced at the deliberate emptiness in his voice.

He stared out over her head, his gaze distant. "When she died, Reaper dropped me off with a friend of hers, Cara. He hit the road and I didn't see him again for years."

As short as his retelling was, it was clear that the untold story floating underneath was both epic and tragic. She decided not to agitate the emotional waves and offered cautiously, "That's rough."

His eyes dropped to hers and he gave a harsh bark of laughter. "That's fucking life, right?"

He'd get no argument there, but there was a simmering fury at the core of the divide between him and Reaper and she was going to see if she could reach it. "Why'd he leave?"

It was Math's turn to shrug. "Don't know, don't fucking care."

Calling him on the obvious lie wouldn't be welcomed so she waited for more.

He aimed his gaze at the far wall. "When he was gone, I took over, did the best I could. Wasn't enough." The hand against her spine fisted. "Ended up on my own a couple years later when Cara was killed by a strung-out street thug." He dropped his gaze to hers, his eyes hard. "I made sure she was the last one he hurt."

She could see that. "Is that when the Strix found you?"

"Yeah." He fell silent, lost in memories, as his hand absently played with her braids. "Finally found something that made sense. Got a new family, a new sense of direction."

"And became a master ninja-spy." Her comment earned a tiny smile, but she could remember the driving need to find her own place, her own tribe, because it was what she eventually found in the Vultures. "You got lucky."

"Yeah, I did."

When he didn't say anything else, she wondered if this was as far as the sharing thing would go. The thought pinched.

"Thing is," he said, easing that discomfort even as he focused on something she couldn't see, "without them, I wouldn't be who I am today. I was so pissed at Reaper for bailing, so pissed at the world for taking my mom, taking Cara, all I wanted to do was make everyone else hurt." He looked down, dropped his hand from behind his head, and traced a finger along her jaw. "The Strix, they gave me a reason to see beyond all that shit. Changed the path I was on."

His barely-there touch raised goosebumps along her spine, but she fought back the revealing shiver, cleared her suddenly dry throat and managed a husky, "For the better, I'm guessing?"

"Yeah." He flashed a small grin. "Not sure how many could say joining a league of assassins was the better path, but in my case, it definitely was."

"I can see that."

"Can you?"

She arched a brow. "A little hard to stay angry when you're working your ass off." Something she learned after joining the Vultures. During that first year, Reaper and Havoc ran her and Ruin ragged, testing how much the twins would take before cracking. Except she and Ruin didn't crack because they knew a good thing when they fell into it, especially after their time with the Portland crew.

Math tapped her nose. "Not as hard as you think." He tucked his hand back behind his head and stared at the ceiling. "Anger is a great incentive, but it's hell on your self-control. My trainer thought I'd never get that through my thick skull."

"But you did."

"Eventually."

She decided it was time for a little wave. "If you're so Zen with your anger, then why the exchange of fists with Reaper in my living room?"

"That's a standard form of greeting for us." Lines dug across his forehead. "When I ran across Reaper right before Greer hit us, it ended up going pretty much the same—he lost his shit, got in my face, opinions were shared, accusations were thrown, and fists followed."

She considered that a great form of sibling therapy, but she sensed Math and Reaper's issues fell well beyond that, which sucked. "You ever see that changing?"

"I don't know." He looked at her, a grim mix of anger and misery swimming in his eyes. "Logically it should, we're two grown men. Unfortunately, every time I'm in a room with him all I can think is he bailed when I needed him. Why should I give him another shot? He'll just leave again..."

His raw honesty snuck under her guard and brushed against that ugly part she tried to deny existed. The angry, bitter girl who lost everyone—even Ruin to some extent. Especially now that Charity was in the picture. Not that she begrudged her twin his happiness, or Havoc's his with Mercy, but the two women shifted the dynamics of their tribe, leaving Vex to feel as if she was being shoved to the outside. It was an uncomfortable sensation, and she laid her head against Math's chest to avoid his gaze, but his admission clawed through her brain, unearthing her earlier conversation with Ruin and how loving someone—even a brother—was a two-way street. Her voice was low when she said, "I get it."

Math's chest shifted under her cheek and his hand bunched in her braids, tugging until she tipped her head back. With no choice she stared into the drowning depths of dark blue and worried he saw more than she wanted.

Without releasing his hold, he rolled her to her back, and she clutched his shoulders as the world spun. He braced on one hand by her head, carefully untangled his hand from her hair, and cupped her face, his thumb brushing over her lower lip.

His simple touch set her body alight. Slumbering aware-ness flared awake and left her wanting, her heart racing. She wasn't the only one affected. An answering flush rode under his cheeks and his lids dropped to a sexy half-mast. He lowered his head in slow motion and replaced his thumb with his lips.

The kiss was strangely chaste, just a heated press of lips against lips. Still, it sank deep and for a breathless moment, something infinitely fragile sparked between them, a connec-tion she never encountered. It slipped through her fractured emotional armor and triggered a nearly imperceptible, slow moving chain reaction that left her shaky.

He pulled back, his gaze holding hers captive while a million and one emotions washed through his face too jumbled for her to decipher. His thumb swept along her jaw. "This is a bad idea."

On more levels than she could count, but she still leaned into his touch. "Yeah." Even as she agreed, overwhelming hunger made it hard as hell to pin down why.

Lust roughened his voice. "Tell me to stop."

Like hell. She lived with regrets. What was one more? She would take this—take him—regardless of the outcome. "No."

She gripped his shoulders and using the leverage to her advantage, rose up to tease his mouth with hers, nibbling along his lips. It was something she wanted to do ever since their heated exchange during his impromptu haircut. She licked along his lower lip and took her time exploring his kiss as she sank into the rising wave of need that crashed through her.

"Vex, dammit, woman." He gave in with an audible moan and chased her mouth with his. This time there was nothing chaste about his kiss. His hand slid from her cheek to the base of her skull and he cradled her head so he could lick across her lips with a stark carnality. Difficult though it was, she played hard to get until he tugged on her hair and his low, warning growl vibrated against her lips.

She nipped his lower lip in retaliation. "You called?"

He lifted his head, lust burning dark in his gaze as he studied her. Whatever he saw had him saying, "Fuck it."

Lust, need, and desire rose in a tidal wave and before she could reconsider, she shot back, "Rather you fucked me, hot shot."

At her challenge a wicked eroticism colored his features, and he took her mouth with a rough tenderness. Their tongues tangled and danced in a sensual duel. The dark, decadent enticement of his taste raced through her, like a lit fuse. Detonations followed the wave of heated arousal. Skin became sensitized, the ache for his touch going bone deep until she craved more. The speed of her arousal ignited miniature starbursts behind her closed lids and left her trembling.

He left her mouth to explore, and she could barely breathe as he nipped her chin before trailing a series of open-mouthed kisses up her neck until he could nuzzle behind her ear. Shivers broke along her spine and spread over her arms as she held on desperate to stay above the storm. His name was both a plea and a curse. "Math."

A brief punishing nip to her ear was soon lost under a wash of blinding desire as he retraced his path along her neck.

When he hit a sensitive spot, she arched with a soft, needy cry. Caught under him, legs tangled, she used her position to shamelessly writhe against him. Her hips rose and fell against the hard, hot length of him as he matched her movements. Despite the layers of clothes still between them her body went into a supernova meltdown.

Determined to get to his skin, she tugged on his shirt and dragged it up his back, breathlessly chanting, "Off, off, off."

"Patience—" his voice was husky with lust as he licked her neck, "—is a virtue." He made his point by setting his mouth against the sensitive tendon and sucking sharply.

"You have me confused with someone with virtue." Her protest lacked her usual snark as she continued to rid him of his shirt.

His dark chuckle was muffled as together they managed to get the stubborn material off.

As soon as his shirt was gone, she fed her craving for his skin. Slowly she dragged her hands up and over his torso, careful of his ribs, before trailing them back around and down his hips to meet under his abs. The bumps and valleys of various marks rose and fell under her palms—like a textured map of his life etched into his skin. She peppered the scars with soft, wet kisses and licks.

"Vex."

She rolled her eyes up to find him watching her tease him and his eyes burned with a need she recognized. His low growl escaped when he caught her gaze. She ignored his warning and continued her carnal exploration, her fingers dipping under his waistband to tease. She dragged her tongue along the midline of his torso and his big body stilled, then shuddered, sending a visceral thrill through her.

Braced as he was above her, he rolled his hips, pressing the hard length of his dick against her aching heat. The sensation short-circuited her nerve endings, and she clutched his waist and threw her head back as her mouth opened in a soundless gasp for air. When she finally found it, she managed a husky, "Do it again."

His grin, filled with wicked intent, came slow. "Like this?"

He flexed hips, and despite the barriers of their jeans his hard cock slid against her with torturously slow intent and earned a rough, needy moan from her. "Oh, yeah…"

He did it again and her body hurtled towards the edge. She dug her fingers into his ass and arched her back in a desperate attempt to get closer. When he pulled back, his unexpected move left her off balance, and she held tight. "Math, what—"

He cut the rest of her question off with ravenous kiss. He took her mouth with a stunning savagery that seared away every last thought and left her with drowning in pure sensation. Lightning lit every inch of her body and left behind an electric demand. He shifted their positions until she was on top, then he drew back and stared into her eyes. "My turn."

Dazed, she blinked and tried to process the fact she was now blissfully straddling him.

"Arms up, babe."

This time his words penetrated, and she managed to follow his directions as he whipped her shirt up and over her head, before making quick work of her binding, leaving her naked to the waist. His hands cupped her breasts, his thumbs brushing the tips as he brought them to aching points. "Fucking beautiful."

His praise slipped through and sank deep, but the feel of his calloused palms against her sensitive flesh dominated, and she arched her spine, forcing her breasts deeper into his palms. Under her restless hips his cock jerked, and she decided this position was a definite go. She leaned forward, braced her hands on his chest, and slid along his hard length until it was cradled where she wanted it most. Clearly, she wasn't the only one happy with the new position.

"That's it, babe." Math's face darkened, and his clever fingers created a beautiful chaos, trailing down the slope of her aching breasts before slowly circling back to the crest where her nipples throbbed. "Tell me what you want."

"Suck them." It was both a demand and a plea. She couldn't tear her gaze away as he cupped her breasts and lifted them to his mouth. When he curled his tongue over one aching tip and suckled, she nearly sobbed. "More." He took his time, lavishing her breasts before he stopped playing and got serious. Her hands flew to his hair and held him close as he used his hands and mouth to torment her until she was undulating against him. Her enjoyment was cut short when he pulled back. "Don't stop."

"Oh, don't worry." His hands slid down her torso and went to her jeans, working the button. "Get these off." He did an ab curl, forcing her to lean back, and as he tugged her pants down, he laid a trail of open mouth kisses down her stomach.

"You too." Order given, she used his shoulders to rise to her knees and shift to the side. In under a minute, she got rid of her boots and pants and came back to find him gloriously, wonderfully naked.

The picture he presented hit all her buttons. Lost in a needy haze, she wrapped her hand around his erection and slowly stroked. He arched into her touch, head thrown back, eyes closed, and the muscles in his torso locked, his hand clutching at the blanket under them. She leaned over and took him deep, relishing the taste of him. He was thick, hot, and hard, his taste an addicting mix of salt and spice.

She lost track of how long he let her play before he stopped her with a hand in her hair. "Enough, babe, don't want to go without you."

Giving him one last, luxurious lick, she let him go. "You better have a condom."

He twisted away, snagged his pants, dug around, and came back with one. "All yours."

She grinned, took it from him and teased them both as she unrolled it over his thick length. Once he was covered, she reclaimed her previous position, but he stopped he by using his hand in her hair to bring her mouth to his for an incinerating kiss. When he finally let her up for air, she was on her back, her legs spread.

He settled between them, his cock in hand as he dragged the turgid tip through her slick wetness. She found it darkly erotic to watch him tease them both and her hands curled into his shoulders as the relentless ache spiraled out of control. "Math, please!"

He stopped his torment and leaned over her, his chest pressing into hers. "Tell me what you want, Vex."

Undaunted she met his gaze. "I want you to fuck me, dammit."

"As you wish." His grin was fierce.

He followed her orders and her back arched as the thick heat of him drove through her tight channel. As he began to move, she wrapped her legs around his waist, dug her heels into his ass, and rose to meet him. He set a fast, hard pace, driving her far beyond anything she'd ever experienced before. Curled into the mix of fear and anticipation was an unexpected depth of intimacy. Instead of shoving it away, she embraced it and the man in her arms. It didn't matter if it didn't last. Right now, it filled the empty spaces inside her. Spaces that had been empty for too long.

His hands cradled her hips, shifting her until he was riding her with an exquisite intensity. Everything inside her tightened as together they raced towards the firestorm tearing through flesh and bone. He echoed her cries as they hit the peak and for one infinite moment her world crystalized.

When it shattered, they fell over the edge together.

seventeen

Math laid on his back and stared unseeing into the dark, his body sated, his mind churning. Overhead shadows from the barrel fires in the street danced across the pitted ceiling, but the earlier clamor was nothing more than an occasional burst of faint noise. Cradled against his chest Vex slept, the whisper of her breath warm against his skin. He ran his hand softly through the tangled silk of her hair and tried to figure out what the hell just happened.

What started as a way to ease the near-constant ache in his dick had shifted into a mind-blowing experience. He could excuse the first time on taking the edge off, but the second? When they slowed things down and took their time? When her smile made him feel ten fucking feet tall and her touch left him craving more? When holding her, pleasuring her, fed something he long thought dead?

Mind fucking blown.

Considering the depth of history he had for comparison, that was saying something. Not that he was complaining, but he couldn't shake the premonition that she managed to crawl under his skin deeper than he intended. Especially since his normal, steady control was shot to hell the minute she ignited his desire.

"Fuck." His whispered oath barely ruffled the quiet. When Vex shifted restlessly against him, he murmured, "Shhh..." hoping she'd get a few more minutes of much-needed sleep.

Hell, he wished he could do the same, but instead of enjoying the post-orgasmic bliss, his head chose to pick through this. When she settled, he returned to the turmoil in his head.

Why was this time different?

He enjoyed women, but none before tempted him to move beyond a good time between the sheets. Vex did. Straight up, he liked her. She presented a curious puzzle—stubbornly loyal, fiercely independent, lethally competent—but under it all, there was something fragile. Most would never see it, but he had, during the rare moments when she interacted with the motley group she considered family. Not that he would ever tell her that because she would claw his eyes out.

Those tantalizing glimpses left him fighting an urge to keep her out of the line of fire. Which he knew was stupid. Vex could more than take care of herself and had been doing so long before they met. Yet, he couldn't shake the inclination off, which messed with his head.

And that pissed him off.

His focus needed to be on Cam, not on whatever this was, because until Cam was safe, Math couldn't dedicate the time to untangle the mess that was him and Vex. And after Cam? He still had Greer to deal with. No matter what Vex could offer him, he couldn't let Greer slip through his fingers.

Grimly resolved, he closed his eyes determined to sleep. He was drifting off, when Vex stirred and her low moan drifted through the room, guttural and rough. His arm tightened, holding her close. "Vex?"

Still caught in her nightmare, she began to struggle in earnest. "No! Don't!"

He managed to avoid a flailing fist and wrapped his arms around her, locking her arms against her sides. Her hair whipped across his face, the beaded ends leaving behind a stinging bite. He lifted his chin to avoid the brutal jerk of her head, but she still managed to graze his chin hard enough for his teeth to knock together. He tightened his hold and trapped her restless legs. "Vex, babe. Wake up!"

Her nails raked along his arm. He hissed, squeezed, and rolled her face down into the pallet, coming over her like a naked, weighty blanket. Trapped under him, she managed to turn her face to the side and snarl. Dangerous though it was, he put his mouth next to her ear and kept his voice hard, hoping to cut through her demons. "Dammit, Vex! It's me! Stop it!"

With a startling abruptness, she stilled, but he didn't make the mistake of relaxing, and instead asked, "You with me?"

With nothing but skin between them, he felt the shudder run through her but her stiff body didn't relax. "Yeah." It came out hoarse. "I'm here."

He carefully loosened his arms, pushed up and shifted to the side. She stayed on her stomach, her arms curled tight to her chest. He gave her time and brushed a hand down her spine, keeping his touch soothing. It wasn't a hardship, despite a few scars, her back was long and sleek, and curved into a mouthwatering ass. Little by little, her stiffness melted as he continued to stroke. "Can you tell me?"

He wasn't surprised when she didn't answer. He sighed.

"Her name was Marnie." Vex's voice was quiet. "Met her in Portland when Ruin and I joined Rally's crew. Never clicked with anyone like I did with her." Under his hand, her shoulders shifted as if shrugging off water. "Ruin swore it was because we were the only females on the crew. That might be how it started, but it became more." Her voice softened. "She was so fucking sweet, the kind of person who just made everyone smile when she hit a room. I have no idea how she managed to survive out there. The streets will rip you apart, laughing the whole damn time. But Marnie, she..." Vex trailed off.

There was something in her tone, in the way she picked through her words, as if this was the first time she voiced them. So, he waited.

A few heartbeats passed before she picked back up. "For the first year or so, Rally treated both of us like one of the guys. We ran our cons, picked our way through pockets, did our drops, just like the others. Most of the time, unless it was a con involving a female bait, we were just one of the guys. The status quo worked for us. The last thing either of us wanted was to be seen as different. Unfortunately, our bodies decided differently and screwed those plans to hell."

Not wanting her to shut down, Math was determined not to react and kept his breathing even. It wasn't hard for young girls to pass as boys on the street. Hell, it was one of the safest plays they had. Some of the Strix had grown up in the same environment, so he had an ugly suspicion of where Vex's story was heading.

Under his hand a fine tremor of tension ran along her spine. When she spoke, her voice was an emotionless void. "It didn't take long for Rally to decide to put Marnie and I to work another way."

His hand froze mid-stroke, and it took considerable effort to force it back into motion, but he wasn't fast enough.

She braced an arm and twisted her head to look over her shoulder. It was hard to read her face with the shadows, but a thread of faint humor broke colored her explanation. "Bait, Math. He used us as bait, not whores."

He didn't think the difference was that significant since

bait meant the girls were in as much, if not more, danger. For a mark, a whore would keep their promise, but bait? Well, bait lured you in, kicked you in the balls, and took whatever you had, including your dignity. Victims got angry, and sometimes, they got even and the way they did didn't bear thinking about. Girls went in, got close to their mark, and turned over information to their crew who did the rest. He witnessed that kind of fallout too many times to count. It was risky as fuck and generally the bait paid the price. "Some can't see the difference, babe."

She folded her arms under her head, looked away, and resettled. "Know that better than you."

He tucked her hair to the side, leaned in, and pressed a kiss to the exposed spot on the back of her neck in silent apology. "Can't see Ruin standing by and letting that happen."

"He didn't. Rally waited until Ruin was gone, running another assignment."

The more he learned of Rally, the more Math wanted to meet him. Granted, only one of them would walk away. He fought back his dark reactions and rested his forehead against the back of her head. "What happened?"

She sighed softly. "He sent Marnie and I out to this rival crew that was encroaching on his territory. He figured he'd send us in, let us do our thing, and then take care of the problem." She stopped.

With their legs tangled, his chest along her side, and her head tucked under his chin, he didn't miss the tremors that crawled through her. Hard though it was, he kept his voice gentle and level. "It didn't go as planned."

"No, it didn't." Her answer was choked. She shifted to her side and drew her legs up.

Her pulling away hurt and his newfound urge to protect rushed in. He curled along her back, wrapped one arm around her waist, and rested his cheek against her hair. It was a protective move that was years too late.

She laced her fingers through his and held tight. "I don't know what we did that gave us away, but they made us. They decided to teach Rally a lesson, so they beat the shit out of us, then dumped us back at Rally's doorstep. Ruin found us first. I don't remember much, but Marnie was in worse shape than me. He tried, but she didn't make it through the next day."

At the image she painted, fury coursed through him, and Math closed his eyes. He couldn't escape the careful indifference in her voice. It screamed there was more, so fucking much more, to it. He prayed he was wrong, but the sick pit in his gut churned. Maybe it wasn't his place, but he'd be damned if he would be the one to stop her emotional lancing. God knew how long the wound had festered. "Did they rape you, babe?"

Her nod was a long time coming.

His heart seized and it made him wonder. "Does Ruin know?"

"No." There was so much pain in her one-word answer.

He held on. "Why?"

Her grip on his hand tightened as if she needed the anchor. "After Marnie died, Ruin went after Rally."

"Not surprised."

The pressure on his fingers flexed and eased back a notch. "It was bad."

Next time he saw Ruin, Math was buying him a brew or three. "Did he kill him?"

"No, some of the crew pulled him off Rally before he got that far."

"Too fucking bad." If the dickless wonder was still breathing easy, Ruin didn't go far enough.

"Rally never forgot. He made sure we paid and assigned us the suicide missions. It's how we ran into Havoc and Reaper."

Her fingers uncurled from his and she traced his fingers. "It took Ruin a long time to stop blaming himself. I had—have—no intention of ever adding to it. What happened to me, to Marnie, that wasn't on Ruin."

Listening to her, he realized he wasn't the only one with a warped need to protect someone in the wrong way, because Ruin wouldn't want her to shield him. *What a mess.* Math couldn't decide if he wanted to shake her or hug her. "No, it was on the assholes who hurt you."

"Yeah, I know."

Despite her words, there was a note in her voice that made him wonder. "Do you?"

Instead of repeating her answer, she took her time. "Logically, I get it."

"But?"

"Hindsight's a massive bitch. Hard not to wonder if I'd made a different decision—told Rally to fuck off, waited for Ruin, forced Marnie to run when I knew it was turning ugly, fought harder, something, fucking anything—maybe she'd still be here." There was so much guilt and recrimination in her voice, it hurt just to hear it.

The need to see her face had him shifting so he could get her to roll to her back. He came back over her, and her hands went to his chest. He braced most of his weight on one hand and used the other to cradle her face. Under the faint light from the window, he could see the mix of anger, shame, and guilt that clouded her face. It was not an expression that fit Vex, and it stung to see it.

His voice was quiet but couldn't hide the steel underneath. "What happened to you, to Marnie, is not on you, Vex."

Her gaze rose to his, the normal warm amber dark.

He held it, wanting—needing her to hear him. "I can't tell you I get it. I don't. I can't understand what drives a ball-less bastard to violently steal what should be given. What I can tell you, what I believe beyond any doubt, is that nothing you did, or said, caused this. Be angry, be pissed, you have every right, but don't you dare lower your head in shame. Your choice was taken, and you did the only thing you could—you survived."

Tears shimmered and her nails bit into his chest. Her throat worked, and a tortured admission finally escaped. "Maybe I could've saved her."

He used his thumb to brush an escaping tear away. "How?"

Her lashes came down as she dropped her gaze.

Not willing to let her get away with it, he nudged her chin up. "How?"

She licked her lips. "I don't know, but—"

"Stop." His reprimand was harsh. "You know sometimes there's nothing you can do. Sounds like the situation was fucked from the get-go. That you survived is a damn miracle, that Marnie didn't is a fucking shame, but that is not on you." Maybe if he said it enough, it would sink in.

Her face crumpled just before she buried it against his chest. He wrapped an arm around her, rolled to his back, and cradled her close. He held tight as shudders wracked her body and hot tears soaked his chest. The intensity of her grief confirmed his suspicion that this was the first time she truly faced the fallout. It took a bit for the storm to pass. When a semblance of calm returned, she lay quiet in his arms, the rise and fall of her back broken only by the occasional stutter.

Finally, she lifted her head, and she stroked his stubble-covered jaw. "Thanks." The spent emotional storm left her voice husky.

He searched her face, pleased to see the heavy shadow of guilt and shame had drifted away. Not gone completely because the edges of grief lingered, but it was moving out. "You going to be okay?"

She nodded.

"Gotta know, am I the first one you told?"

Her gaze dropped to where her fingers drifted against his face before she gave another nod.

Her admission boggled his mind and something in his chest went tight and warm. He had no idea why she chose to share with him, but it left him humbled. "Honored, babe. And glad you shared." He gave her a gentle squeeze and waited until her gaze came back to his. "Since you're in a sharing mood, can you answer one more?"

She dropped her hand, took a big breath, and let it out. When she was done, she stacked her hands on his chest and put her chin on top. "Shoot."

"Those bastards still alive?"

She blinked. "Nope."

"You or Ruin?"

That earned a tiny curve of her lips. "Both."

"Good. What about that fucker Rally?"

"No longer among the living—not my doing." The curve bloomed into a fierce smile and something close to her normal irreverence reappeared. "What? Planning on going back and resurrecting the dead, hotshot?"

He tucked a strand of hair behind her ear and brushed his hand down her neck and over her shoulder. "If I thought it would help."

Her smile shifted from fierce to something else, revealing the bottomless well of strength that was Vex. She leaned up and nipped his chin. "Appreciate the thought."

To prove it, she kissed him. Instead of passion and hunger, her kiss carried a generous sweetness, a drugging temptation on its own. He sank his hand into her hair, held her close, and reveled in the offering. They slid closer to the hungry edge only to be pulled up short a fist pounding on the wall outside their room.

"Get yo' asses up, we're out in fifteen."

Vex gave him one last taste, then pulled back, and rested her forehead against his chin. "Sounds like your time's up."

"I'm not done yet." He carefully untangled his hand from her hair, gathered it back into one hand and tugged until she looked up. "After we get Cam and get back, I want some quality time with you." As he said it, he realized it was nothing short of the truth, uncomfortable though it was. Yeah, they had shit to do, but afterwards? He wanted—no needed—more from her, with her—whatever she was willing to give. Maybe then the strange hold she had on him would ease.

There was a flash of uncertainty quickly buried, before she said, "After we get Cam back, we'll make time."

Her cautious agreement soothed the rougher edge of his emotions. He pressed a fast, hard kiss to her lips and took them to solid ground. "Good." He gave her curvy ass a light slap, rolled over, and got up. "Let's get to work."

Math and Vex headed to the questionable elevator and one of the waiting guards got on with them and said, "He'll meet you out front."

As the rickety car dropped down, he and Vex shared a look, but didn't speak. When they finally arrived, the guard waved them through the open doors, pointed to toward the entrance, then left them there to find their way.

The night's earlier activities had died down and now the main floor was quiet, with piles of sleeping or passed out bodies scattered along the edges. Here and there a few stubborn souls were still drinking or tripping or both. As they crossed the main floor, movement caught Math's attention. He pulled up short and grasped Vex's wrist in silent warning, tugging her back behind the partial concealment offered by the ancient video arcade machine.

She stuck to his side and kept her voice low. "What?"

He used his chin to direct her attention to the man striding towards the entrance. "Recognize him?"

She studied the figure when he stopped to talk to one of the door guards. "Nope. Should I?"

"That's the jackass who couldn't take his eyes off you."

The unknown man finished his conversation and strode into the night.

Vex tugged against Math's hold. "Maybe he's our guide."

Math hope to hell not considering the uneasy feeling that crawled over his skin. They continued across the room, passed by the main entrance guards, and stepped out onto the cracked sidewalk.

Math did a casual check and noted the sentries posted on the buildings across the street took their job seriously, their attention still as sharp as it was earlier. He awarded Ori a point for running a tight ship because the well-disciplined fighting force had to be the result of loyalty to Ori not Trip. If he and Vex failed to redirect Greer's ire, that force might be enough to hold off any reprisals. Maybe.

"Took you long enough." The drawled greeting came from the shadows and drew Math out of his grim speculation. A familiar whipcord figure moved forward in a flutter of mismatched material. Light from the barrel fires danced over Bon's face, his grin a slash of white in the mix of dark paint and dirt. "I was gettin' lonely."

"Really?" Vex aimed a pointed glance at the woman who was sauntering off in the opposite direction with a distinctive rolling gait.

Unashamed, the street rat danced between them and threw his arms over their shoulders, becoming the middle to their human sandwich. Math coughed as a wave of nose-wrin-kling odor accompanied the move.

Bon's grin widened. "Ah now, beautiful, no need to get jealous. Plenty of goodness to go around."

Math caught the warning flicker in Vex's gaze and wisely stepped out of Bon's hold to enjoy the upcoming enter-tainment.

Vex snagged Bon's hand and with a quick twist, had him bent over in front of her by a painful wristlock. "Bon, Bon, how many times do I have to tell you? No touching." She patronizingly patted the kid's back with her free hand and released him.

As Bon straightened and shook out his hand, he flashed another manic grin, making it obvious Vex's warning hadn't even dented his attitude.

Math caught the calculating gleam in the kid's gaze and decided it was time to get down to business. "Guessing you're our guide?"

Bon started walking backwards as he led them down the street. "Got it in one."

"You seem pretty damn happy to be doing this," Math commented as he trailed the street rat. Vex move up on Bon's other side.

Bon shrugged, pivoted to face in the right direction and his grin faded around the edges. "Trip reached out. I do him a favor, maybe he returns it, yeah?"

Vex managed a disbelieving snort. "Don't count on it."

A lethal adult peeked out from behind the crazy teen act. "Don't count on much, 'cept me."

"Smart man," Math muttered.

"Stupid gets you dead," Bon shot back, then thumped his chest. "I'm still breathin', my man."

Kid had a point.

Bon turned down a side street that led away from Trip's

place and deeper inside the maze of the Hole. About halfway down the dark road, he stopped and turned. "Since I plan to keep inhalin' on a regular basis like, you should know."

Since Bon wasn't moving, Math and had no choice but to stop. Math took point. "What's that?"

Bon folded his arms across his narrow chest, his face hard to read, but the warning in his voice was clear as a bell. "You ain't the first to wander in tonight. More city rats scampered in a couple hours ago. Thinkin' you might be lookin' at an unexpected welcoming committee."

Vex's shoulder brushed Math's. He looked at her and saw the same grim realization mirrored back. Their shadows had slipped through the Green and arrived, which meant there would be more bodies joining those already holding Cam. He looked to Bon. "Know how many are serving on this committee?"

"At last count? Five, could be six." Bon shrugged. "Hard to tell, they all look the same." He snickered at his own joke.

Vex read Math's frustration and murmured, "They're using him as bait. Still six to three odds aren't bad."

"Count me out." Bon's hands flew up and made warding motions. "I guide you in and that's it. That's all I agreed to. Ain't taking a knife in the back for either of you."

Not keen on dragging along dead weight, Math considered ditching the kid and taking the chance on heading in on their own. They already had enough to worry about. Frustrated at the whole fucked up situation, Math snapped, "Fine, hide in a corner and watch. We'll be sure to tell Trip you did your job."

That earned him a snarled, "Fuck you."

Bon went to lunge at Math only to pull up short when Vex stepped in front of Math, blocking the kid's access. "Step back, Bon," she warned.

The kid spun on a heel and stormed down the street.

"Son of a bitch." Math dragged a hand through his hair

and glared at the ground under his feet. The sensation of time running out wrapped its icy hands around his throat and squeezed.

Vex put a hand on his arm. "You need to get a grip." She waited for his reluctant nod. "We need him, otherwise we'll waste time trying to pinpoint Cam's location."

"If he's going to bail, I'd rather he did it now instead of when shit's going down." One of the reasons why he preferred working solo was it meant the odds of getting stabbed in the back were much less.

"Can't argue with you, but let's use what tools we can, while we can, okay?"

Unable to fight her logic, he reluctantly agreed. "Fine."

She studied him for a long moment, then started after Bon leaving Math to follow.

eighteen

Close to an hour later Vex dropped to the ground, her attention aimed at a crumbling brick structure, and took a position on her stomach, allowing the small overlook's high grass to hide her. To her left, Math did the same, while Bon mimicked them to her right. The moon hung high above, it's light casting a silver glow that was occasionally interrupted by a drifting cloud.

"You see it?" Bon's voice barely rose above the soft rush of dancing foliage and nature's nightlife.

From her position, Vex caught the amber glow that escaped the boarded edge of a first-floor window. "Yeah."

Math touched her shoulder and indicated a shadow that moved out from under the protective reach of an old growth tree. As the details became clearer, she realized it was a perimeter guard, and where there was one, there were bound to be more. Sure enough, another figure came around from the back and the one in front disappeared around the far side. The boots on the ground were alternating their patrols and eliminating possible double ups.

It took her a few more minutes to pick up another one

perched on the sloped roof to the west. Bon had said there were six, so the best use would be to station four outside at the most vulnerable points and keep two positioned insides with Cam. With three down, where was the fourth?

She started to reconsider her assumption as time ticked by and nothing changed, but then Math indicated the half-collapsed building to the east. There, on the flat roof of the stoop, a bit of darkness shifted, providing a glimpse of a man shape shadow before it blurred back into obscurity.

Just once it would be helpful if the enemy was a little less capable.

Vex gave it another handful of minutes for any new players to appear. When no one new popped up, she tagged Bon and Math, and used hand signals to indicate they should fall back. Message sent and received, she carefully retreated to the backside of the overlook and the men followed.

They huddled together out of sight of the guards and Vex kept her voice low and addressed Bon first. "You need to hang here until we're sure this is our target. Can't have you giving the game away." When the teen's expression turned mutinous, she grabbed his shirt in her fist and dragged him close until their noses almost touched. "Not up for a discussion, or the payment promised disappears."

Bon's arrogance wavered, then collapsed with an ungracious, "Whatever."

Vex shoved him back. "Don't forget a return trip was included."

Math closed in, his tone soft, but his threat no less fierce. "You ghost on us, boy, and I'll hunt you down and skin you."

Bon's Adam's apple bobbed and Vex knew the kid was scared enough to stay put. Which was good, because chances were high that they would be running hard and fast when they left here.

Done with Bon, she turned to Math. On their way in, Bon

had led them around their targeted building, giving them a rough view of the sides and back before they took their positions on the overlook. "You pick out an entry point?"

Math crouched at her side, his arms resting on his knees, and nodded. He looked back in the direction of the building, even though it was out of sight. "Second floor, east side. There's a narrow window, board on the bottom is hanging by a thread."

She eyed his broad shoulders and pointed out, "You're a bit wider than a two by four."

"If one board's about to go, you can be sure the others are right behind it."

Math probably had a point. The building was tucked on the edge of what used to be the town and navigating the route to it required a canny survivalism approach. The structure was at least a hundred years old, maybe more, based on the brick exterior and pre-Collapse architecture. "Right, you want me to take care of our friend to the east or our duo making the rounds?"

Math shook his head. "Leave the east guard to me, you worry about the guy to the west."

"And our climber and plus one?" The delay between the eliminations worried her because it meant there was time for an alarm to be raised.

Math was obviously following the same line of thought. "If baby boy wasn't so worried about getting a boo-boo—" he shot a contemptuous glare with a hint of calculated manipulation at Bon, his opinion clear, "—we could take care of all three posts at once."

Bon curled his lip and spat, "Fuck you, asshole. I could gut those wankers in a heartbeat without breaking a sweat."

Math just arched a brow and smirked.

Ben folded his arms and proved just how fragile the male ego was by declaring, "I'll prove it."

Not about to laugh at how easily Math caught Bon, Vex said, "So that mean you're working with us tonight?"

Bon's attention shifted from Math to her, and realization at how he had been played sank in. But instead of blowing up, he set his jaw and glared. "Tonight only. We get clear of this shit, I'm out."

Not about to look a gift horse in the mouth, she murmured, "Good enough." She turned to Math. "Yeah?"

Math's expression remained stony as he studied Bon, but he finally grunted.

Vex took it as his agreement and went back to their plan. "Crow takes east, I'll take west, Bon takes front." She looked at Bon. "You take him out, you don't have much time before his back up comes around."

"Got enough."

She took him at his word and addressed Math. "If Bon's right on the numbers, means you're going to face at least two more inside. They could be hiding anywhere."

"Chances are good they're sticking close t—" he flicked a glance at Bon before continuing, "—the bounty. Our best bet is for you to get inside, cause a distraction, and draw them away so I can get to him. The kid can stay outside, in case others show up."

Bon shifted restlessly. "You expectin' more?"

Vex didn't want him to bolt so she said, "No, but better safe than sorry." She considered Math's suggestion and told him, "I'll keep them occupied, you get to your bounty, and get him out. Preferably through the back."

Math frowned. "Not leaving you behind."

Used to such protective statements from the Vultures, she was unprepared for the tiny kernel of warmth Math's comment generated. She tucked it away and reminded him, "You'll probably have your hands full because there's no telling what kind of shape he'll be in, but I'll be right behind you."

A muscle worked in Math's jaw before he gave her a short nod.

Now that everyone was on the same page, it was time to get a move on. "Right, then let's move."

nineteen

It took a bit of time for Vex to access her target and work her way west around the building. Of the three structures, hers was the shortest with a single level layout. She climbed the thick trunk of a nearby tree and used the protective cover of the heavily leafed branches to reach the other side of the pitched roof. From her position in the branches, she studied the guard's movements.

When his attention shifted to the occupied building, she carefully dropped to the opposite side of the roof and kept low as she picked her way across. Every time the guard's head started to swivel, she dropped to her stomach and prayed the roofline kept her presence hidden. It was nerve-shredding work, but she inched her way across until she was within range of her target.

She had no clear line of sight to where Math should be taking down the east guard thanks to how the buildings were aligned, so she chose to time her attack with Math's entrance. With knife in hand, she waited because no matter what Math said, making the hole wider would cause noise.

It wasn't long before the muffled groan of breaking wood

sounded and the prone guard's head snapped up, giving her an opening. She pushed up from her position, lunged over the roof's peak, and slid down to land on the guard's back. She gripped a handful of hair and yanked his head back as he rolled. He nailed her kidney with an elbow and raked a bruising heel down her shin, but she managed to swipe her blade across his throat. Unfortunately, it wasn't deep enough.

Fuck it.

Caught under his heavier weight she shifted the grip on her blade, drove it in until it sliced through tissue to hit bone with an arm jarring impact. She ripped it free and drove it in two more times. The last strike she twisted her wrist and held the blade steady as his body jerked in her arms. His head slammed into her cheekbone so hard she saw stars and kept her mind blank as his blood dripped over her in a warm trickle. Finally, his body went slack. She shoved him off and crouched next to his lifeless body, relearning to breathe.

Dammit, no way that fight didn't get tagged.

She kept a vigilant eye out, leaned in, and used the relatively clean edge to wipe the worse of the blood from her face. The thin, sticky film on her eyelashes indicated she missed some, but it would do for now. She cleaned her blade on the dead man's pants and stayed low as she crept to the roof's edge to check the way below was clear before she dropped down.

The drifting clouds blew clear of the moon giving its light free rein as the soft scuff of leaves came from the big tree out front. In the uncertain light she was able to make out the pair of boots, soles up, slowly being swallowed by the thick shadows at the trunk of the old growth. *Score one for Bon.*

She waited for the second guard to appear, her ears straining until they rang with the quiet. By the time the night's natural sounds resumed, impatience joined hands with worry. She was running out of time to provide the distraction Math needed. She grasped the edge of the roof and tested it to make sure it wouldn't crumble under her weight. When it held, she adjusted her hold on her blade, slipped over the edge, and dropped into a crouch, her blade at the ready. The insect choir's hiccuped and returned to its melody.

With no choice, she left Bon to watch her back and darted across the yard. She was exposed for only a few feet, but it was enough to have her spine twitching. She crept up the short stoop and hunkered beneath the window. Despite the fact it was boarded up, light seeped around the edges. Not keen on warning those inside she was there, she stayed low, wrapped her hand around the knob, and pressed her ear against the weathered door, all while watching the thin sliver of light.

There was no betraying noise but every instinct she possessed screamed someone waited on the other side. Now, she just needed a clue to their position. She started to turn the knob and the narrow light on the right side of the window just above the ledge flickered.

That would work.

Before whoever lurked inside could shift out from behind the door, she threw it open, and added her shoulder to the impact's weight. The door hit with a sickening crack and elicited a muffled grunt. As counterweight shoved the door back, she rolled out of the way and came up in a crouch, knife out.

A blur of movement was her only warning. She threw up her arm and barely managed to dodge the incoming strike. A stinging line from shoulder to elbow indicated she wasn't the only one armed with a blade. She stepped in close and came up as she retaliated, slicing under his arm and along his ribs as she knocked his blade hand aside with her other arm. They separated and circled each other as she studied the lean guard who handled his weapon with an easy familiarity.

To gain control of his knife, she would have to move fast. She darted in, her blade aimed at his neck. She blocked his return volley with her left arm and earned another wicked slice, even as her blade kissed skin. Unfortunately, he jerked out of weapon range and stumbled back.

She didn't ease back but kept the pressure up. On his next swing, she slapped his blade away, ducked under his swing, and sank her knife into his gut. With a dark growl he wrapped a hard hand around her wrist and the blade in place.

Instead of fighting his grip, she used her free hand to block his incoming strike and loop his arm in a brutal joint lock. She twisted and snapped his arm at the elbow by applying her body weight to the hold. His pained bellow drowned out the sound of his knife hitting the. The grip on her wrist loosened, and she twisted her knife and yanked it free.

She stepped back and the guard clutched his stomach with his uninjured arm and dropped to his knees. To make sure he stayed down, she nailed the bastard with a kick to the temple bringing the short, brutal fight to an abrupt end.

Vex swept up the discarded blade next to the crumpled heap and tucked it into the small of her back. No sense in wasting a perfectly good blade.

With one guard down, she scanned the ramshackle entryway and the rickety set of stairs that climbed to the second floor in the light offered by the solar lamp that hung from a nail on the wall. With no one running to the fallen guard's rescue, either Math neutralized the other interior guard, or she was about to start playing a deadly game of hide and seek. Since Fate was a fickle bitch, it was best if Vex got a move on.

She bypassed the room to the left, which was clearly empty since no one rushed out of it and started to clear the rest of the bottom floor. She slipped by a couple of empty doorways that guarded more empty rooms and crept down the dark hall toward the room at the back. She was closing in on the last shadowed room when the creak of wooden floorboards drifted from above.

Shitshitshit! They were upstairs.

She turned and rushed toward the stairs, clearing the first set in a matter of heartbeats. When she reached the first landing, she found a hole dominated one side of it. She did a weird hop-leap combination to gain the second flight and winced when the stair's tread protested with an audible creak. The narrow space was unforgiving and forced her to slowly pick her way up as she avoided more holes and rotten steps.

When she reached the second floor a line of sweat cooled along her spine, and she stared into the long, equally narrow hallway lined by rooms, some with doors, some without. At the end of the hall, it branched off, but what got her pulse thumping was the light that slipped across the warped floorboards.

She crept down the hall, testing each spot as she inched along. No sense in making her presence any more obvious, not until she was certain all possible threats were out of play. By the time she reached the end, her pulse had settled into an anticipatory beat.

With her spine pressed against the dubious protection of the wall, she snuck a peek around the corner. Light spilled from a room tucked halfway down and was joined by the quiet rumble of conversation that was too low to identify the speaker. The back of her neck itched in warning. She took a deep breath, prayed the speaker was Math, adjusted her grip on her blade, and worked her way forward as she monitored potential threats.

She got to the doorway without incident and was careful not to reveal her presence and cross the spill of light. Her nerves should've chilled with the minor success, but they kept jumping. She repeated the back to the wall move and managed a quick look inside. The room was empty except for the familiar set of Math's shoulders and a sprawled body off to the side. She rushed in. "Math."

He turned his head and the naked fury and grief in his face about knocked her on her ass before it disappeared under a stony mask. Then he indicated the body on the floor. "Found your admirer."

She made her way to the corpse and used the toe of her boot to kick him over. Sure enough, the man from the Hole, who headed out earlier, stared back with unseeing eyes. Looked like Trip owed them one for taking out a rat. She stepped over the informant's body and went to Math's side.

In front of him, bound to a chair was a badly beaten man. Looked like Math had found Cam. She winced at his condition. Head bent, barefoot, stripped to the waist, and wearing only a grungy pair of pants, she thought he was dead until she caught the faint rise and fall of the burnt and scarred chest. The light provided by the small camp lights set on either side spilled over hair that may have been blond at one point, but now bore the distinct rust color of old blood.

Based upon the signs of both recent and repeated torture she marveled at the will that kept this poor soul breathing. "Shit, and I thought Si looked bad after his time with the Raiders."

Math cut through one of the thick cords wrapped around Cam's waist. "Get his wrists."

"Got it." She moved around Math, crouched at Cam's side, and slid her blade between the rope anchoring his arms to the chair's rear legs and his torn wrists. As she worked, she kept his arms still with a gentle hand. Only when they were free did she carefully let them hang at his side.

As she rose from her crouch, Math asked, "Can you hold him up, while I work on the rest of this shit?"

"Yeah." She tucked her blade into a boot and considered

how to hold Cam without hurting him which based upon the amount of visible damage, might be a hopeless endeavor.

To give Math access to the rope wrapped around Cam's waist and torso, she moved behind the chair to get a better hold. When the mess that was Cam's back came into view, she bit off a curse. It looked like so much raw meat. The prospect of moving Cam in the shape he was in and getting out of the Hole was looking decidedly grim.

She shoved that worry back for later and got as close as she could without putting pressure on the chair's spindled back. Then she leaned over and carefully crossed her arms over Cam's battered chest, holding him up without pressing him back. It was awkward and left her muscles screaming, but she remained steady as Math sliced through the thick rope and tossed them aside. Cam groaned and Math winced, his eyes flicking to Cam's face.

Vex's position made it difficult to tell if Cam was aware or not, but Math said, "I know it hurts, man, but hang in there."

When the last piece loosened, Cam's weight sagged in her arms, and forced her to shift her weight awkwardly to keep him from falling into Math. Off balance, she was slow to react when Cam's arm jerked out of her hold and his fist swung out.

"Math!" Her warning coincided with Cam's fist nailing Math's cheek.

Injured or not, there was enough force behind it to knock Math sideways. He cursed and caught himself with his hand against the floor.

When Cam drew back his fist for another swing, Vex grabbed his wrist. Not an easy feat from her position but hung on determined not to hurt him.

"Cam!" Math crowded Cam, cupped his friend's face, and forced him to listen. "Cam, it's Math. Stop, man. Don't make me hit you. Do you hear me, Cam?"

Cam's arm went limp, his hand uncurled, and his voice was a hoarse croak. "Math?"

Vex slowly tugged Cam's arm back down and then let it go before going back to bracing his shaking shoulders.

Math didn't let go of Cam's face. "Yeah, man, it's me."

"Took you fucking long enough, bastard."

Weak though it was, his complaint made Math's lips curving. "Sorry, had to pick someone up to help save your ass."

Cam lifted his head, turned to Vex, and swayed a bit. "Well, hello."

She looked into his battered face, one eye swollen, the other streaked with red, broken vessels, his nose out of joint, and his cut lips trying to curve. She gave him a small grin. "Hey there, handsome."

Cam turned to Math, his body tilting heavily to the side. "At least you didn't come barreling in on your own." Math and Vex caught and kept Cam upright as he hissed in pain, then said, "You finally wising up, bro?"

Math shifted until he could help Cam stand. "I'm not the one playing punching bag for a bunch of third-rate heavies."

With a great deal of cursing and a few groans, they got Cam to his feet. Math held Cam's arm over his shoulder with one hand, curled his other arm around his friend's waist, and then craned his neck to Vex. "Let's bail."

She took point position and skirted the body on the floor. Behind her, Cam asked, "How many did you eliminate?"

She half-turned to see Math lead the wounded man around the corpse as he answered, "Two. That one and one outside."

Both men looked to Vex, who added her tally. "Two, one exterior, one interior. Think our lookout got one."

Cam grimaced. "If he didn't, you'll be missing one."

"Just one?" Math asked as they continued to the doorway.

"Yeah." Cam leaned against the doorframe. "Earlier

tonight, this guy showed up. Didn't catch much, but I think he lost his partner in the Green. He argued with that bastard —" he indicated the body behind them, "—then left."

The men fell silent as Vex moved down the hall to check the first turn. Nice to know their shadows had been halved. While she would love to assume Bon managed to take out the other outside guard, luck never stuck around in situations like this. Since Math was busy with Cam, it was up to her to get them out without getting killed.

She studied the dark hall and stretched all her senses, looking for anything out of place. Although her nerves still hummed and her neck still itched, nothing moved, and they couldn't stay here forever.

Good enough.

Vex motioned them forward and they made their way downstairs without incident. The crumpled heap of her attacker lay where she left him to bleed out. She stepped around him, chanced a look back at the shuffling duo and warned softly, "Watch your step."

Light played over Cam's sweat-streaked, grey face and she worried he wouldn't be able to stay upright for much longer. Based upon Math's grim mask and the fury flickering in his dark gaze, she figured he shared her concerns.

Hand on the knob she waited for the two men to join her. She kept her voice low and met Math's gaze. "I'll signal you."

He looked to the door, then back to her, and gave a short nod.

She took a deep breath, opened the door, and slipped into the night.

twenty

Math followed the dust trail from Vex's bike and steered the modified off-road buggy they liberated from Gus's shop around the sharp hairpin curve that took them further up the mountain. He did a quick check on Cam, who was strapped into the passenger seat. He was aware, but barely hanging in there.

Math switched his attention back to the road and hoped to God they were close to wherever it was that Vex was taking them. After Bon admitted to only taking out one guard, it became crucial to remain unseen. Not an easy task when you were dragging a half-dead man along. The trip from where Cam had been held, back through the Hole, and to Gus's shop had been nothing short of an endurance test, even with Bon utilizing every shortcut he knew, and Math had to admit, the kid knew his shit.

They reached Gus's deserted garage about an hour before dawn. Bon disappeared, off to collect the stashed bike they promised him as payment and Vex went on a hunt for a vehicle they could use to get Cam out.

While she did her thing, Math did his best to treat the

worst of Cam's wounds. It wasn't much more than field dressing and a few quick stitches, but it was better than nothing. Although, if he wasn't slipping in and out of consciousness, Cam might disagree. Vex displayed the depth of her talents when she liberated a modified buggy hidden in the back of the garage. Together, she and Math got Cam belted in, and then Vex tossed in a cracked helmet from one of Gus's dusty shelves.

When Math raised a brow in question, she explained, "No shocks equal a rough ride. You'll be too busy keeping wheels on the ground to keep his head from slamming into the frame."

Fifteen minutes later they were on the road back towards Pebble Creek. Or so Math assumed, then Vex turned off the main route, and took them into the higher elevations outside the settlement. As they wove deeper into the foliage he was forced to slow. She finally stopped, and Math did the same, but left the buggy's engine running.

She got off her bike and walked over to him. The buggy's engine was so loud, she mouthed, "Follow me." To ensure he understood, she pointed towards what looked like a thick weave of trees and brush.

He gave her a nod and watched her move to the grove of trees. She tugged and pulled at the heavy foliage revealing a dark opening. He slowly eased into the shallow cave and when the front bumper kissed the back wall, he shut off the engine. The early morning light barely penetrated, so there wasn't much to take in other than rock walls and a dirt floor. He got out and rounded the buggy to unbuckle Cam, while Vex rolled her bike closer.

She looked over and warned, "Careful, Math, not much room to maneuver."

She wasn't lying. His back scraped the cave wall as he squeezed between it and the buggy. He got to Cam and started to undo the seat straps. "Thought we were heading to Pebble Creek."

"Considered it," she said. "But if we missed one of Greer's men, the first place they'll check when they get word out is Pebble Creek."

The certainty in her voice stopped him and he looked at her. "You think Trip will give us up."

She pulled their saddlebags off the bike and her mouth curved with a cynical twist. "Don't think it, know it."

Math undid the last buckle and barely caught Cam when his friend slumped forward. The impact of Cam's heavier body provoked a muffled grunt from Math and a groan from Cam.

Vex stepped forward. "Need help?"

Math shook his head and adjusted his hold on a barely conscious Cam. Since he knew the injured man was operating purely on instinct, Math added the whip of command to his voice. "On your feet, Cam."

Thankfully it worked. Cam moved with Math, who got his arm around Cam's waist, carefully steering clear of the raw rope marks, and locked his hand just above Cam's torn up wrist. Together, they half-stumbled, half-shuffled alongside the buggy as sweat rolled down Math's spine. As soon as they were clear, Vex wheeled her bike into the narrow space.

Math guided Cam out of the cave and lowered him to the ground next to a thick tree. Vex replaced the cave's camouflage and worked her way back to them, doing her best to erase the tire tracks.

Next to Math, Cam lifted his head, and tried to look around, but with one eye swollen shut and the other blood-shot, Math figured his friend was basically blind. Cam dropped his head as Vex came over and sank into a crouch next to Math.

"Where are we?" Cam's question was slurred.

Vex answered, "Just outside Pebble Creek." She exchanged a worried look with Math over Cam's bent head. "We don't have far to go, maybe another fifteen, twenty minutes."

Math frowned. "Where are we going?"

Vex looked back up the mountain, then back to him. "There's a farmstead up there. The family knows me. They'll give us a place for Cam to rest while I send one of them to Pebble Creek for Mandy."

"Mandy?" Cam's head lifted, his gaze confused, his face flushed. "I know her," he mumbled.

Considering Cam was about to keel over, Math ignored his ramblings and stuck to the conversation with Vex. "Works for me." He pushed to his feet and ignored the protests of his aching body. He raised his arms above his head, stretched his spine, dropped his arms, and rolled his shoulders. "Okay, let's do this."

Together he and Vex got Cam upright between them. Vex used her head to indicate the direction. "There's a deer path behind the cave. We follow it up to the top of the next rise, then east. The farm won't be far."

Repositioning his hold on Cam, Math asked, "Did you catch that, Cam?"

Cam's head-shake was weak. "Missed it."

"Time to suck it up, you're almost home free." Determined to get Cam to the farm, Math worked with Vex and hauled Cam up the mountain.

WHEN THE FLAT roof of the farmhouse came into view, Math considered dropping to his knees and shouting hallelujah. Cam managed to stay mobile for the first ten minutes, but injuries overrode instincts and he turned into dead weight. Math viewed Cam's unconscious state as a mixed blessing.

As he and Vex stumbled across the clearing towards the front porch, the door flew open. A gangly boy pushed through the weathered screen door and crossed the porch. Once recognition hit, he was rushing down the steps and out to meet them. He only slowed when he got close and caught a better look at Cam.

His eyes widened as his gaze jumped from Cam to Math before landing on Vex. "What happened?"

Vex slowed, forcing Math to do the same, even though he worried if they stopped, he wouldn't be able to start again. She managed a weak but reassuring smile at the boy. "Hey, Daniel, need to get him inside."

The boy's throat worked as he swallowed hard. "Gotcha."

He did a quick about-face and led the way back to the house. He held the screen door open as Vex and Math shuffled Cam up the porch stairs. They stopped just inside the door and Math noted the neat, but sparsely furnished, living room with a tidy kitchen just beyond. Another room filled with mismatched cloth was tucked over to the left and a narrow hall divided the house into two.

"Where's your aunt?" Vex asked the boy.

Daniel squeezed by Math to move in front of them. "She's in Pebble Creek for Market Day. She had a bunch of finished blankets and stuff she wanted to sell."

"Damn," Vex muttered. "I lost track of the days." She eyed Daniel. "Our friend is going to have to stay a couple of days before he can make it into town. You sure your aunt would be okay with that?"

The kid gave a jerky nod. "She'd kick my butt if I didn't help you, you know that." He stepped out of their way and waved in the direction of the hall. "You can take him to the second room on the right."

Math eyed the hall's dubious width and looked over Cam's head to Vex. "I'll go first."

She nodded.

Together they managed a weird side shuffle down the hall. Finally, they got Cam in the room and eased him down to the simple quilt-covered bed. Daniel followed with a glass of water, that Vex took while Math lifted Cam's legs to the bed. Vex roused the injured man enough to get some water down him, before Cam weakly pushed her arm away. She set the glass down on a nearby stand, then sank next to Math who sat on the floor, his back and shoulders against the bed's edge. For a few blessed minutes, they simply sat there.

"Brought you some water." Daniel entered and crouched in front of them, two glasses extended.

Exhausted beyond politeness, Math took his glass, drained it, and then handed it back to Daniel. "Thanks."

The kid took his empty glass. "Want another?"

When he nodded, the kid rushed out of the room.

Vex nudged his foot with hers. "Why don't you go get cleaned up? I'll talk to Daniel."

"You sending him down for Mandy?"

She nodded. "Cam's going to need some serious medical attention, not to mention antibiotics, and she's our best bet. I'll also have Daniel reach out to Charity or Havoc. Whoever he runs across first."

Sounded like there was a story here with the kid. "Why not send him straight to Reaper?"

Vex raised her brow. "Reaper scares the kid spitless."

"He tends to have that effect on people."

Vex's voice softened and dropped low. "Daniel knows Charity and Havoc. They were there when he showed up at Pebble Creek after Raiders took out his family."

Math winced. The Raiders called the desert ruins of Las Vegas home but ranged further afield when the price was right.

They ran weapons, drugs, flesh, and anything else that sold. In their wake they always left carnage. "That was right after the Raiders killed Crane and took Simon, right?"

She looked away, but not before he caught the shadow of memory. "Yeah." She raised her almost empty glass and drained it.

The Raiders reminded him of their other problem—the mole burrowed somewhere in Pebble Creek. Now that Cam was as safe as he could be for the moment, Math needed to fulfill his promise to Reaper. He scratched at the heavy scruff on his jaw. "Daniel's got to stay low key." He didn't want to put Cam, or the kid, at risk.

Vex's grin was faint but amused. "He knows the drill. I'll have Daniel bring whatever medical supplies they have on hand, so you can take care of Cam. While you're doing that, I'll clean up and put some food together." She leaned her head back against the bed's edge and closed her eyes. "Figured Cam'll be more comfortable if I wasn't hanging around."

Under the thin layer of dust and grit, he didn't miss her exhaustion-lined features, the purpling along her cheek, or the bloodied piece of cloth wrapped around her arm where one of the guards managed to slice her up good. The personification of a badass female sat right next to him, and yet, when she turned her head and looked at him with those unusual amber eyes, he saw beyond the tough exterior to the worry and compassion she tried so hard to hide. That glimpse sucker-punched his heart.

Fuck, he was in so much trouble here. Strangely unsettled, he looked away and coughed. "Yeah. Sounds like a plan."

Daniel returned with a refilled glass in hand. He offered it to Math, who took it.

Vex used the bed's edge to get to her feet. "Daniel, can my friend use your bathroom? Maybe take a shower?"

"Sure." He jerked a thumb over his shoulder. "It's the

door at the end of the hall. Clean towels are in the linen cabinet."

Math raised his glass. "Much appreciated." He brought the glass to his lips.

Vex threw an arm over Daniel's narrow shoulders and led him out of the room. "Want to help me get some med supplies together?"

"Yeah, my aunt has stuff stashed. I'll show you."

"Cool, then I have a favor to ask."

Their conversation turned indistinct as they walked away. Exhaustion settled over Math as every bruise and cut decided to chime in. He set his glass on the floor next to his thigh, laid his head against the bed, and closed his eyes, just for a minute. He must have drifted off because the next thing he heard was Vex's soft, "Hey."

He blinked his scratchy eyes opened and scrubbed his hands over his face, forcing his brain into gear. When he dropped his hands, Vex was crouched in front of him, a small frown marring her forehead. He managed a weak smile. "Hey."

"Come on, hotshot. Let's get you on your feet." She reached out and grasped his arms. Automatically he returned her hold as she pulled him up. "You think you can manage a shower without falling asleep?"

"Maybe," he muttered.

When she moved to his side and curled an arm around his waist, he settled his arm over her shoulders. Together they headed for the bathroom.

She gave him a sidelong look as they moved along, hips bumping. "Don't need you going down in the shower."

"Aww, babe," he teased as he stepped into the small bathroom, "if you're that worried, you could always join me."

He set the temperature on the water for the shower, and turned to find her leaning against the doorjamb, her gaze leveled on his ass. When her eyes rose to his and color swept under her cheeks, he gave her a wicked grin and started to strip off his grimy t-shirt. He sucked in a sharp breath when his abused ribs protested and got stuck with his shirt halfway up.

The air shifted as she stepped in close, then her warm hands slid against his chest, not to help but to tease. Laughter lurked in her voice. "Need a little help?"

"Please." It came out rough as her touch snagged his body's attention. It didn't help when she moved in, standing so close he could feel every inch of her, from the soft press of her tits against his arm as she stretched against his front to help lift the shirt free, to warm breath against his bared skin. By the time she was finished "helping", his dick wanted some attention of its own.

She wadded up his t-shirt and went to step back. He caught her hips and held her in place. Their eyes locked as he dipped his head and pressed a soft open mouth kiss against the base of her throat. Her lashes fluttered as her head dropped back and a soft groan sounded as she lobbed the t-shirt to the corner before linking her arms around his neck. He traced a line of tiny kisses up her neck and over her chin before settling his mouth against hers.

Her hands slid into his hair, holding him close as her mouth opened, letting him in. He traced her lips before luring her tongue into a leisurely dance. Thoughts disappeared replaced by pure sensation. Lost in their shared desire, they moved in sensuous accord, lust and need combined into a voracious hunger that fueled a passionate storm.

All spiced heat and exotic promises, her taste sank deep, encouraging his lazy exploration, even as his body demanded more. She shifted restlessly against him, her hands sweeping from his hair, down his shoulders to drift over his chest with destructive intent. When her hand closed over the hard length of his cock and gave a gentle squeeze, he growled, thrust against her palm, and nipped her lower lip in punishment.

He lifted his head, took in her kiss-swollen lips, the twin flags of color riding under her skin, and the hazy heat of her eyes. *Damn, she was stunning.* Unable to resist her siren's lure, he brought his hand up over her ribs, determined to enjoy every inch of her. He cupped her breast through her shirt, pleased at how it fit his palm.

Her hand curled around his neck as he dropped his head to capture the turgid tip with his mouth and held him close. He teased her, taking savage delight when her hand flexed on his cock and a breathy moan escaped.

Daniel's abrupt, "I'm heading out, Vex," was followed by the slamming of the screen door that cut their carnal interlude short.

He reluctantly released her breast and rested his forehead against hers, their heavy breaths mingling. "Dammit."

The hand curled at his neck squeezed, then slowly let go even as her lips curved. "Play time's over." She gave his cock one last gentle squeeze before stepping back. Her hands went to his chest and gave him a small nudge. "Go, shower. I'll get some water boiling for Cam and find us something to eat."

He let his gaze go hooded. "I know what I want to eat."

Her smile took on a wanton curl. "Food, Math." She turned, moved into the hall, and threw over her shoulder, "The other, we'll deal with later."

"Promise?" he called back as he tried to adjust himself.

Her answer was a husky laugh.

twenty-one

Math's shower was short and cold, but took the edge off his aches and pains, and cleared some of the cobwebs from his brain. He draped the damp towel over his bare shoulders as he padded barefoot down the hall. Somehow Vex found a clean pair of jeans, that while a bit baggy, worked.

At the door to Cam's room, he turned to the kitchen and called out, "Shower's free!"

After getting her muffled response, he went to Cam's side and noted the pair of sweats sitting on a pile of blankets at the foot of the bed, which is where they would stay until he got his friend cleaned up. On a low side table, medical supplies were neatly arranged, and steam curled up from a water filled pot sitting on the seat of an empty chair. Noises from the kitchen indicated Vex was working on food and wondered how well she cooked. He'd find out enough.

Math sucked in a bracing breath as he took in Cam's battered body and wondered where the hell to start. The cuts and burns created a cruel map on his skin, and there were a couple of concerning bruises, which might mean something more serious lurked underneath. Unfortunately, since it would take a few hours, if not more, for Mandy to arrive, he needed to treat what he could now and pray the doc got there before things got ugly.

Math pulled off his towel, dipped one end in the water and let it soak while he cut Cam's pants off. By the time he finished, Math's jaw ached. Removing Cam's ragged pants wasn't easy as it stuck to various wounds and working them loose left Cam twitching and groaning.

Minutes ticked by as Math kept up a running monologue while cleaning Cam's battered skin. At one point, as Math worked on a particularly deep burn scoring Cam's hip, Cam took offense and punched Math in the side of the head. Math snarled, caught Cam's wrist, and forced it to the bed. Then he rubbed his ringing ear while a mix of frustration and fury roiled through him. "Dammit, you sure as hell stepped into it this time. What the hell were you thinking?"

"Was trying to stop a shipment." Cam's unexpectedly lucid response brought Math's head up. Despite the haze of fever and pain, there was no way to miss the sharp intelligence lying deep in the dark green eyes.

Math dipped the washcloth back into the water for another round. "Of?"

Cam tried to shrug but stopped with a pained wince. "Thought it was kids. Turned out to be one poor bastard."

Math was one of a few who knew the details of Cam's harsh history, so he knew exactly why his friend rushed to the rescue. "What happened?" He went back to his cleaning and tried to be as careful as possible as he worked his way down Cam's legs.

Cam's gaze went to the ceiling and only the occasional flinch revealed his discomfort. "I was working an angle on Greer, ran across whispers there was a deal going down."

"What kind of deal?"

"Repayment. Details were sketchy as shit, but did a little

digging, found out the repayment included some kid, couldn't be more than sixteen, maybe younger."

Math frowned and tried to slot in Cam's information into what he knew of Greer and how the bitch worked. "What's so special about this kid?"

"Dunno," Cam answered. "Was trying to find out and walked into an ambush."

Math gave him a sharp look as the dots started to line up, because if Cam had a hot button, it was abused kids. "A trap," he corrected his friend. "Designed specifically for you."

"Yeah," Cam agreed grimly.

"Greer's got her claws in deep somewhere," Math muttered, bending back to his painstaking work.

"Not a surprise." Cam's abused vocal cords turned his normally smooth voice rough. "You and I both know if you wave enough money around, leave a few hard-to-miss examples around, and follow up with more threats, someone is always willing to spill."

Knowing that didn't make it easier to swallow. "Did you overhear anything while they had you?"

Cam frowned. "A couple things. Not sure what they meant, if anything."

"Every piece of information means something. It's just a question of where it fits." Math finished cleaning the raw marks around Cam's ankles and threw the stained washcloth into the murky water. He dried his hands on a clean hand towel, moved the pot with water to the floor, and dragged the chair to the edge of the bed. He rested his arms on his knees. "Okay, you've got two choices, my friend. I sew up what I can on front, or you roll over so I can clean your backside, then I sew. So, heads or tails?"

Cam grimaced. "Shit. Heads. Get it over with." His eyes rolled to the door. "What's a man got to do to get a drink around here?"

Math tipped a glass of water to Cam's lips and when he was done, asked, "Ready?"

Cam nodded. Math used needle and thread and made the first of many punctures as Cam's jaw flexed, and his hands curled into fists.

Math kept an eye on Cam as he worked. "Tell me what you heard."

Sweat beaded Cam's brow. "Greer's still pissed about what went down in Salt Lake."

Math snorted and paid attention to his stitches. "No surprise. She's always had a hard-on for the Vultures." Especially Reaper, but that was a worry for later.

"Brother, she's out for blood. Yours and the Vultures." Cam's teeth snapped together as Math set another stitch. Once Math tied it off, Cam continued. "She won't stop until she destroys you both."

"Me specifically?" He busted his ass to keep his identity hidden, even during the chaotic events when he blew Greer and her men to kingdom come in Salt Lake. To find out it had been pointless would piss him off. He bent over the next deep wound and set his needle against ragged skin.

"Not yet, but she's closing in." Cam caught Math's arm with his other hand, and Math met his gaze and the ominous weight there. "She came by just after they caught my ass," Cam warned. "Never seen her so worked up. Swear to God, she's like a rabid dog with a bone."

Math searched Cam's face, easily reading his concern. "She's always been like that, Cam. You cross her and she'll scorch the earth to ensure you don't do it again. That hasn't changed." He tugged against Cam's hold in a silent request to be released. Cam's fingers uncurled, freeing Math. He searched his friend's face as his mind raced. "You're sure she doesn't have my name?"

Cam's cut lips pressed together as he studied Math, but he

finally blew out a breath and answered. "Just a vague description—tall, long dark hair, beard—nothing more that separates you from any other man." He eyed Math's hair and offered a half-assed grin that eased the tension. "Like the disguise, by the way. Very..." He waved his hand around in the air. "Not you."

"Yeah," Math muttered and went back to sewing up his friend. "It was Vex's suggestion."

"Vex, as in Fate's Vulture's Vex?" Speculation colored Cam's voice.

"The one and only."

"Huh, guess that means you finally took my advice."

Math shot his friend a look. "What advice would that be?"

"Stop trying to go it alone."

For some reason, Cam's stark answer arrowed deep, and snapped steel band around Math's chest, stilling his hand.

"It's about time," Cam said, blissfully unaware of Math's sudden shift in worldview. "I was getting worried you'd try taking Greer on all by your lonesome on some martyr-suicide bid and leave me all alone in this big, bad world."

Cam's half-serious comment broke Math's strange spell and he sucked in a quiet breath, before resuming his work. "I have no problems risking my ass to take Greer on, but to save your sorry ass required more than my humble skills, so I reached out."

"Glad you did. Just wish it hadn't taken me getting captured for you to take that step." Cam hissed in a sharp breath. "Hey, man, it's my skin needing stitches, not my bones."

"Buck up," Math shot back without pity, strangely stung by Cam's opinions. "Strix aren't team players."

"Strix are history." Cam's quietly serious response made Math pause. When he looked up, Cam kept going. "There aren't enough of us to survive, not like we were."

His matter-of-fact tone carried an edge of apology that pissed Math off. "So what? You want to walk away?"

"Fuck no. I have every intention of gutting Greer for what she did, but when she's no longer the mission? Then what? The only constant in this world is change, and for us—you, me, Mercy, and the others—we need to carve out our place in it. That means stepping out of the shadows and working with other like-minded groups—like the Vultures, or Dogs of War. Otherwise, the Strix will be nothing but a memory." By the time Cam finished, his face was pale, and his breath choppy.

Math let the silence settle between them, as he turned Cam's words over and over in his head, unable to escape his point. Greer's attack years earlier hadn't just devastated the Strix's ranks but left huge cracks in the foundation of what they were. Too much closely guarded information died with those who held it. Greer had been the surviving Strix's main focus for so long that picturing a future beyond her was difficult. What would they do? Settle down and play nice? *Fat chance in hell.* "Fuck, when did you get so smart?"

Cam's chuckle was rough as Math went back to work. "Always been the brains, my man. You were just too focused on the end game. Consider it my contribution when playing your wingman." His voice tightened as Math hit a particularly bad spot. "Gotta admit though, it'll be fun to watch you with Vex. She's definitely not your normal type."

Math snorted. "I don't have a type."

"Uh, yeah you do, man."

"One-night stands don't constitute a type."

"They do when they're all waiting for you to ride to their rescue." Cam's dry chuckle was shaky.

Math noted that although aware and talking, Cam's skin had taken on a pasty undertone and his breathing was erratic. He laid a hand on Cam's forehead to check his temperature.

It didn't stop Cam from talking. "Thing they never seem to realize is that you're not the knight they're waiting for."

Math set the last of his stitches in place. "If I'm not the knight, then what the hell am I?"

"You're the fucking dragon, devouring maidens and spitting out their bones. You, my friend, are easily bored and need a challenge."

Since Vex was pure challenge and currently embedded under his skin, Math figured Cam's observation skills were spot on.

Not done sharing his pearls of wisdom, Cam added, "Besides, you need a partner who's willing to come to your rescue occasionally. Especially when you're playing your stubborn ass solo hero routine."

"Appreciate the approval, now I can rest easy." Math set aside the needle and thread and picked up the jar of healing ointment. He carefully covered Cam's wounds with a thin layer, not missing the cool and clammy texture of his skin. "Come on, let's get you turned over before you pass out."

With a few curses and some groans, they got Cam on his stomach, and once he was stretched out, small shivers created mini earthquakes along Cam's muscles. The trauma was taking over and leaving Math little time to get whatever information he could out of Cam. "You got anything more on Greer?"

"When that last guard arrived last night—or was that this morning?"

"Doesn't matter." Math cleaned Cam's back, grateful the wounds were shallow.

"He mentioned Greer was expecting news, and they should be prepared to move in the morning." Cam's voice was fading.

"What kind of news?"

"Don't know, like I said, I only got bits and pieces."

Math worked on Cam's mangled back and his brain picked over the pieces Cam offered. Minutes swept by and the faint sound of the running shower played in the background. Math finished with the last bit of cleaning. "Hope to God Doc Mandy has some damn strong antibiotics, otherwise you're going to be in a world of hurt."

Cam's half mumbled, barely there, "Know that name," froze Math in his seat.

It was the second time he said that, and instinct whispered it wasn't just random mumblings. An ugly suspicion crept in and dragged cold fingers of dread along Math's nerve endings. He leaned closer to Cam and prayed he was wrong. "What name, buddy?"

But Cam was well and truly out.

Sitting back in his chair, Math listened to the shower shut off and thought of the woman in the bathroom and the brother in Pebble Creek with the mole problem. "Fuck."

twenty-two

Vex walked out of the bathroom on bare feet as she tied off the damp ends of her braid. Daniel found her a faded t-shirt and baggy pants that were comfy and clean, and from the size of them, weren't his. She was betting they once belonged to his older brother who died in the Raider's attack a few months back. The poor kid had lost his parents, older brother, two cousins and an uncle. Now it was just him and his aunt, Sara, struggling to keep the farm going.

She moved down the hall as the quiet of the house followed her. *What the hell had she been thinking bringing Cam here?* Especially with Greer and her men breathing down their necks?

Danny and Sara didn't need to be looking over their shoulders or praying they wouldn't get caught in the fallout of Vex's decision. She paused at the door to Cam's room as guilt poked and prodded and stuck her head in to see if Math was still with him. Cam was alone, passed out on his stomach, with a blanket resting at his hips that left his raw back exposed as it rose and fell with his breathing.

She stood there for a moment, just watching him breathe.

With each breath, her nibbles of guilt faded. The trek back from the Hole had been brutal and worry that Cam wouldn't make it kept her bike's throttle wide open. Strangely her worry wasn't so much for Cam, but for Math.

She didn't want to consider what would have happened if they hadn't found Cam alive, or if they lost him on the way in. She did know it wouldn't have been pretty. A loss like that would be the final nail in Math's coffin of sanity, and it would leave her in a world of hurt. So, yeah, she was glad Cam was still breathing.

She shook her head and headed to the kitchen where she found signs of Math's presence in the pot that rested in the drying rack and the small pile of soiled clothes that sat outside the small washroom door. Yet the man himself was nowhere to be found.

The savory scent of the soup heating on the stove caused her stomach to wake with a growl. She walked over and turned down the heat since the soup was for Cam. She required something a bit more substantial. After rummaging through cupboards and the fridge, she set out sandwich fixings.

For the first time in what seemed like forever, she wasn't occupied with dodging fists or knives, or covering Math's ass. Which was great, until all the messy emotions she shoved aside roared forward and demanded her attention. She cringed under the internal onslaught.

First was her uncharacteristic lack of control when it came to Math. Scratching an itch was one thing, but what was happening with Math was a different animal altogether. There was no way to deny that sleeping with him went beyond a simple itch. Emotions got involved, before and after, and defenses fell under the unrelenting barrage. She knew better.

Bad Vex!

There was no happy ending to this scenario. With Cam out of immediate danger, the only thing keeping Math around was his promise to Reaper to unearth the mole. Not just because he was a man of his word, but because keeping Reaper in his debt gave him leverage. Once that debt was paid, he'd be gone like the wind, leaving nothing but dust in his wake. He sure as hell wouldn't stick around for her.

And his request for time to see what would happen didn't mean anything. She chalked it up to the afterglow of getting laid. Resentment sank her good mood and left her irritated.

She grabbed a knife and started to cut up a tomato, doing her best to focus on anything other than why it upset her to think of Math leaving. Unwilling to go there, she considered the turbulent relationship between Reaper and Math because that was a puzzle.

Reaper wasn't one to walk away. Hell, if he was, he would have left Vex and Ruin in Portland. Their first couple of years with Reaper and Havoc were far from smooth because they pushed every known button to see what it would take to make the two older men turn their backs.

But they never did. Which made her wonder, what went down between the brothers to get Reaper to walk away? Because there wasn't much to hold on to in this world, except family, be they tied by blood or bond. Thanks to Math's sharing session at the Hole, her curiosity burned bright even as logic warned no one could help bridge that gap. Especially not her.

And that bothers you, why?

I don't like seeing him hurt.

He's a big boy. He doesn't need you.

Yeah, he does.

What makes you so sure?

Because I need him.

Her hand jerked at the simple answer that resonated with a sense of inevitability. She hissed as the blade kissed her finger and left tiny drops of red to seep along the thin cut. She dropped the knife, stuck her finger in her mouth, and went to the sink to rinse it off, mentally cursing a blue streak.

She ran her finger under the cool water and stared blindly out the window. Inside, where it could no longer be ignored, the truth of what she reluctantly admitted settled.

Dammit, she was falling for Math.

Worse, she wanted him to stay even though she didn't want to be in the position of having to choose between her love for Math and her unwavering loyalty to Reaper. She blinked back the ache that pressed against her tired eyes, turned off the water, dried off her finger, and finished her sandwiches.

It took a few deep breaths before the shaky storm that rocked her world retreated and left a bemused calm behind. Okay, so Math meant something to her. *Fine and dandy.* It didn't change what came next. Not really. She'd enjoy him as long as she had him. When the job was done, he'd leave.

She'd survive it.

She ignored the hollow ache in her chest and quickly finished her meal prep. Once everything was put away, she piled the two sandwiches on a plate and headed for the front porch. As she moved through the front room, she tried to tell herself she wasn't avoiding Math. Not that she knew where he was. Maybe he was lying down in another room, or something. Regardless, she pushed through the screen door only to come to a stop.

Sprawled in one of the wide rocking chairs, a shirtless Math turned his attention from the front yard to her. Curled at his feet was a herding dog, who lifted his head at her entrance. Math caught sight of the plate and offered a tiny smile. "Hey, one of those for me?"

She held out the plate. "Sure." She looked to the hopeful canine at his feet. "Sorry, you're out of luck."

Math chuckled and took one of the sandwiches.

She stepped over Math's legs, avoided the dog, and settled into the empty chair beside him. With her feet propped on the lowest rung of the railing, she took the edge off her hunger, and deliberately kept her eyes off Math's naked chest. It wasn't easy.

Next to her Math chewed and appeared to be deep in thought. Instead of adding to her tension, his stillness eased it. She settled back and worked her way through her sandwich. When she was halfway through, she paused, and asked, "How's he doing?"

Math frowned down at his sandwich. "Right now? Fine, I think."

She noted the worry darkening his features and decided he'd do better talking it out instead of brooding over it. "Any internal injuries?"

He shook his head. "I managed to stitch up the deepest of the cuts and got ointment on the burns. His bruises don't worry me, but avoiding an infection is going to be a challenge."

His concern was valid. Infections ranked right up there with viral outbreaks on the mortality scale. "Danny should be hitting Pebble Creek about now, so hopefully Mandy will be on her way soon. She's got some serious antibiotics in her arsenal, so I'm sure he'll be okay."

Her reassurance had the opposite reaction, seeming to darken Math's mood. "Yeah, about that," he muttered.

She waited for him to continue as a sense of foreboding set up shop. She held her tongue as he deliberately took another bite, his gaze aimed out into the front yard as he chewed. When he stayed silent, she set her half-eaten sandwich down. "What?"

He swallowed and turned his attention to her, meeting her gaze. "Think I know who your mole is."

For a moment his words didn't make any sense, but when

they did, she sat there stunned, and blinked in shock. "Wait! What? How?"

He held up a hand to forestall her questions. "There's a chance I'm wrong."

Although his words said one thing, his tone and expression said something different. She shook her head. "But..."

A muscle jumped in his jaw as his gaze shifted away. "I don't think I am."

When he looked back, she caught a flash of reluctant pity that left her hands curling into fists. This wasn't going to be good. "It's bad, isn't it?"

He nodded.

Her voice came out tight. "Who?"

"Mandy."

"Mandy?" In the shockwave of his answer, disbelief crowded in. "Are you fucking kidding me?"

When he remained grimly silent, she dropped the rest of her sandwich to the mutt since this discussion was ruining her appetite. She shoved out of her chair and stalked to the end of the porch.

No fucking way.

Mandy would never sell out Pebble Creek. That kind of betrayal required a cold, selfish heart. Mandy's was protective and loving. She was fiercely loyal to those in her community, especially those who had been abused. It was why she was in charge of the kidnapped kids rescued from the Raiders. Everyone trusted her. Reaper trusted her and he wasn't anyone's fool.

She hit the end of the porch and kept her back to Math, as she tried not to let her temper overtake logic. "Tell me why you think it's her."

He didn't answer her question, instead he asked one of his own. "What do you really know about her?"

Her stomach knotted as she braced her hands on the

porch railing and stared unseeingly out over the side yard. She shoved her emotions down and forced her brain to work.

What did she know about Mandy's history? Not much. Most of what she knew came from Ruin and Simon, who both seemed to hold a special place in Mandy's heart. Maybe because they were always getting patched up. Their acceptance and Mandy's care of the two men managed to get her an in with Vex, who wasn't inclined to accept others easily.

"According to Ruin and Si, about a decade ago, her entire family was wiped out by Raiders. One of Crane's patrols found her among the remains of their burned-out homestead and brought her to Pebble Creek." She turned and leaned back against the railing, her arms crossed over her chest. "She's been Pebble Creek's doc ever since. Crane, Simon, and Boden, they all use her as a sounding board. They trust her." She shook her head. "She's the heart of Pebble Creek, Math. I know it doesn't mean much to you, but Reaper trusts her. It's why he and Simon gave her the kids to take care of. There was no one else any of us would have trusted those girls with." She held Math's gaze. "You've got to be wrong."

Instead of arguing with her, he said, "Maybe, but Cam recognized her name."

Vex threw out a hand in frustration. "Cam's injured and probably delirious."

"Cam's a Strix."

"So, what? He's immune to making mistakes?"

"No, but a Strix's strength lies in the information they hold. We excel at stitching the tiniest pieces together to create an accurate tapestry." He held her gaze. "Cam isn't making it up."

Math was so sure she wanted to hit him. "She's not the only Mandy out there."

"Think about it for a second." He didn't relent and kept his voice level. "You know the mole has to be someone the

Vultures and Simon trust. Too much critical information—including Crane's movements the day of the attack and details on shipments—are only known to a few." As she shook her head, trying to refute his words, he kept going. "Since Crane's death, other than a couple of runs at the supply shipments, has there been anything more serious?"

"No," she gritted out.

"If it is her, chances are, after what went down with Crane, she's keeping a low profile."

"She wouldn't do it." Even she could hear the underlying plea in her voice.

"If someone has something she wants, she might."

She spun away from his too insightful gaze and curled her hand over the railing. Images of Mandy with the traumatized girls, Mandy sipping tea and laughing with Worth, Mandy taking care of Simon, of Ruin, ran through her mind. It was beyond difficult to believe the woman Vex knew would betray those she called family and friends.

Difficult, but not impossible.

Vex knew everyone had an Achilles' heel, that one vulnerable spot where if enough pressure was exerted, could break a person. *What was Mandy's?*

Vex hated the fact that Math's accusations were taking root. She sucked in a breath and fought to keep her voice even. "What possible reason would she have for betraying Crane?"

"I don't know, but whatever it is, it has to be important enough for her to risk everything." He paused, then asked, "You said Raiders attacked her homestead? Where was it?"

Vex turned and slowly made her way back to her chair as she combed through the bits and pieces she knew of Mandy's story. If Crane's patrol found her, it meant her home was somewhere along the main route. That route stretched from New Seattle, down to northern Arizona, and into Utah, which covered a lot of territory. It was the main artery between Lilith's domain in Colorado and Michael's on the west coast.

Vex settled into the chair and said, "I couldn't say, other than it had to be on the main route."

"That's a lot of distance, but there are a variety of strategic points, bigger and more critical than a single homestead, that could be hit." He watched Vex closely. "So why pick Mandy's homestead? What made her place so special?"

"Who the hell knows why Raiders do anything?" Vex rubbed at the ache rising behind her eyes as Math's question tumbled over and over in her mind.

The Raiders hit Pebble Creek and took out Crane to disrupt the main supply routes between territories. The only reason their plan didn't succeed was that Fate's Vultures had been working with Crane and were close at hand when the hit went down. Not close enough to stop it, but they did minimize the fallout, thanks to their personal tie to Simon. As soon as shit hit the fan, they set out to rescue Simon so he could lead Pebble Creek and keep it stable.

She drummed her fingers on the chair's arm. "We know they took out Daniel's family simply because they were close enough to raise the alarm in Pebble Creek."

Math leaned forward and braced his arms on his knees. "Exactly. So why hit Mandy's homestead? If it wasn't close by, but simply along the route so a patrol could find her, what does taking out a single, out of the way, homestead accomplish? What was so important about Mandy?"

"I don't know." She held his gaze and fought past the ugly thoughts slipping in.

What if Mandy was a sleeper? Planted there to gain a position of trust and moved when the time was right?

Vex's chest hurt, physically hurt, as if she had taken a hard punch. She needed answers. Answers that would come from only one person. She swallowed down the metallic taste of betrayal. "What do you want to do?"

"When she shows up, we ask her."

Vex's laugh was harsh. "And, what? Expect her to answer honestly?"

He shot her an unreadable look. "Are you going to torture her for the truth?"

The thought of hurting Mandy left Vex ill. Before she could answer Math, she caught a trail of dust heading towards the ranch. Straightening, she muttered, "Incoming."

twenty-three

Math rose to his feet and moved to her side. He curled his arm around her waist and pulled her close, even as he stayed silent. It wasn't like there was anything he could say to make this easier.

Despite her emotional upheaval, Vex rested her head against Math's shoulder, needing the comfort. "How do you excuse a betrayal like this?"

The arm at her waist tightened and he brushed his chin against the top of her hair. "I can't."

Together they watched two bikes roar into the yard, the lead one was Ruin's, the second was Charity's bike. When the dust settled, Ruin got off, and waited for Charity and the older woman coming up behind her. The trio headed towards the porch.

Vex took a deep breath and strove to keep her voice casual. "Hey, Ruin! Charity! Mandy! You made good time."

Ruin answered first. "Reaper sent us out the minute Danny shared."

Afternoon sunlight glinted off Mandy's glasses as she looked to Vex. "Heard you needed my services." The dark-haired, reed-thin woman pulled a small pack off her back as she mounted the steps. She flashed a smile. "Where's the patient?"

Without stepping away from Vex Math motioned inside. "Down the hall, second room on the right."

Ruin sent his twin a curious look as he clocked her cozy position. Vex gave him a short shake of her head and a pointed glance at Mandy. Thankfully he didn't need much more than that to understand her silent request. He turned to Charity. "Babe, you mind helping Mandy? Need to catch up with baby sis."

Charity's gaze narrowed at the subtle undercurrents, but she played along. "Sure." She held the door open for Mandy. "Come on, doc, let's see what we're dealing with."

"There's soup on the stove if he's awake," Vex said as the two women started inside.

Charity let Mandy pass through and studied the three on the porch. "I'll make sure he eats something." Then she followed the doc inside and let the door close.

Ruin waited until the sound of Charity and Mandy drifted away. Then he turned, settled his shoulder against one of the porch columns, and faced Math and Vex. "You two don't look especially happy for pulling off a rescue. What's going on?"

Vex studied her brother, reluctant to share because Ruin adored Mandy and was extremely protective of the older woman. No way could she just blurt out Math's suspicion. She looked back to the screen door, then back to her brother. With a tilt of her head, she stepped away from Math and moved out into the front yard and out of possible hearing range.

She picked her way over the scrubby grass and gravel and stopped near the bikes. When Math and Ruin joined her, she took a bracing breath and said, "We might know who the mole is."

Ruin's face turned into a ruthless mask and his spine straightened. "Who?"

Vex shared a glance with Math, then shared, "Mandy."

For a long moment Ruin simply stared at her, uncomprehending. Then anger swept in and darkened his face. Recognizing the signs of his impending temper, Vex crossed her arms and waited for the explosion.

Ruin didn't waste time closing in and hissing, "What the fuck are you talking about, Vex?" His gaze slid to Math and narrowed. "What kind of shit are you playing at? Because this has to come from you."

"Take it down a notch, Ruin." Vex eyed the screen door then came back to her brother. "Before you lose your shit, just listen."

Ruin pivoted on his heel and stalked away. His shoulders rose and fell as he fought back his temper. When he returned, she didn't flinch from the storm in his eyes. His voice was arctic as he stared down at her. "Start talking."

She started with, "Cam, Math's friend, overheard Greer's guards mention a Mandy."

"A Doc Mandy," Math corrected.

Ruin glared at him. "Doesn't mean shit."

"You're right," Vex agreed. "But can we risk it?"

Ruin's gaze dropped to her. "You really think that the woman in there betrayed Crane? Betrayed Simon?"

Vex didn't miss his unspoken, "us," and her heart ached. If she was reeling from the possibility, she knew Ruin was hurting too. Hell, probably even more so since he let people in more than she did.

"I don't know," she answered. "I wish I could swear on all that's holy she would never do anything like that, but that's a risk we can't take."

"She would never work with the Raiders. Not after what they did to her family." Ruin pointed out.

"If Cam's right, it's not Raiders she's working with," Math explained. "It's Greer."

"Sure, it is," Ruin shot back, his sarcasm loud and clear. He turned to Vex. "What possible reason could she have?"

Vex stared into angry, familiar amber eyes and felt frustratingly useless. "I don't know."

Ruin spun on his heel, giving them his back, and ran a hand through his hair. Minutes ticked by as he struggled with their speculation. "What's your plan?"

Vex shared a look with Math, then told her brother's back. "We ask her."

When Ruin turned back around, his emotions were tucked away, but a hint of contempt lingered. "You're going to accuse her of betraying the community that saved her, all on the word of some asshole you hooked up with?" He shook his head. "What the hell, Vex? You love 'em and leave 'em. What's so special about him?" He jerked a dismissive hand at Math. "He have a magic dick or something?"

"Never had any complaints," Math offered unhelpfully.

"Shut up!" Vex and Ruin snapped in unison before returning to glaring at each other.

Ruin's scorn sliced against Vex's heart as she struggled with her own guilt for suspecting Mandy. As twins, they shared the same, lethal temper, but rarely had she ended up on the receiving end. Ruin's accusation stirred up a storm of fury that buried the hurt. That he would question her judgement made it that much worse.

She closed in and used both hands to shove Ruin back a step. "Fuck you, Ruin! I didn't question which head you used when you hooked up with Lilith's damn 'Hound."

Undaunted, Ruin shoved back. "Charity has nothing to do with this!"

His hit rocked her but with Math standing solidly at her back that's all it did. "Bullshit! If she came to you with this, you'd have her back. But me?" She got in Ruin's face, forcing him to lean back. "I bring this to you and suddenly I'm so desperate for cock I can't be trusted?"

His face twisted and he crowded her back. "Careful, you're starting to sound jealous."

Jealous? For a second, she could only stare at him, stunned. *Was he out of his tiny, demented mind?*

With a short scream of frustration, she grabbed her hair so she wouldn't deck him. "It's not jealousy, dumbass!" She dropped her hands and drilled a finger into his chest. "It's fucking frustration that the one person who knows me best doesn't have my back."

Ruin wrapped his hands around her arms and held her in place. "I'm not the one determined to punish anyone who gets close." He shook her, his frustration and temper at an all-time high. "What the hell did I do that you can't forgive?"

Any semblance of control Vex held shattered under his accusation. "You left!" The retaliatory truth she'd never dared voice broke free. He had backed her into an emotional corner by starting this conversation and after too many years of silencing her younger self all that buried resentment and pain spilled free. She stared into his stunned expression and choked out, "You left us—me and Marnie."

Ruin didn't get lost with her sudden shift in the argument but followed her unerringly into their shared history. Emotions played out over his face, a familiar mix of guilt and grief, years in the making, mixed with his current temper, until what was left was an exasperated frustration. He loosened his grip on her with a studied carefulness. "I can't change that, Vex. All I can do is apologize."

"I don't want an apology." She forced her voice past the constricting weight of suppressed emotions.

"Then what do you want?"

She heard the hurt under his frustration and struggled for a way to ease it. She came up empty.

His expression shifted, his hurt disappearing under a scowl as his voice went hard. "How long are you going to use that excuse to hold everyone back? God, it's time to grow up, Vex."

Ruin's verbal slap poured steel into her spine. She drew back only to come up against Math as her emotions iced over. Her voice was flat and empty as she held Ruin's gaze. "I grew up a long time ago, Ruin. Right about the same time I was raped, and Marnie was murdered. Always did think she was the lucky one."

Her revelation wiped Ruin's face clear of all but shock. He reached for her, but she stumbled out of reach, forcing Math back a step even as his hands went to her hips to keep them upright.

"Goddammit, Vex." Ruin's hands curled into fists and his voice was heavy with unrelenting. He looked away, his throat working. Seconds stretched before he spoke again, his voice rough, his gaze on the ground. "I think I knew. Somewhere, but..."

"You didn't ask." Somewhere inside the frozen wasteland of her heart his pain resonated, but she couldn't feel it. Not yet. Behind her, Math shifted, pulling her close, his hands folding at her stomach.

Ruin held up a hand and corrected, "I couldn't. When I got back and saw you, the bruises, and broken bones, and then Marnie..." Whatever he saw in her gaze made him flinch and look away. His hand went to the back of his neck and held on, guilt riding his shoulders into a curve. A breath passed, then another before he lifted his head. "I'm sorry, Vex. More than you'll ever know. I should've pushed it, but..." His shoulders straightened and his chin lifted. "Whether you shared or not, isn't important. I shouldn't have left you two. Rally couldn't be trusted, and somewhere, deep down, I knew he sent me on that job to get rid of me."

As she listened to her brother try to claw free of the past, the ice inside her chest cracked and the emotional storm waned. Needing an anchor, she wrapped her hands over Math's and held on. "If you hadn't gone, he'd have killed you."

"We'll never know." Ruin's chest rose and fell in a deep breath. "Afterwards... it made me sick that I couldn't fix it, so I did the only thing I could. I hunted the assholes down."

The defeat on Ruin's face left her stomach in knots. "It helped."

Ruin searched her face, his doubt clear.

She wasn't sure what to say to make him believe her, so she kept going. "It did, Ruin. Maybe I should've said something, but you had your own steaming pile of shit to deal with." The tension riding her muscles ebbed away as the last of the upheaval retreated, leaving her tired—physically and emotionally. "I shouldn't have shared like that, but you pissed me off."

"No, I hurt you, which makes me a shitty brother." Ruin offered her a half-hearted grin. "It earns you a free hit. Want it now?"

Her laugh was shaky. "I'll take a rain-check."

"Figures." Ruin looked to Math. "Sorry, shouldn't have dragged you into this mess."

Vex felt Math shrug. "Do I get a free punch?"

"Hell, no." Ruin rubbed his jaw, his eyes dropping to where Math held Vex. He aimed a pointed look at his sister. "You know what you're doing?"

Vex's brain was slow thanks to the emotional overload, and she frowned. "With?"

Ruin lifted his chin toward Math. "Him."

Her temper stirred and she narrowed her eyes in warning.

A warning that bounced right off of Ruin's thick skull

because he kept pushing. "He doesn't strike me as the bendable type."

Behind her, Math asked, "Bendable?"

White teeth flashed in his beard as Ruin grinned. "As in, she won't be able to wrap you around her finger."

Her brother's quirky humor made Vex huff, even as heat rode her cheeks. "Maybe we can stop poking around my personal life and focus on the problem at hand."

Ruin's humor drifted away, and he looked towards the house, his face reverting to inscrutable lines. "All right." He turned to Math. "Explain to me why you think Mandy's screwing us all over."

twenty-four

Math watched the sun flirt with the horizon as he sat on the porch and picked through the unsettling mix of emotions caused by the woman curled in the chair at his side. Everything about her was unexpected and kept him continually off balance. He never thought he could enjoy such a wild and bumpy ride, but now that he had a taste, he was addicted to the rush of slipping down every rabbit hole she presented. Maybe it wouldn't last, but the ride—damn, the ride might be worth it. Admitting that was a kick in the balls.

Never again did he want to witness a confrontation as painful as the one between the twins earlier, but listening to her relive it, he saw how deep the damage went. For her to drag the whole sordid mess out into the light and share with her brother took courage, and there was no denying he was proud of Vex's bravery.

And that other emotion, the one he couldn't pin down? The one that burrowed deeper each time she stepped into him, like he was her anchor? Nope, he wasn't ready to go there. Not until there was no other choice.

"I don't like this." Ruin's voice was low, as he half-sat,

half-leaned on the railing in front of them and hitched his hip on the railing's edge, eyeing the screen door.

Vex stirred in her chair, untucked one leg, and set a bare foot on the porch. "Not sure any of us do, but we need to know. One way or the other."

Ruin's gaze shifted and Math craned his neck to see Charity slip out the screen door and head straight for her man. Ruin adjusted his position and made room for her to slide her curves close. She tilted her head back and touched his jaw with her lips. "Hey, babe."

Ruin brushed the back of his hand over her cheek. "Hey, you."

Charity turned back and her gaze settled on Math and Vex with a disconcerting shrewdness. "You guys look awfully serious."

It had been years since he first saw her, but Math recognized the woman who was Lilith's 'Hound and she wasn't one to miss details. Of course, those details often determined your ability to live out another day when you played master spy to the Rocky Mountain Queen. Before she could share their previous connection with Ruin and Vex, he asked, "How's Cam?"

Amused recognition danced in her eyes, but she played along. "Sleeping. Mandy managed to get antibiotics and soup down him. She's monitoring his temp in case it spikes." She twisted to look at Ruin. "What don't we like?"

Ruin grimaced. "Heard that, uh?"

Charity didn't answer but waited in silent demand. Ruin sighed and recapped their concerns in low tones as he kept one eye on the screen door.

Math gauged Charity's reaction. Not only would she provide an unbiased assessment, but her job required an enhanced skill at reading people. If their assumptions about Mandy were off base, Charity wouldn't hesitate to set them straight. After Ruin finished, she looked away with a frown, folded her arms over his at her waist, and dropped her head to rest against his shoulder.

Her reaction left Math uneasy. "You don't seem surprised."

Charity's shrug was half-hearted. "Not much surprises me anymore."

"We're talking about Mandy," Ruin argued.

Vex stayed quiet, her thoughts hidden, and her focus on Charity.

"I get that." Charity tipped her head back and caught the way Ruin's jaw tightened before he looked away. "Hey." She caught his face and turned him back to her. "I do. But I don't have history with Mandy."

The lines in Ruin's face eased at whatever he saw in her face.

Math leaned forward and braced his elbows on his knees, gaining their attention. He met Charity's somber gaze. "Do you think we're reaching?"

She thought it over and eventually shook her head. "No." She shot Ruin an apologetic look. "Sorry, babe."

The emotion burning in Ruin's eyes didn't leak through his impassive mask, but his voice was grim. "Yeah, me too."

Charity took a big breath and resettled against him, once again facing Math and Vex. "So, what's next?"

Vex finally spoke. "Reaper will be here soon."

And won't that be fun? It was a close call, but Math managed not to roll his eyes because when Reaper heard their suspicions his reaction wouldn't be pretty. Shit would get said, and some of that shit would land on Math. Since he already survived one sibling blow-up for the day, maybe it was best he go in and keep an eye on Cam and Mandy. He pressed his palms against his thighs to do just that but Vex caught his arm and held him in place.

"Going somewhere, hot shot?" Despite the exhaustion on her wan face, wry humor peeked through, as if she knew exactly why he was leaving.

Still, he gave it a shot. "Figured I'd check on Cam and keep an eye on Mandy."

"Uh-huh, so you're not trying to steer clear of the blast zone?"

He gave in and grumped, "That a problem?"

She patted his arm. "Don't worry, I'm sure he'll pull his punches.'

"Ha-fucking-ha." He tugged his arm away. "Aren't you a riot?"

"That reminds me," Ruin started. "What is the deal between you and Reaper, anyway?"

Math held Vex's gaze as the teasing glint disappeared and was replaced by understanding. "Might as well tell him," she warned in a soft voice. "He'll find out sooner or later."

He knew she was right, but dammit, when would all this sharing shit stop? It had to end, right? What lay between him and Reaper stretched long and deep, and he didn't want to dive into the emotional pit of resentment and love that would leave him a bloodied mess. At least, not today. He turned away from Vex only to catch Charity's tiny nod of agreement.

Ruin didn't miss the silent interplay. He straightened and lost all signs of his earlier casualness to demand, "What the fuck? Am I the only one who doesn't know? Tell me."

For fuck's sake! Can't anyone mind their own business anymore? "Reaper's my brother."

Ruin's reaction was a long, slow blink, followed by a slow, wicked grin. "No shit!" He threw his sister a speculative look. "You're so in for it."

Vex's lips thinned, and her chin lifted. "What?" The belligerence in her question carried a world of guilt she couldn't hide from the others.

Ruin's grin widened. "What do you mean 'what'? You're hooking up with Reaper's brother. You think he's going to throw you a party?"

When Vex's chin notched higher, Math couldn't help his spurt of amusement. Any higher and she'd tumble her chair backwards.

Clearly unwilling to give Ruin an opening, Vex haughtily informed him, "Not his business."

Undaunted, Ruin asked, "You a Vulture?"

Vex's nod was reluctant.

"Then, he'll make it his business." On that note, Ruin turned to Math and his grin went from wicked to downright evil. "I can't wait. This is going to be fun." He squeezed Charity. "We're going to have front row seats to the best show in town."

Charity smiled. "You're way too happy about this."

"Yep." He popped the 'p' as his evil grin widened.

Math resorted to a time-honored response and flipped Ruin the bird. "Like Vex said, not his business." Hell, Math's life hadn't pinged on Reaper's radar for years, and there was no reason for to start doing so now.

"Even if you're messing with one of his Vultures?" A snarky internal voice asked.

Okay, point, but Vex was a big girl. Reaper would have to deal. Math ignored the resulting snicker in his head.

Ruin tugged on Charity's hair until she tipped her head back to look at him. He frowned down at her. "You knew this?

Her expression was pure cat-and-canary. "Uh-huh."

Ruin narrowed his eyes. "Why's that?" When she didn't say anything, he shot Math a dark look, then went back to her. "You two know each other." It was a statement, not a question and it came out on a near growl.

Charity angled her head until her hair slid from Ruin's hold, then turned to Math with a silent question in her eyes.

Holding her gaze, Math gave the tiniest of shakes, and answered Ruin for her. "Our paths crossed." He looked to Ruin and caught the hint of jealous speculation. Normally that would be funny, but right now, not so much, so he elaborated. "Once."

"Or twice," Charity corrected.

"Really?" This time it was Vex asking.

There was something in her voice that urged him to explain. "Not surprising, considering our career choices."

Color flagged Vex's cheeks, but that disconcerting note disappeared when she muttered, "Yeah, go figure."

"A spy and an assassin walk into a bar..." Ruin started in a singsong voice only to trail off when the rumble of an approaching bike reached them.

The bike came closer until the rider was easily recognizable. Reaper pulled in, alone. No sign of Danny or Havoc. The four on the porch waited while he shut down the bike, dismounted, tugged the bandana protecting his nose and mouth down, and then lifted a hand in greeting.

With his dark hair pulled back, his bandana below his beard, dressed in black cargos, gray t-shirt, and leather jacket, he was an intimidating figure. Add in the aura of menace he projected and there was a reason his name was feared among the degenerates he hunted. He shrugged off his jacket, tossed it over his bike, stalked over, and his boots hit the steps. He exchanged nods and greetings, then picked a spot next to Ruin and Charity to settle in. He braced his elbows on the railing, leaned back, stretched his legs out and crossed them at the ankles.

His dark gaze drifted over Vex, then to Math where it stayed. "How's your man?"

"Alive."

Reaper lifted his chin at the news. "Good to hear."

Vex drew Reaper's attention by using her foot to set her chair in motion. "Where's Danny?"

"Left him with his aunt at Grave's Hall," Reaper shared. "Worth's putting them up for the night." He gave Math a mocking glance. "Didn't want to risk them getting hurt if you were tailed."

Math refused to rise to his brother's bait, and when Reaper's eyes lit with silent laughter, Math gritted his teeth, determined not be the one to start shit. This time.

Reaper's humor disappeared as studied the faces around him and clued into the underlying tension on the porch. He turned back to Math. "You don't look like a man who just pulled his guy out of the Hole and lived to tell the story." He shifted his attention to the others. "None of you do. What don't I know?"

Math bit back his need to comment about what his brother didn't know.

Vex held up a hand. "Hang on, where's Havoc and Mercy?"

"With Simon," Reaper said. "No sense in tipping off our rat that shit might be going south."

As an opening, it was a big one, and when Ruin, Charity, and Vex all turned to Math, he mentally cursed, then muttered, "Yeah, about that. Might have a lead."

Reaper didn't move, but the air chilled. "Explain."

Ruin moved closer to the door, looked to the screen for movement, and then nodded to Math.

Math shared an abbreviated version with the same logic he used with Vex. By the time he was done, Reaper had turned away his grip on the railing tight enough to delineate the muscles in his corded arms in stark relief. He stared over the yard, his shoulders rigid, and his profile a granite mask that effectively hid his thoughts. Math expected a demand for details, instead an ominous weighty silence settled in.

When Reaper finally spoke, his voice was cold and empty. "Where is she?'"

"Inside," Vex answered.

Reaper's head turned slowly, and his dark gaze landed on Charity. "Get her."

Charity nodded, touched Ruin's hand in passing, and headed in. Once inside she disappeared into the house's dim interior.

Math gave his brother credit, Reaper had sent in the one person guaranteed not to tip off Mandy.

Reaper straightened and motioned to Math. "Up."

Math didn't argue with Reaper, not with his current mood coiling around the porch like a snake waiting to strike. Instead, Math got up and went to stand by Vex. She shifted in her seat and made room so he could hitch a hip on the chair's wide arm. He laid an arm over the chair's back and Vex settled against him. He looked up to find Reaper watching them. Math met Reaper's dark gaze in silent challenge, not about to hide whatever it was that he and Vex had going on.

Reaper snorted, grabbed the now empty chair, and spun it around so it sat in the middle of the porch. Then he and Ruin shifted back to the railing and waited for the two women to appear.

Feminine murmurs drifted towards them and then Charity was pushing through the screen door. She spotted the rearranged chair and her lips tightened, but she held the door open for Mandy to follow.

The older woman stepped through and came to an abrupt halt when she realized everyone was staring at her. "What's wrong?" Her gaze jumped around the group, but there were no answers to be found in the ring of emotionless masks.

Reaper made a sharp motion to the empty chair. "Sit."

Mandy heeded the whip of command in his voice, slipped around Charity, and sat. "What's going on?" Although she tried to hide her worry, it was evident in the tightening around her eyes and the whitening of her knuckles as she clutched at the chair's arms.

Reaper didn't answer, instead he moved in front of her, dropped into a crouch, and grabbed the chair arms, caging her in. His gaze was hard, and he didn't screw around, but got right to the point. "Doc, going to ask you some questions." There was no mistaking the pitiless tone in his low voice. "Whatever you do, don't lie to me."

Unable to escape the threat in front of her, Mandy sat in the chair, her eyes wide and staring behind her glasses, like a rat with a viper. Whatever she saw in Reaper's eyes leeched the color from her skin. Her mouth opened, but nothing came out. She swallowed hard and tried again. "About?"

"You." Reaper didn't give her a chance to process his answer before he started in. "You lived on a homestead out on the line between here and Denver?"

Her nod was jerky, and she cradled her stomach with her right arm as her left hand rose and absently rubbed it. "Settlements are few and far between there, but there were families spread throughout a nearby valley. We had a small farm and provided medical assistance for those traveling or living nearby. Especially when they couldn't get to Denver or one of the bigger towns." Her tongue darted out over her lips. "Wha... what's going on?"

Reaper ignored her question and continued in the same low voice. "Raiders hit your homestead?" He waited for her nod, and when it came, he pressed, "Why?"

Mandy watched Reaper warily. "I don't know.' It came out shaky and she sucked in a stuttered breath before adding, "We didn't have anything, other than some medicines. Nothing worth ki... killing for." Behind the lenses, her lashes fluttered, and a single tear escaped to trail down her cheek.

Next to Math, Vex shifted. Unlike Math, she was

undoubtedly moved by Mandy's distress. He squeezed her shoulder in warning and she settled, but a frown marred her forehead.

"One of Crane's patrols found you?" Reaper let go of the chair arms but held his position.

Mandy managed another nod. "Raiders torched the farm." An audible hitch broke her voice. "The patrol spotted the smoke."

Reaper reached out with infinite care and gently pushed her right sleeve up past her elbow revealing burn scars. He trailed a single finger over the raised, shiny white skin that dripped down her arm. "You were the only survivor?"

Her quiet sob was followed by another nod.

Reaper stopped touching her and rested his arms on his knees. "How?"

Witnessing the depth of bitter anger and endless grief wasn't easy, but Math reminded himself of the death and destruction this woman had caused, including how she put Vex and Reaper in Greer's crosshairs.

"Dumb luck." Mandy said the words like a curse. "A burning beam fell, knocked me out, and trapped me underneath the rubble. The patrol combed through the ruins and found me." Small tremors ran through her.

Her obvious distress didn't stop Reaper's inquisition. "And your family?"

Mandy's frame shuddered as tears fell, and a stifled sob escaped. She never looked away from Reaper as anguish and pain, fresh as the day it happened, reflected on her face. Math recognized the guilt under it, and so did Reaper, who covered Mandy's clenched hands with his.

At the railing, Ruin shifted and opened his mouth, but Charity set a warning hand on his chest and shook her head in silent reprimand. His mouth closed and his lips tightened into a thin, tight line.

Yeah, Charity saw it too.

Mandy stared down at where Reaper held her hands. "There were remains." It came out in a choked whisper. "When I finally woke in Pebble Creek, they told me they buried what they could, but there wasn't much left." She lifted her head, tugged her hand out from under Reaper's hold, and angrily brushed away the revealing wetness. "Why is this important?"

Reaper answered with brutal honesty. "Because I'm trying to figure out how they got to you."

twenty-five

At Reaper's accusation, Mandy's spine shot straight and her mouth fell open. Her shock was clear, but there was a skitter of panic sliding under it. She shook her head once before she choked out, "Got to me?"

Reaper ignored her question, and any earlier sympathy was gone, replaced by a flat, cold tone. "You know what bothered me most about the Raiders' attack on Pebble Creek? They were focused. It may not seem like it, the way they butchered Danny's family on the way in, but that was tactical—a way to make sure no one raised the alarm before they struck. But when they hit Pebble Creek, they caused a shit ton of problems at the front gate and dropped a few bodies, all while a smaller group slips through and heads straight for Crane. Just as if they knew exactly where Crane would be. They take him out and bail."

He didn't look away from the now nearly translucent Mandy. "That's not typical Raider behavior, that's surgical, strategic. They blitz, take what they want, and then raze shit to the ground. And, just like your family, they tend not to leave witnesses."

He leaned in and Mandy inched back. "Knowing that, I have to wonder, who knew Crane's movements well enough to share?" He kept his gaze on Mandy, but raised his voice to ask, "Charity, which name hits you first?"

Soft, but sure Charity answered, "Boden."

Mandy flinched as if hit.

Reaper shook his head. "Nope, not Boden. He was holding the fuckers back at the front gate. Plus, if he wanted Crane out of the way, he would do it himself. He sure as shit wouldn't endanger anyone else."

"There's Simon." Ruin offered, even though it was obvious from his torn expression, that he didn't want to, he followed Reaper's play.

Reaper gave another slow shake of his head. "Not, Si. He chased the bastards into the mountains and got nailed to a wall." His voice got soft. "So, who does that leave, Mandy? Who else did Crane rely on? Who did he trust?"

With each question Reaper put to her, Mandy flinched, until she was cowering in the chair, her arms crossed protectively over her stomach.

Reaper didn't relent but got close and held her eyes with his. "That would be you."

Mandy's hands went to her face in a last-ditch attempt to hide, but it only muffled her denial. "I... I... d... didn't..."

This time it was Math who flinched, because lying never went over well with Reaper. *Bad move, Doc.*

His brother's face darkened with temper and fury. He grabbed the chair arms so hard the wood creaked under his grip. "Don't." It came out in a vicious snarl. "I don't want to hurt you, but if you lie..." He let the threat hang in the air. "Tell me why."

Mandy's quaked in her seat, her fists curled in her lap, and choked out a whispered admission. "She has Drake, my son."

Her revelation hit the group and left a stunned shock in its wake.

For the first time Reaper looked away from Mandy and his jaw flexed as he visibly fought for control. When he looked back up, his voice was as hard as his expression. "Who has him?"

"Greer." Mandy leaned forward and lifted her hand as if to touch Reaper, but she stopped, pulled back, and tucked her hands back into her lap.

Her confession added fuel to Math's smoldering fury with Greer, and under his arm, Vex leaned deeper into his side as if to comfort. *Greer was a bitch, but to use a child?*

Reaper turned to Math, his eyes stormy and his jaw tight as he struggled with some unnamed emotion. Math held his gaze and wondered what pissed off his brother more, the fact that Math was right, or that Greer got to one of his own.

Reaper turned his attention back to Mandy, and Math did the same, noting her body language said there was more to her story. A hell of a lot more.

Reaper must have seen the same because he ordered, "Start at the beginning."

Mandy sucked in a big breath and gathered her shaken composure. "After the Raiders, I spent a year looking for my kids. It didn't matter what anyone said because if no one found actual bodies, it meant if I could survive, there was a chance, a slim one, granted, that so could they." The last bit came out rushed.

Math understood her logic—no parent would willingly give up hope on their kids' survival, no matter how tiny that hope was. Hell, kids were the same, they wouldn't stop believing until there was nothing left to hold on to. He was proof of that.

Mandy stumbled over her explanation. "Every time I got a

lead, I followed it up. I couldn't risk not doing so, and each time, it went nowhere. But I couldn't stop."

Reaper shifted back and sat on the porch in front of her. "Did Crane know you were doing that shit?"

She dipped her chin. "He knew if he didn't let me go, I'd leave, and I was in no shape—physically or mentally—to be on my own. It took time and a lot of patience, from Crane and Worth, before I stopped jumping every time someone claimed to see my kids. Years passed and the leads trickled to an occasional rumor. Most weren't worth chasing, but there were a few." She worried her bottom lip. "After every dead end, I promised myself it would be the last time." She looked at Reaper. "But I couldn't ignore that stupid, useless promise that this time it would be different."

Whatever she saw in Reaper's face made her lift her chin defiantly as she looked to the others. "About seven, maybe eight months ago, I was in Kennewick restocking medical supplies, and someone sent me a notice about an underground auction, said what I was looking for would be there."

"You went?" Ruin's question carried bucket loads of disbelief and equal parts censor.

A bit of Mandy's spirit broke through her guilt and fear. "Of course."

"By yourself?" Ruin shot back, totally ignoring Charity's dirty look. "Are you stupid?"

Charity's dirty look morphed straight into 'shit-you-best-duck-for-cover' territory. When Vex aimed a similar look at her brother, Math figured Mandy's story was making a dent with the women. However, he silently agreed with Ruin. It was downright stupid to follow up some anonymous lead—especially into an underground auction.

Before Mandy could respond, Reaper cut in. "Did you find him there?" When Mandy turned to him, he clarified, "Drake. Did you find him?"

"No," she answered. "But what I found, wasn't good." Based upon the sick fury coloring her cheeks a hectic red and the anguish darkening her eyes, whatever Mandy saw had left a hell of an impression.

Math's memories of such events were far from pretty, so he could just imagine what a woman like the doc felt when faced with the depravity of a human auction.

Vex leaned forward and got Mandy's attention. "What happened?"

Mandy's gaze unfocused as she recalled that moment. "There was this vile man dragging a little girl on a leash. She couldn't have been more than seven, and so scared." Her throat worked, and her voice went husky. "She was nothing more than bones, barely able to keep up, and he was dragging her through the filth, laughing while she cried. I couldn't stand by and watch."

It was a familiar scene at such auctions, and as difficult as it was for Math to stand aside when faced with such a scene, as a mother and a healer, it would have been hell for Mandy.

"I lost my temper—my mind—and went after him." The defensive note in Mandy's voice remained strong. "The fight I started spread to others and they pulled me off of him, but the little girl..." She blinked and looked down at her hands. "She didn't survive." Those healer's hands curled into tight fists and her voice was harsh with self-recrimination. "My fault. If I hadn't gone after him—"

"She'd still be dead," Charity cut in not unkindly. "Maybe in a worse way."

Charity's strange comfort earned her a grateful look from Mandy.

"Who's 'they'?" Reaper asked.

Mandy did an awkward mix of a shrug and head-shake. "Some type of guards, private, I think. Maybe hired by whoever ran the auction. They were monitoring the crowd, the payments, all of it."

Guards, my ass. Math had no doubt those so-called guards were actually mercenary enforcers, paid to ensure the exchange of money and flesh was kept as bloodless as possible. If a single person, especially someone like Mandy, managed to cause a mini riot, they must have sucked at their job.

Mandy wasn't finished with her story. "They took me to a holding cell, told me I would be charged with attacking that... that man and fined for loss of property." Her lips twisted into a bitter curve and her voice was harsh. "They called her, 'property'." She blinked away the moisture in her eyes. "They threw me in, locked the door, and after a few hours, when I figured I was pretty much screwed, she showed up."

"Greer?" Reaper clarified, drawing a leg up so he could rest his arm on his knee.

Mandy gave another one of her nods. "She claimed to be in charge of New Seattle's militia and started in on the questions—who I was, why I was there. There was no reason not to tell her, so I did. When I finished, she explained the charges against me, how I could find myself sentenced to a labor camp or serving as a replacement for the property the man lost." Her gaze dropped away, and her teeth worried her bottom lip, as she smoothed her palms over her thighs.

Reaper studied her. "Then she made you an offer?"

Mandy swallowed and looked up. "She said she'd be willing to talk to the slaver, get him to take a deal."

Math could see it all so clearly. Greer, probably thrilled beyond measure to find an unexpected gift, would move quick to sink her nasty ass claws deep into a possible inside source to Crane. His conclusion solidified as Mandy kept going.

Mandy solidified his assumption when she said, "She told me she'd ask around, see if she could find out, once and for all, if my children had survived. Put my mind at ease."

"And what did she ask for in return?" Ruin asked.

Mandy turned to him. "Nothing." She rushed on at Ruin's disbelieving look. "I knew when she made me an offer with no strings attached, that it was too good to be true, but I wanted out. I wanted to go home. I was willing to pay later so long as I didn't rot there." She turned back to Reaper and pleaded. "I'd spent years chasing whispers and got nothing. Why would it be any different from her? I figured she'd come up empty. I'd be off the hook. Once I was out of the cell, she had no leverage."

Mandy's desperation as she tried to convince not just Reaper, but herself, of her logic, created a small flash of pity in Math. Mandy wasn't like him, or Charity, or the Vultures who watched her. She wasn't one to come up swinging when life decked her, not anymore. Life had dealt her a brutal blow and she barely walked away. If forced into a corner, she might fight —might being the operative word. All of that made her the perfect choice for Greer.

"What changed?" Whatever Reaper thought of Mandy's explanation was hidden behind an expressionless mask.

"I came home, tried to pretend it never happened. Prayed I'd never hear from her. Then a month or so later, she reached out—told me to meet her in Kennewick. Said she had something I'd want to see for myself. So, I went." Her smile was small and wobbly. "He was there, Drake was. A little worse for wear, but alive and breathing. She had him working with her men, training. She made him part of her guard."

"Did he recognize you?"

Mandy swallowed hard and nodded. "I got to hold him, talk to him. Not for long. She watched the entire time, made it obvious she was the one in charge."

Call him cynical but Greer finding a boy supposedly taken by Raiders almost ten years earlier, in a month's time? Yeah, Math found it awfully convenient.

Obviously, the irony didn't escape Reaper either. "How, exactly, did she explain finding a boy you couldn't?"

"She said she used her resources to track down one of the Raiders involved in the attack. From there it was a matter of following the money." Mandy turned away and closed her eyes. "Initially he was sold into a brothel, then again to a private owner, and most recently to a Cartel-held farm for labor. Greer paid his owner and put him to work under her." Her eyes opened, blurred with tears. "She told me she'd give me his papers free and clear, once I did her a favor." Her voice faltered to a halt and she swallowed, hard.

"Let me guess," Charity spoke up. "She wanted information on the supply runs."

"Dates and routes, mainly." Mandy took a bracing breath, her shoulders shuddered, and lifted her head. "I pushed back, told her I wasn't comfortable betraying Crane. She gave me this look—," her hand went to the back of her neck as if still feeling it, "—and informed me it was Crane or my son. Which would I rather lose?" Her hands went to her lap and her fingers laced tightly together as she held Reaper's gaze. "Crane had you and Simon and Boden to protect him. Drake only had me. I didn't have a choice."

"You could have come to us." Vex's voice carried a whip of castigation.

Mandy flinched. "Maybe, but at the time I couldn't risk Drake." Her voice dropped to a husky whisper as she held Reaper's gaze. "I'm sorry."

Maybe she was, but Math knew the words meant little to those watching. Her actions, on the other hand, spoke volumes.

Reaper stared at her and said nothing. He got to his feet and went to the railing, his back to the porch. Mandy twisted in her chair and watched him. Silence stretched, until the crickets filled it. No one spoke, leaving Reaper to pass judgement. When he turned and finally spoke, he held Mandy's gaze, even though his comment wasn't directed to her. "Charity, take her inside and check on Cam."

Mandy scooted forward and half rose from her chair. "Reaper, please."

He held up a hand, stopping her. "Don't. Inside."

Charity gave a soft sigh, moved away from Ruin, and went to Mandy. "Come on, doc."

With slumped shoulders and bowed head, Mandy followed Charity into the house, leaving the shattered remains of the Vultures' trust behind.

twenty-six

Vex was torn between pity and anger as she struggled to come to terms with Mandy's confession. No one spoke, but the emotional storm hovered over the porch and raised the fine hairs on her arms. The only one who appeared unaffected was Math who sat so close his solid presence kept the bone-deep chill at bay. He kept her tucked into his side with his arm around her shoulders, and she rested her forehead against his scruffy jaw, taking his scent deep.

Ruin turned and stared into the night-shrouded yard. "Fuck."

"You can say that again," Vex muttered without moving from her position. Math's hand on her shoulder tightened as she blew out a breath, lifted her head, and turned to Reaper. Even after years of riding at his side, his intimidating mask gave her pause. She got it. Betrayal left scars, but there was no getting around the need to discuss what Mandy shared.

The Vultures rode the roads as judge, jury, and, when needed, executioners. Never before had her responsibilities been so difficult. This situation hit so close to home she wasn't sure she could do it.

Judge, jury—no problem. Executioner?

The possibility left her stomach in knots and snaked emotional fissures through the core of her. She carefully maneuvered around her internal struggle and kept her voice level to ask Reaper, "What do we do with Mandy?"

Reaper leaned against one of the porch's posts, his arms folded over his chest, and his gaze directed out into the night like Ruin's. "That's Simon's problem." Fury sharpened his rough voice. "Ultimately Pebble Creek's his responsibility. She's one of his."

Ruin gripped the railing, his arms flexing. "Hell of an intro to the big leagues, don't you think?"

"Crane's gone." Reaper's response was a simple statement of fact, hard and unforgiving. He met Ruin's gaze. "He's going to have to pick that mantle up sooner or later. We promised Si we'd stick around until he was back on his feet. He's upright and breathing. We aren't sticking around much longer." He turned away. "And not just because of this shit."

"You forgetting something?" Ruin snapped.

Reaper stilled and aimed a glare over his shoulder.

Not heeding the silent warning, Ruin pushed. "You promised Lilith we'd stay and keep things steady until the dust settled." His lip curled. "Ain't seeing nothing but dust storms on the horizon, brother."

Vex braced when Reaper's eyes narrowed, and his expression darkened. Clearly, he hadn't forgotten a damn thing, including how Lilith manipulated him to give that promise.

When he spoke, his voice was cold enough to freeze her brother's balls. "Promised her I'd hold it—temporarily. Time's up."

It sucked, especially for Si, but Vex agreed with Reaper. Things in Pebble Creek got shaky after Crane's death because the only two men available to step into his shoes were Boden and Simon. While Simon recovered from the Raider's brutal handling, keeping things running required more than Boden's hand on the reins. So, the Vultures had stuck around to help until Simon got back on his feet.

It was all copasetic until Lilith got involved, and since she held territory that stretched from Colorado, through New Mexico and into Texas, she was a power to reckon with. Much like Michael in the Northwest.

At Lilith's request—okay, more like order—the Vultures agreed to stay put and keep the routes open and moving until further notice. But Simon was back in action, which meant he and Boden could not only manage without the Vultures but handle the fallout from Mandy's duplicitous role.

Vex could predict Reaper's next steps—the Vultures would get Mandy's son, go after Greer, and eventually deal with her handler, Michael. Not items the Vultures could accomplish if they were stuck in Pebble Creek. No matter what Reaper decided, he would ensure Si and Pebble Creek stayed clear of whatever trouble he caused.

Math shifted in his seat next to her and gained Reaper's attention. "You got a plan?"

Reaper's expression was half hidden by the shadows falling from the porch roof as he studied Math, and by extension, Vex. There was a shift in the air around the big man that made Vex want to squirm, but luckily Math's hold kept her still.

"First," Reaper said, "we get the boy and to do that we take on Greer."

Math tensed and Reaper's chin suddenly acquired a stubborn jut. "Just because you were right about this, doesn't make you right about all of it," he snapped. "Greer belongs to Michael, which means his hands could be dirty."

Sounding just as surly, Math shot back, "Maybe, but Michael's not your immediate problem."

"Yeah, fucking got that." With that, Reaper pushed away from the post and started to pace, one hand going to his neck.

Fury and frustration shimmered in the air around him as he paced and fumed.

When he stalked by Ruin, her brother risked Reaper's temper again. "We gonna tell Mandy we're going after her boy?"

His question brought Reaper to an abrupt halt. He turned on his heel and shot Ruin a dark look. Before the big man decided to take his frustration out on her beloved twin, Vex intervened. She scooted out from Math's hold and perched on the edge of her seat, elbows to knees. Math's hand settled at the small of her back and she fought back the resulting shiver by focusing on Reaper. "So, plan?"

Their fearless leader's attention bounced between her and Math. "Any idea on how soon your boy is mobile?"

Vex turned her head in time to catch Math's shrug. "Have to check with the doc, but I'm thinking two, maybe three days."

Reaper rubbed his chin. "So, he's out."

With obvious impatience Ruin stepped closer. "Details, brother?"

"We can leave Cam here with Sara and Danny, but we keep it quiet. Can't bring this farmstead any further into this mess. Work for you?" He aimed the last at Math and got a nod in return. Reaper continued, "You and Vex need to head out before sunrise, want you at Stone Pen before the sun's up."

Stone Pen was a collection of ancient buildings that once served as a prison. Located on a bend of the Boise River, it was tucked behind overgrown trees and vegetation. Most of the structures were one strong wind from crumbling into piles of rubble and dust. But there were a couple that weren't going anywhere any time soon. Even better, it was far enough away from the Hole to escape Trip's notice.

Reaper turned to Ruin. "Once doc says Cam's stable, you

and Charity get her ass into town. Doc needs to reach out to Greer."

Ruin nodded. "Want us visible or shadows?"

"Visible. No reason to hide yet. Far as Greer is concerned, we still trust Mandy, so you two escorting her into town won't raise any alarms. Just give the doc enough room to make contact."

"You think that's smart?" Math cut in.

A muscle jumped in Reaper's jaw. "Chances are damn good Greer got wind you snatched Cam, so she's most likely hauling ass to Boise as we speak."

Of that, Vex had no doubt. Especially since one of the men who held Cam managed to get away.

"We need Mandy to reach out. Fastest way to do that, get her close and have her make that contact." Reaper crossing his arms over his chest and his face fell back to its familiar hard lines. "Mandy's going to offer the bitch exactly what she wants, us—" he pinned Math with a look, "—and you."

"We're bait." Math made it clear he wasn't asking.

Reaper's lips curled into a nasty smile. "She wants us, so fuck yeah."

"And the boy?" Ruin asked. "How do we get to him?"

"Doc's going to make one demand, Greer brings her boy out. Gets him somewhere she can see him. Easy enough to hide a face in a marketplace crowd. Once she has eyes on him, she'll lead Greer to us. The boy will be dragged along as insurance for doc's good behavior."

"So what?" Ruin groused. "Charity and I are just supposed to play stupid?"

"Yeah." Reaper shot back. "Make it believable."

Unlike Reaper, Vex wasn't so sure it would be that simple. Granted Greer wanted blood, but would she really be arrogant enough to believe her greatest wish would fall right into her hands? Vex asked Math, who seemed to have a better grasp on Greer's mental state, "Will that be enough for her?"

His gaze was steady and clear. "My guess? Yeah." He looked to Reaper and warned, "But she's going to double cross your ass, and you know it."

"Not stupid," Reaper growled. "Which is why we're picking the place."

Math didn't back down. "Greer will bring reinforcements."

"Figured she would," Reaper snapped clearly losing patience with Math's persistence. "Got an idea how heavy?"

Math took his time answering. "She's arrogant enough to believe Mandy's trapped under the thumb, so she might be convinced the doc wouldn't double cross her. Still, she doesn't go far without her handpicked guard. Guessing ten, but no more than fifteen. She likes to use two-man teams."

"Doable," Reaper said. "There's seven of us. As soon as Havoc and Mercy arrive, we'll ride out and hook up with you at Stone Pen."

Vex admired Reaper's ability to think outside the box, but with this, there were a hundred things that could go horribly wrong. Even if they made it through, there was one more concern overshadowing all the rest. "We take her down, there's going to be blowback."

"We'll do our damnedest to keep it contained," Reaper responded, but didn't bother to elaborate.

Vex wasn't so sure considering their odds of coming out of this breathing were iffy. But if that's how Reaper wanted to play it, then she'd keep that worry for after. For now, there was another cause for concern because too many times, it was the bystanders who got burned when things went to hell. "Not sure taking it to Boise is going to keep Simon off the radar."

"Chance we have to take," he said. "I'm doing my best not

to bring attention to him. Hence the reason why I'm not having doc go back and make the call from there."

Math eyed Reaper, clearly catching something Vex hadn't, because he stated, "You think the doc's not the only set of eyes and ears in town."

Reaper gave an arrogant shrug. "Said it yourself, Greer's not stupid, so yeah, got to factor that in."

God, this was such a mess.

Vex couldn't shake the unsettling doubt that wrapped tight around her heart. Maybe it was because Mandy's betrayal had blindsided her, left her reeling. But Ruin and Reaper's reactions proved she wasn't the only one feeling it. Everyone was off balance. Not a good thing when you were getting ready to walk into a mess. Math was the only one that appeared to be holding rock steady. Probably because his life-long goal was within reach and his friend was alive and breathing.

She stifled her sigh, laid her head against Math's shoulder, and hoped a little of his confidence would seep into her. When his arms curled at her waist and his lips brushed her hair, she closed her eyes and held that small, soft touch close. She really hoped he would stick around once this was over, because she wasn't ready to let go.

"You two a thing now?"

She opened her eyes to find Reaper watching her and Math, his face inscrutable. Behind him, Ruin was fighting a grin. She shot her brother a glare, but before she could give Reaper a response, Math sent her world reeling.

"Yeah."

Stunned by the surety in his answer, Vex floundered under her unexpected reactions. A cautious hope colored by an unusual joy, and threaded through it, a hard-to-pin-down fear. There was no time to come to terms with any of it before Reaper pushed off the railing and closed in.

Math's arm disappeared as he rose to meet his brother's advance. Vex's mouth went dry as the two men went nose to nose.

"You playing games with her?" A dangerous edge rode Reaper's question.

"You know better." Math didn't back down an inch. "She's worth more than that."

At that one simple declaration, Vex knew she wasn't falling for the man standing at her side, she was well and truly gone.

Dammit.

Math wasn't done. "Case you need reminding, I'm not the player in our family—that's you, brother." His lips curled into a sneer. "I see something worth taking a chance on, I'm not screwing it over and then throwing it away."

Oh shit, this would not end well.

Vex got to her feet, sent Ruin a frantic help-me-out-here look. Instead, he mirrored her worry at the turn the conversation was taking.

A sound that was suspiciously close to a growl escaped Reaper. "Getting sick of your digs. Didn't throw you or ma away."

"Didn't you?" Math shot back, completely unmoved by his brother's fury. "You walked the fuck away without looking back. At first, I figured maybe I did something, then you did it again, years later. That's when I realized, it's just you."

Whoever, or whatever, Math referred to, found its mark. The air around Reaper turned dark and cold. "Drop it, boy." The bigger man drew up stiffly and took a deliberate step back, putting much-needed space between them. "She has no part in this."

Math held his position, barely suppressed rage running through his lean frame. "Keep telling yourself that, but I call bullshit." His hands curled into fists and his coiled tension ratcheted another notch. "You missed Greer because you're still so tangled up with her and what happened, all you see is him."

Vex didn't think Math's 'her' had shit all to do with Greer. *But then who was it?*

Proof that the two furious men shared blood came when Math's voice went arctic in a strange mimicry of Reaper's. "Ready for your world to go dark again, brother?"

Reaper's head snapped back as if Math's question was a punch.

"Because if you don't open your eyes, you're going to lose them—" Math shoved a hand in the direction of Ruin and Vex, "—just like you did her."

It was crystal clear Math was not talking about Greer. Despite the volatile situation, Vex's curiosity was killing her. Who was the 'her', because damn, whoever she was, she left some serious damage in her wake, and considering who carted that damage around, that was saying something.

With a muted roar Reaper lunged at Math, who met him halfway. Vex stumbled back out of the way as the two collided, the impact echoing through the wooden slats under her bare feet. A hand caught her elbow and Ruin dragged her back, keeping her clear of swinging fists. She stood beside Ruin and watched with a bit of amazement as Math and Reaper went at each other. The fight was fast, and it was savage.

She winced when Reaper shoved Math against the thick post and nailed him in the ribs. Math came back with a vicious knee, followed by an even sneakier hook. They spun away from the railing and stumbled down the steps to the front yard. She and Ruin followed, staying at the top step as the two men continued to pound on each other.

"Definitely brothers," Ruin muttered as Reaper sent Math to his knees with a kick.

Math blocked the next incoming kick by locking Reaper's

thick thigh with his arm and sinking his fist into the sensitive nerve running along Reaper's other leg. Then he shoved him away. Off balance, Reaper fell back, and Math followed him down.

"We should probably stop them." Vex cringed at the thick sound of flesh impacting flesh. Between the shadows and the weak reach of the porch light, the fight became a tangle of limbs, but the sounds testified it wasn't losing any of its intensity.

"Not feeling like looking for my damn teeth in the dark," Ruin drawled as he crossed his arms over his chest. Math managed another hit and Ruin sucked in a breath. "Yeah, that's going to hurt."

The twins watched another minute or so before the hits slowed and started to miss their intended targets. A sure sign it might soon be safe to interrupt. "Vex?" Ruin called softly.

"Hmm?" She didn't look away as Reaper rolled to his back and trapped Math under him. When Ruin didn't say anything more and Math fought his way free, she looked over to find her brother watching her.

"You sure about him?" From Ruin's quiet question, Vex understood this was coming from her protective brother's heart.

She shifted over until their shoulders brushed. "Yeah."

Ruin's voice stayed low. "Rough road."

"Hasn't stopped me before." And that was the God's honest truth. Didn't matter how bumpy the ride got, she was determined to take it, with Math. "Know it's quick, know it doesn't make sense to anyone watching outside, but—" She rubbed a hand over her chest, "—all those hollow spots? He fills them."

Ruin brushed his cheek against her hair and sighed. "Happy for you, sis, but fair warning." He waited until she lifted her head. "He hurts you, I'm taking him down."

She flashed Ruin a grin and aimed her thumb at the two men going at it in the yard. "You might have to get in line."

"Right." Ruin straightened, and Vex did the same, both of them eyeing the two punching bags circling each other in the yard. "Which of us gets to step in?"

As the worst of whatever triggered the brothers drained away, Vex decided to call it a night. "That'd be me."

She made her way down the stairs, taking her time so when Math circled around, his back was to her. She found her opening and took it. Trusting Reaper to keep his shit tight, she slipped in front of Math, and gave Reaper her back. Math's hands went to her arms to put her aside, but she stopped him by pressing her hand to his chest. "Enough, hot shot."

The hands on her arms tightened and she wondered if she'd be carrying his bruises tomorrow, but she didn't move, just waited him out. Math's tension leaked away and the coiled muscles under her palms eased. He sucked in a deep breath, then another, before he looked away from Reaper and down at Vex.

She took in the new marks left by Reaper's fist, sighed, and cupped his face. "Day three, fight number four."

A flash of amusement pierced the darkness of Math's eyes and he turned into her touch. "You keeping count?"

"Someone has to." She was relieved to see the worst of his anger slithering away. She gave him a small nod, then turned to face Reaper. He winced and wiped away the blood trickling from a cut above his eye. When he finally met her gaze, she asked, "Feel better?"

Reaper shot a dark look at Math, then dropped it to Vex. "Hope you know what you're doing."

Since he was half hidden by shadows it was difficult to read him, but she didn't miss the protective note under his warning. Because of that, she kept her voice gentle, despite the rasp of irritation that he and her brother kept questioning her decision. "I'm a big girl, Reaper."

He moved towards her, trapping her between him and Math. His gaze was filled with a difficult mix of emotions. Hard as it was, she held it recognizing the depth of love, pride, and worry, so much like what she saw in Ruin's eyes, that her throat grew tight. His hand rose and brushed her cheek with a startling gentleness before dropping away.

He switched his attention to Math, his softer emotions disappearing under a hard glare. "Hurt her, and I'll make sure you feel it."

Yep, Ruin would have to wait in line.

Reaper stalked by Math, deliberately knocked his shoulder into Math's in one final, silent warning, and then he headed up the steps to disappear inside. Ruin silently followed, shaking his head.

It was the closest thing to a blessing that she would get from either of them. Not that she needed it, but she wanted it. They were family. Family mattered.

She helped Math onto the porch and into a chair. Now that the immediate storm had blown over, her mind kicked into high gear. She wanted to poke at Math's claim and make sure it wouldn't disappear like a soap bubble.

Too soon?

Probably, but it was so pretty.

Math shifted and released a quiet hiss, the sound dragging her out of her head. "How bad?"

"Bastard has a heavy fist." Math grimaced and gingerly touched his battered lip. "But I'll be fine."

"You want to go in?"

"Nah, rather sit out here for a bit."

She settled in next to him, close, but not so close as to aggravate his aches and pains. In order to ease into their various conversational options, she decided to tackle the mysterious 'her' first. There was something important there. "So, who is she?"

"Who?"

"The 'her' Reaper threw away."

Math sighed, then looked at her. "Lilith."

Struck speechless, Vex blinked. Lilith was one scary ass woman. Vex met her once when she came to Pebble Creek to reclaim her kidnapped daughter, Tabby. The incendiary way she and Reaper interacted left no doubt they had a shared history. Like two rabid dogs vying for the same juicy bone. No one dared get between them. But Vex never guessed it was the kind of history Math's accusations indicated.

Holy shit. Reaper and Lilith? It almost boggled the mind. Almost as much as Lilith having a daughter. Her brain screeched to a halt. "Wait, is—Tabby—Reaper's?"

Math's lips thinned. "That's not my story to tell, Vex. Bad enough I shared the who. If I give you more, tonight will look like a cakewalk."

"Understood." And she did. Despite her pesky curiosity, she couldn't deny that Math's reluctance to share his brother's story, despite their differences, proved how deep his honor ran. She studied his battered and bruised profile, and her next question slipped out without permission. "You serious about us?"

That earned her an unreadable look, almost as if he was concerned about her reaction. "Is there any reason I shouldn't be?"

Since he and Reaper just finished pounding each other into the ground, partially because of their history and partly because of her, she figured her biggest concern had been answered. Even if her family thought it ill-conceived, they would stand by her and help pick up the pieces, if necessary. It was up to her to either crawl back behind the crumbling wall she erected, or woman up, step out of that dubious protection, and grab Math's hand to see where this road led. "Some think I'm too high-maintenance."

He curled a hand around her neck and drew her close. She braced a hand on his chest and let him capture her lips in a kiss. She lost herself in his taste and touch, finding a sense of peace despite the storm waiting on the horizon. When he finally drew back, her body ached to follow through on the promise of his kiss, but she was more than happy to sit on a porch and just be.

They sat there, letting the quiet soothe the rough edges. But shaking years of experience was difficult and she couldn't help but voice her worry over what the future held. "What happens now?"

Math's chest rose and fell under her hand and the arm around her shoulders tightened. His chin brushed across the top of her head. "Got enough to worry about right now. Best not to borrow future trouble. We'll deal with it, if or when, it hits. You good?"

Trouble was coming, but she held his words tight in her heart and gave back a soft, "Yeah."

twenty-seven

The next couple of hours, Math listened to his brother hammer out the details of his risky plan. Vex shared that she and Math had run across Bane in Boise but couldn't say if he remained nearby or not. Ruin promised to keep an eye out, because it would be good to have an extra pair of hands if available.

Reaper's loss of trust with Mandy was made clear when he refused to bring her into the conversation until the very end. Even then, he gave her only what she needed to know, and nothing more. Once their roles were set, Math and Vex disappeared into one of the bedrooms to grab a couple of hours sleep before hitting the road. They would be the first ones to head out as they needed to the cover of darkness to hide their trip to Stone Pen from any watching eyes.

The dead of morning pressed heavy and deep against the windows when Math managed to untangle himself from Vex's warm body without waking her. He dragged on his jeans and padded down the hall to Cam's room, where he found Reaper keeping vigil. He stopped in the doorway.

Reaper slowly got out of his chair and came over. Together

they stood there looking to the man sprawled on his stomach in the bed.

Reaper spoke first. "His fever broke few hours ago. Doc said he needs rest but should be back on his feet in a day or so." He turned to Math, who must not have been hiding his worry as well as he thought, because Reaper said, "You did good. He'll make it."

Math dipped his chin in acknowledgement as something deep inside relaxed. Hearing it from doc was one thing, but from Reaper, who never pulled his punches—physically or verbally—was another.

"Going to grab some coffee. I'll be back." Reaper gripped Math's shoulder, then walked away.

"You going to stand there and stare?" Cam winced and shifted so he could see Math.

"Just letting you get your beauty rest." Math walked over and took the chair Reaper left. He studied Cam's battered face as a caustic mix of anger, guilt, and shame churned in a noxious brew in his gut. Was the end result worth it? Would it bring him peace? He swallowed the bitter taste of doubt and managed to keep his voice steady. "How are you feeling?"

"Like shit."

"Good, because you look like shit."

"You're one to talk," Cam teased. "Did Vex whip your ass for sassing her?" His brief flash of humor drained away as he took in Math's expression. "Fill me in."

Without hesitation, Math shared everything, including the Mandy and Greer situation and the brotherly quarrel. Then he moved on to Reaper's plan.

Cam frowned. "A lot of ways for it all to go to shit."

"Not telling me something I don't know," Math agreed. "As whacked as it is, it's our best bet."

Cam didn't say anything for a long moment. "Dammit, don't like you going in without me."

Math understood Cam's frustration and didn't hesitate to share his. "Just saved your ass, brother, not real keen on exposing it again."

That earned him a telling gesture and glare.

Math's lips twitched. "Love you too, man."

Cam heaved a sigh. "Dangerous game you're playing."

It's the closest we've been to the bitch in a while." Math rested his arms on his knees and held Cam's gaze. "I hate to lose this opportunity."

"I get that, but..." he trailed off.

"What?"

"Okay, got to put this out there. I'm glad you're finally dealing with your brother." Cam ignored Math's glare and kept going. "No matter how much you try to deny it, you two were close once. Blood is blood, and despite how much anger sits between you two, that bond isn't going away. So yeah, fucking ecstatic you're reconnecting there." There was a shift in his expression and sly humor crept under his worry. "Even better, I'm beyond thrilled you finally got yourself tangled up with a woman, but—" humor shifted into something more serious, "—you're so focused on getting payback, you're risking what you just found."

Cam's words got in there and shifted something heavy that left a strange emptiness in its wake. "I hear you, but I've waited—hell, we've waited—a long damn time for this." Then because he needed Cam to understand, he added, "She gets it and she'll stand." Even as he said it out loud, he couldn't muffle the whisper of doubt that crawled deep in his heart. Vex wasn't the type to patiently take second place in someone's life, and she made it clear she was looking for a partner, not a part-time protector.

"Have no doubt on that, considering she's yours." Cam held his gaze. "But, just saying, don't be stupid, man. When it comes down to it," he paused and sucked in a breath. "And you and I know it will come down to it, you better make the right fucking choice." Then he lightened the mood with a cocky grin and offered his hand. "Besides, might take me a bit to ride in and save your ass."

"What the fuck ever, man." Math grasped his friend's hand and gave him a mock scowl. "Be seeing ya."

"Yeah, you will."

With that, Math pushed to his feet and left.

<h1 style="text-align:right">twenty-eight</h1>

The one-two hoot of an owl broke through the quiet night and drifted into the small stone building half-hidden by old growth trees and draped in long, verdant cords of vines and leaves. In the dim interior, huddled under a heavy, bloodstained blanket meant to disguise her form, Vex's chest stilled, and her ears strained to catch what should be Mercy's response. A heartbeat passed before it came and Vex took another shallow breath.

This was the part of Reaper's plan that was ripe for trouble. Maybe she should have protested more when Reaper informed her, that her role was to play a supposedly dead Cam. Not that it would have done any good. Once Ruin and Charity brought back Mandy and lunch, Reaper wasted no time refining tonight's entertainment.

First up, Havoc and Mercy. They waited outside for Greer's approach. They finished setting the various traps around the abandoned building minutes before Greer's initial scouts arrived, and then spent the afternoon playing a waiting game with those same scouts.

Mandy's part was to step outside with Math and inform

him that his friend wasn't doing good and might not make it. This served as groundwork for Vex's dead body role. Mandy and Math continued the conversation, ensuring the scouts got the picture. Then Mandy went back inside, while Reaper came out and the brothers got into a low-voiced argument. During that act, Ruin did a couple of stints, ostensibly checking the perimeter. All of it to make sure the scouts clocked the players.

An hour ago, when night fell, Charity slipped out to join Havoc and Mercy. Ruin would follow shortly with another round of perimeter check, putting all four deadly shots in outside sniper positions.

Vex tried to point out that they were limited to the few guns they carried—all pistols, no rifles. Reaper countered by explaining those four could pick off Greer's men and confiscate their weapons while Reaper, Math, and Vex kept Greer busy inside.

Which brought her to now, curled on her side with her favorite blade cradled against her stomach, she nudged the edge of the blanket that covered her from head to toe enough to allow a limited view of the room. Not that there was much to see. Mandy, Reaper, and Math sat around the only lamp in the room, throwing heavy shadows.

The scuff of boots over stone preceded Ruin's voice. "Doing another check, be back." The door swung open, and the cooler night air swirled inside as he walked out. He didn't pull the door all the way closed—creating a deliberate invitation that those inside hoped would soon be accepted.

Ruin hadn't been gone more than a couple of minutes before the soft chirp of a mockingbird trilled.

Vex braced.

A heavy foot hit the door and slammed it back on its hinges, a rush of displaced air sweeping through the room.

Their guests had arrived.

Math, Mandy, and Reaper jumped to their feet while a clamor of voices shouted, "Get down! Get on your knees!"

Chaos reigned as Greer's men moved into the room. The shadows in front of her shifted as Reaper and Math stepped back towards Vex's position, forcing Mandy to follow. Tension tightened Vex's muscles, and she did her best to maintain her corpse pose as heavy boots moved closer.

"Fuckin' drop!" The harsh command was followed by the sound of something solid impacting flesh.

A groan that sounded like it belonged to Math followed. The shadows shifted as he dropped to his knees. Vex bit her lip and gripped her blade tighter.

Still on his feet Reaper tugged Mandy closer as if trying to protect her. "What the hell?" His question was a furious growl.

An ominous click sounded as another order was barked. "Get your hands up, asshole!"

From where she lay, Vex could see Reaper uncurl his hand from Mandy's wrist and lift his arms. "Who the fuck are you?"

"On your knees." Black boots, military in style, closed in. "Now."

Reaper took his time and dropped to his knees, hands held high.

"You too."

Mandy was slower to go down, staying between Math and Reaper as the last in a flimsy barrier of flesh between Vex and the soldiers. Then it was her turn.

"Who's that?"

Mandy's voice quavered as she answered the soldier's question. "He's dead."

Vex sensed someone getting closer and fought her instincts because although she knew they were looming over her, she couldn't predict their next move. Something hard slammed into her hip with bruising force. She nearly bit through her lip to stop her gasp as her leg went numb, then pain started to sing along angry nerve endings.

Tension rode through the room and snapped when Math snarled, "What the fuck is wrong with you?"

The sounds of a struggle broke out and the soldier standing over Vex turned away to watch. Whether intended or not, Vex used Math's distraction to suck in a couple of deep breaths and force the pain back to a tolerable level.

"Enough!" barked the voice. One last thud sounded, before all that remained was harsh breathing. "Give the all clear."

Boots all but ran out. Inside no one moved. A faint hoot came, and gravel crunched underfoot before more feet came inside. Deliberate steps drew close and finally stopped.

"Interesting company you're keeping, doc," drawled a cold feminine voice Vex knew would haunt her nightmares. "So nice to see you're a woman of your word."

"What the fuck, doc?" Reaper played his role to the hilt.

"So... sorry, but I had to." Mandy's voice was shaky as shit and layered in misery, totally selling her part.

"Told you, man," Math's voice was tight. "Trusting people is bullshit."

"You would know, wouldn't you, boy." Greer's arrogant amusement scraped over Vex's nerves. "Thought you would've learned that lesson by now, Math."

Math groaned and Vex would have given anything to be able to see what was happening, but she was stuck listening and what she heard was far from comforting.

"Got to give you credit, didn't quite put it all together until you showed in Salt Lake. Call me curious, but how did you survive the purge?"

"Luck." His one-word answer emerged on a hiss.

"Maybe." There was a shift in the air and the hair on Vex's arms rose in warning. "But it seems your luck's run out."

"Crane saved you, gave you home and safety." Reaper's ploy to redirect Greer's attention was aimed at Mandy. "And you betray that for what? What the hell does this bitch have on you that's so damn important?"

Greer answered in Mandy's place. "Told you years ago, Reaper, everyone breaks."

The hostile familiarity between the two added another layer Vex's tension. *More bad blood.*

"Told you then, you're full of shit." Venomous scorn laced Reaper's voice.

"You sure about that?" Something ugly crept into Greer's tone. "I've learned even the most stubborn of people can break. You just have to find their weakness. Like family for instance."

Vex couldn't see what happened, but she heard the sharp, pained inhale. Instinct screamed it belonged to Math and everything in her demanded she move, but experience and her faith in Reaper held her still. She was so focused on what was happening, she almost missed the trilled warning. Her hand tightened on her blade's hilt as a muted gunshot sounded from outside.

Inside, all hell broke loose.

Vex sprung up from her position and threw the blanket over the nearest soldier. He yelled and lifted his gun blindly, spraying bullets across the ceiling. She sank her blade into his gut with one hand and caught his rifle with the other. He fell back and she went with him, twisting her blade and yanking on the rifle. As they hit the floor, his grip loosened. She left her knife in his gut, took control of the weapon, and smashed his face with the butt of the rifle. A sickening crunch of breaking bone dropped him.

She scrambled over the body, pushed to her knees, twisted with the rifle in hand, and aimed, and nailed a soldier near the front door. She selected her next target and fired. Unfortunately, so did he. His bullet left a line of cold fire along the top of her shoulder. Her bullet landed in the middle of his chest. His knees folded and he toppled over.

The barrel of a rifle swung her way and she ducked. Reaper's hand wrapped around the rifle's barrel and forced it up as he sank a knife into the soldier's eye. A hoarse scream ripped through the chaos. Reaper shifted his grip on the rifle and smashed it across the screaming man's face, laying him out.

Gracelessly, she clambered to her feet, and came up at Reaper's side. The repeated gunshots in the enclosed space left her ears ringing. A muted yell caught her attention and she turned to see Math slice a soldier's throat, then drop him to the ground.

Something heavy hit her, slamming her into the ground. It took her a minute to realize it was Reaper. When she finally sucked in a lungful of air, she tried to push against his weight. "Reaper, let me up."

She felt, more than heard his groan, before he rolled off. Worried, she got to her knees and leaned over him, trying to see if he was hit. There was blood high on his chest and panic tried to take hold. "Reaper? You with me?"

"Yeah." It came out on a groan, but hearing it pushed her trepidation down.

"You're going to be okay." It helped that his blood was seeping, not pumping out, under her hands as she put pressure on the wound. She looked around frantically. When his hand covered hers, she looked into his face. "You're going to be okay." It was more a plea than a promise.

Suddenly Math was on Reaper's other side, pushing her hands away and shoving a wad of material against Reaper's shoulder. "Hold this."

"Got it." Reaper suited action to words. "Help me up."

Together Math and Vex got Reaper to his feet and

propped him against one of the walls. Math looked to Vex. "What the hell happened?"

"I don't know."

Reaper answered. "Greer was dragging doc out the door, the solider covering her took a shot at Vex." Despite being pale and sweaty, he managed a grin. "I got in the way."

At hearing Reaper's retelling Vex reeled but there was no time to find her balance.

"I always said you were clumsy." Math's gratitude snuck through the jibe.

"You two need to haul ass. Get doc before Greer kills her," Reaper ordered.

Math was on his feet and running towards the door when Vex pushed the rifle she held into Reaper's hands. "You sure you'll be okay?"

"I'm breathing. Now, get your ass moving."

She took him at his word and followed Math into the night.

Sporadic gunshots and screams rode the air but Vex focused on Math's back as she dodged between shadows. At one point Math bent down and came up with a rifle. The sound of her name hitched her stride and she twisted to see Ruin off to the side, a crumpled heap at his feet. She motioned back to the building. "Reaper! Go!"

Ruin deciphered her shorthand, spun, and darted towards the building. Ahead of Vex Math disappeared in the trees. Muttering a curse, she hurried to catch up. She barely side-stepped a bike lying on its side, tires slashed, and the choking scent of corn fuel hovering like an invisible cloud.

Looked as if Mercy and Havoc knocked Greer's rides out of commission.

She slipped into the surrounding foliage and left the fight behind, her focus centered on the flashes of Math's back. Hopefully he was following an actual trail and not just stumbling about. They covered a few more yards before he halted and held up a hand for her to do the same. She stood at his side and tried to slow her breathing as her chest heaved and her heart raced.

A muffled cry sounded off to their right. They chased it, slower this time, as they took care to keep their approach quiet. Their caution paid off.

Out of the trees emerged the dark outline of a building. Vex stayed on Math's heels as they crept closer. Nearby something brushed over stone indicating they were on the right trail.

They closed in and used the shadows as they took positions on either side of the opening. Math's fingers flashed in a countdown.

Three, two, one.

She followed him inside. It was difficult to make out the interior, but there was no missing the half walls that turned the room into a lethal maze. A muffled whimper drifted from the back.

They moved forward in a leapfrog pattern and pushed deeper into the room. Rotted boards turned the floors into a dangerous version of Swiss cheese and slowed their progress considerably. The holes looked endless in the dark and Vex assumed there was a basement somewhere below. While the fall might not kill her, it would take her out of the game and with Reaper sidelined, they couldn't afford to lose another player.

She and Math hit a staircase and stopped. Overhead wood creaked. They shared a look. It was suicide to go up. Greer's guard would be waiting at the top and they would walk into a hail of bullets. But based upon the grim determination on Math's face, he wasn't about to let that stop him.

Vex silently cursed because the lure of finally getting his

hands on Greer was fucking with his head. Which left it up to her to be the sensible one. *Man, they were fucked.*

Determined to walk away from this with Math alive, she motioned him ahead.

He raised the rifle to his shoulder and inched his way up, pressing against the wall. She stayed on his heels and with each step, waited for a bullet to hit. Her wariness increased as it remained quiet.

They edged by the first landing. Math set his foot on the first step of the second set of stairs and shifted. The wood shattered. Vex grabbed the back of his shirt and yanked him back.

Bullets rained down, pinning them down. She hissed as one managed to kiss a line of fire from her elbow to her wrist. At this rate, she'd be carved into a bloody mess. Math grunted and tried imprint his spine in the wall.

A rifle clicked on an empty chamber, and they charged up the stairs. Math leapt the last few feet and collided with the solider at the top. The two men fought for control of the rifle, but Math had the advantage and used it ruthlessly. They stumbled into the narrow hall and ricocheted off the walls, teeth bared as they tried to end each other.

Vex edged around them, her goal the end of the hall and its scant coverage. Once clear of the struggling men, she crouched, and poked her head around the wall's edge. The stairs emptied into a large open room that led to another room that sported a huge gaping hole on the other side. Not much existed in-between.

A shift in the shadows near the opening that probably once held a large window morphed into two figures. A breeze ruffled the leaves and moonlight slipped through. The soft light glinted off of familiar lenses. Vex jerked her head back and let it fall against the wall.

Dammit. Greer was working her way back towards the opening and using Mandy like a human shield. Vex stole another peek. *Double damn.* Mandy's stiff movements meant Greer had a weapon trained on her.

Mentally cursing a blue streak, Vex ran through her limited choices. Behind her an ugly grunt sounded. She turned to see Math rising from a crumpled body.

He came up behind her, staying close to the wall, and mimicked her position. His lips brushed her ear as he whispered, "Where is she?"

"Other side of the room. Problem is getting across. No floor."

He rose to a half crouch, used her shoulders for balance, and looked back down the hall.

She did the same as she tried to follow his mental path. The hall held a couple of doors that led God knows where.

Math turned back to her. "Has to be another way around."

Maybe, maybe not. Still, it wasn't like they had much of a choice. "What do you want to do?"

"I'll keep her busy, you get behind her."

Stupidest plan ever. But with nothing better to offer, she nodded. They switched places and Vex worked her way back down the hall. Hopefully one of the rooms would connect across.

Math made quick work of gaining Greer's attention. "Doc, you okay?"

Mandy's voice was shaky and high-pitched. "Ye... yes."

"You want her to stay that way, back the fuck off, Math," snarled Greer.

"You know I can't do that, and you know why."

Vex slipped into the first room and was grateful to discover most of the floor was intact. Another doorway stood on the far side. She dashed across and winced when a board creaked underfoot. She held her breath and waited for an outcry. Instead, she was barely able to make out Math's deeper tones and Greer's nastier ones but couldn't catch the actual words. She rushed the doorway and rocked to a halt, the night air nipping at her skin.

The small space in front of her had been left exposed to the elements. The protective roof was long gone. A thick tree branch sprawled over what looked like an old tub. Moonlight hit the tarnished glass shards to her left and illuminated the gap between where she stood and the next room.

She needed to jump. Hopefully they were so caught up in their pissing contest they wouldn't hear her land. Then she prayed the other side wouldn't crumble out from under her. She blew out a breath, got a running start, and sprung into the air. Her heels hit the other side with a dull *thunk* that was followed by a sharp crack as the wood underfoot gave way.

Shit, shit, shit!

She threw her weight forward, landed on her hip, and rolled to her feet. No way Greer missed that. With no time to waste, Vex pushed her pain aside, sprinted across the room, and peeked through the doorway.

Relief filled her when Math's assumption was proved correct. The doorway dropped her behind Greer's line of sight. That was the good news. The bad news? To get to them, Vex needed to navigate around the precarious floor, which left her exposed.

From her new position, Vex saw the gun Greer had dug into Mandy's side. The way she kept the doctor in front of her meant Math didn't have a clear shot. Which left it up to Vex to get him one.

She inched out and did her best to stay quiet. She used the debris and shadows to camouflage her movements as she worked her way closer. She left her questionable protection and moved into the room. Sweat coated her spine and her nerves vibrated like an over-tightened wire.

If Greer turned, just the tiniest bit, she'd see Vex.

Her heartbeat filled her ears and made it hard to catch the back and forth between Greer and Math. She crept closer and eased into a crouch as she shifted her grip on her knife. Throwing it was out. Too risky. Better to go with a blitz attack.

Before she could move, Greer shoved Mandy aside and lifted her gun, aiming at Math. Two shots rang out, so close together they blended into one. The doctor stumbled forward coming perilously close to the ragged edge of the floor.

Vex ignored Greer and lunged for Mandy. She caught the doc's wrist, and yanked her forward, hissing, "Run!" before she propelled the older woman away.

A weight slammed into Vex and drove her face down into the floor, her chest compressed, squeezing the air out of her lungs. Somehow, she kept hold of her knife even as the skin of her knuckles tore away. A hand grabbed her hair and jerked her neck back painfully. Greer's snarling face filled Vex's vision. Vex slammed her blade back and drove it into whatever she could hit. Repeatedly.

Greer screeched and ripped her hand free, taking some of Vex's hair with her. As she tried to get evade Vex's knife, she shifted her weight. Vex shoved up, twisted, and forced Greer's weight off of her. She rolled from her hands and knees to a crouch, pivoted, and barely blocked a vicious kick. The bone-jarring impact sent Vex tumbling back on her ass. She scrambled to her feet, only to stop as the floor behind her began to crumble.

In front of her Greer rolled to her feet, teeth bared, blood spreading beneath her shoulder, and cocked her leg back. Something heavy landed nearby and caused the floor to quake. Vex didn't have time to worry about it, as she braced for Greer's unavoidable kick. An angry roar sounded and then Math ploughed into Greer, forcing her away from Vex.

There was no chance to enjoy her rescue because the floor under Vex decided it had enough.

twenty-nine

Driven by rage and a decade's old need for vengeance, the world around Math narrowed down to one thing—ending Greer. He rode the arrogant bitch to the floor and wrapped his hands around her neck. Violent satisfaction coursed through him as his grip tightened. *Finally, fucking finally,* he had his long-awaited dream in his brutal grip.

"Math!"

Vex's frantic voice snapped his head around and his heart seized. Cracks ran like fault line through the boards under her feet, the fractures gaining speed as he watched. In less than a heartbeat, his priorities shifted. He slammed Greer's head into the floor and barely registered her body going limp. He let go of sure revenge and dove forward. "Vex!"

The last of the boards fell away and left her windmilling and teetering over empty air. He skidded the last few inches on his stomach and reached out. His palm hit her wrist and their hands locked. The abrupt drop of her body weight shot agony through his shoulders. Desperate not to follow her into the hole, he dug the toes of his boots in, finding crevices. He blocked out the warning groans from the remaining boards, including those directly under him, and looked down into her pale face as she swung in the air. "Hey, babe. Don't let go."

"Not planning on it." Her voice was steady, but her hands curled tight around his wrists. "Going to hang around a while."

He gritted his teeth and started to inch backwards, his arms screaming in protest. His back spasmed and every inch was a battle. Focused on pulling Vex up, he only had the widening of her eyes as a warning before the sharp retort of a rifle sang out. A pained grunt and the sound of displaced air followed.

Stuck holding Vex, he couldn't see what happened.

The floor vibrated as someone rushed to his side. An arm appeared, then Mandy was there, stretched out beside him and taking hold of Vex's arm. "Let me help."

Together he and the doc managed to get Vex up, and all three cautiously backed away from the ragged edge of the hole. When they were out of harm's way, he turned to where he left Greer only to find her gone. He stared at the now empty space, his mind skipping. "Where is she?"

"I shot her." Mandy's admission was shaky as she huddled next to Vex. "She fell out the window." Tears and dirt streaked her face, and her glasses had a decided crooked tilt. She raised trembling hands and took them off. When she used her shirt to clean the lenses, Math noticed they were missing a side piece. She resettled the broken frame with care and met his gaze. "I didn't have a choice. She was coming after you."

Math pushed to his feet and tried to process her answer.

Vex asked, "Did you hit her?"

"Yes." Mandy's response was sure.

Stunned that it was really over, Math went to the window frame. Behind him Vex called his name. He turned to see her struggle to her feet. She got close, her eyes dark but steady. "She was hurt." When he simply stared at her, she clarified,

"Greer. She had a gunshot here." Vex touched her chest near her shoulder. "She was bleeding bad."

As soon as Vex was within touching distance, he wrapped his arm around her waist, and pulled her close. She put a hand to his stomach and dropped her forehead against his chest. He dropped his head over hers, closed his eyes, and breathed her in. A tremor ran through him.

Too fucking close.

For a minute they stood there, holding each other. Finally, he loosened his arms so Vex could put a couple of inches between them. "Math?"

"Need to see her body." His voice was hoarse.

She nodded. Together they moved to the opening, stood on the edge, and peered down, trying to see through the foliage and shadows to the ground below. The wind had picked up stirring the nearby trees into constant motion, their leaves murmuring in a soft rush. He blinked but it didn't change the picture. "She's not there."

"She was shot twice," Vex murmured. "I'm thinking she won't get far."

He stood there, shocked he wasn't filled with gut-churning anger at the idea of Greer being once more in the wind. Instead, there was a giddy sense of relief, as if he escaped losing something vitally important. It was such an unexpected reaction, he had to figure out what changed, and when.

A warm hand cupped his face and turned his attention to the woman at his side. "You okay?"

And like that, he found his answers. He stared into her amber eyes and couldn't mistake the depth of emotion that stared back. For him. She didn't hide it and it sank through his emotional numbness, to resonate and settle deep. He covered her hand with his, turned his head, and pressed a kiss to the center of her palm. "I will be."

MATH LAID ON HIS SIDE, head braced in one hand, and brushed his other over Vex's bare skin, careful of the deep bruise that spanned her hip and thigh. He nudged the t-shirt she wore higher. It was one of his, but he liked the look of her in it better.

She murmured in her sleep but didn't wake. Not a surprise considering the last handful of hours were spent cleaning up the mess at Stone Pen before they rode hard to the farmstead outside of Pebble Creek. Once he and Vex got Mandy out of the crumbling house, he had Vex take the doc back to the others while he tried to follow Greer's trail. There was a blood trail that indicated Greer had taken serious damage and he held to the hope he would stumble across her corpse. Unfortunately, fate decided differently. Now it was a waiting game—would she surface, or would she do everyone a favor and crawl into a hole and die? He hoped for the second but expected the first.

"Hey, you." Vex watched him as he stroked her, her face soft. She sank her fingers into his hair and tangled her legs with his. "Did you get any sleep?"

He shook his head.

She frowned. "What's wrong?"

He bent down and dropped a kiss on her stomach, just above the edge of her panties. "Nothing."

Her hips arched, not much, enough to let him know she wanted more. Then she tugged on his hair and forced him to look at her. "Uh-huh, hotshot. That kind of answer is my thing, not yours. If we're doing this, got to be honest."

Amused, he slipped his hand under the t-shirt until he could tease the supple curves of her unbound tits. "Says who?"

Those lush lips curved. "Every woman ever. 'Nothing'

belongs to us." She shifted to her side and faced him, mimicking his pose. Her free hand played along his scruff-covered jaw. "So, spit it out. What's bothering you?"

He nipped her fingers. "Nothing's bothering me, I'm just considering my options."

She did a piss poor job of hiding her reaction and there was a tiny hitch in her movements while the skin around her eyes tightened in the smallest wince. "So, you're heading out to New Seattle in the morning?"

He drew his hand out from under the shirt and caught her chin, forcing her to meet his gaze. "Who said I'm leaving?"

"Look, it's no big. You made it crystal clear what you wanted." Her unspoken "and it wasn't me" came through loud and clear, and he wanted to shake her. She gave him an empty smile and tried to pull away, but he refused to let her go.

Since actions spoke louder than words, he bent his head and caught her mouth with his in a fierce kiss. She didn't make him fight for it. Her mouth opened and her tongue met his stroke for stroke. Want and need lit his body up like a torch and he came over her, needing to feel every inch of her, He took her to her back until he could sink against her. Her hands curled over his shoulders, dragged him close, and her leg curled around his waist as he ground the aching length of his dick against the heated softness she offered.

He gave her everything, pouring his need, his frustration, his desire, hell his fucking heart and what was left of his soul, into the kiss. And she answered. Taking what he gave and giving what he demanded until he nipped her lips, then trailed a soft series of kisses along her jaw to the base of her throat. When he lifted his head, he found her watching him, her normal walls shattered and gone, exposing a world of emotion in her eyes. "I'm not going anywhere, Vex."

Her tongue darted out in a nervous touch against her bottom lip. "What about Greer?"

"What about her? One way or the other, she's going to show up. When she does, we'll deal with it."

Something fragile and bright seeped around her brittle mask. "We?"

"No way in hell I'm walking away from you or that asshat brother of mine. God only knows what kind of world-ending trouble the Vultures will cause trying to take out that bitch." He lost his teasing tone and got serious. "I'm not walking away from you. I'm not ready."

She didn't shy away from the hard question. "Why?"

"I almost lost you last night." He cupped her face and rested his forehead against hers. "I can't close my eyes without seeing it, and every time, every fucking time, my heart shatters." He lifted his head and laid it all out. "There's not much left of it, but if you'll settle for damaged goods, it's yours."

A brilliant grin broke free as she rose to rub her nose along his, her mouth moving across his cheek until she could whisper in his ear, "I'll take it, hotshot, but fair warning, I've got a strict no return policy."

He turned and whispered back, "Works for me," before he sealed their deal with a hell of a lot more than a kiss.

thirty

"Glad to see you listening to Mercy." Sprawled in a chair on the porch, Cam scooped another bite of vegetables and rice from the bowl balanced on his stomach. Early evening was setting in. Sara and Danny were tucked inside, giving the small group on the porch much-needed privacy.

"Me too," Mercy agreed from her position in Havoc's arms as the couple leaned against the porch railing.

Math sat with his feet propped on a stump that served as a stool, his arm around Vex's shoulders, as she curled next to him, slowly eating dinner. "Working with Reaper to take on Michael is a no-brainer."

"How do you figure?" The question was Havoc's.

"Michael's not an easy target," Math said. "Which means Reaper's going to need all the help he can get." Vex was right, it was time to leave the past in the past, and move forward. Besides, someone needed to watch Reaper's back. Especially now.

Cam scraped up another bite and lifted his gaze, his voice careful. "We pulling the Strix out of hiding?"

Math didn't hesitate. "Yeah, we are."

"You sure that's wise? We don't know if Greer's still breathing."

"Doesn't matter. After last night, there's no more hiding. If she's alive, she knows I'm hunting her."

"True," Cam murmured. "I'll reach out and start bringing our birdies back to the nest." He cocked an eyebrow. "You got any idea of where that nest is going to be?"

Math didn't get a chance to answer as the rumble of pipes announced the impending arrival of Reaper, Ruin, and Charity. The three went on to Pebble Creek, escorting the doc and her boy to Simon. Reaper caught Simon up on what happened while Ruin and Charity collected the rest of the Vulture's stuff because the Vultures' time in Pebble Creek had run its course.

Everyone watched the three heavily loaded bikes pull into the yard and stop just shy of the porch. Reaper stomped up the steps, exchanged a manly shoulder bump-slash-arm-shake with Havoc, a chin dip with Mercy, and a quick eye meet with Cam, Vex, and Math.

Vex waited until Reaper joined Havoc and Mercy at the railing. "Mandy and Drake?"

"With Simon."

"How is he?"

"Pissed," Ruin answered as he and Charity came up the steps. "But he's dealing with it." He sank down on the top step and braced his back against the post. Charity took the step below and leaned against him.

"You ready to ride?" Reaper asked Cam.

He licked his spoon and said, "Yep."

"Good, because we've got news." Reaper's ominous announcement gained everyone's attention. "Dog got word to Si, bounty's already out." His dark gaze shifted to Math.

"They got names—yours, mine, Ruin, Vex, Havoc, and Mercy."

Math shot Cam a look. "Guess you're not important."

He snorted. "More like they think I'm dead."

Vex looked to Charity. "How'd you luck out?"

The blonde shrugged. "Not sure, but I'll take it."

Math looked at Reaper. "So, what's our next move?"

Reaper arched a brow. "Our?"

"Yeah, our."

Reaper's gaze drifted to Vex and then went back to Math. "That enough reason for you to see this through?"

Math choked back his automatic response to rip into his brother. Getting along with Reaper was going to take practice. Lots of practice. He tightened his hold on Vex. "More than enough." He held Reaper's dark gaze and took the first step forward. "But it's not the only reason."

"Yeah?"

"Yeah," he returned softly. "Taking on the King of the West Coast is going to be fucking brutal, brother." In more ways than one, since no one could gut you faster than family, or in this case, the man you once considered a brother. The history between Reaper and Michael ran deep, and the scars it created still caused pain. But now wasn't the time to get into it so he shifted the conversation. "Where are we going?"

A muscle worked in Reaper's jaw as he stared at Math. Finally, he answered, "We're getting out of Michael's reach."

His tone didn't bode well. There was only one place Michael couldn't touch and it was the last place Math thought Reaper would choose considering how ugly things could get. "You've got to be shitting me."

There was nothing happy in Reaper's grin, in fact it was more a bearing of teeth. "I wouldn't shit you, you're my favorite turd. It's time to strengthen our fucking alliances."

"Oh shit." Charity echoed the sentiment. "We're going to Lilith's."

Dive in to the thrilling conclusion when Reaper is forced to turn to the woman who walked away in FEAR THE REAPER.
Now available at your favorite bookseller!

the collapse: fate's vultures

Meet a new breed of warriors, Fate's Vultures, a mercenary band who live by a code in a world gone to hell — loyalty to each other, but for the right price, they'll be the shield for those without. In the ravaged aftermath of the post-apocalyptic these evocative couples will stop at nothing to claim their future.

Binge the world of The Collapse, now available at your favorite booksellers!

LYING IN RUINS

Charity & Ruin

On a shared mission of vengeance, what will destroy them first—their suspicions or their enemies?

BEG FOR MERCY

Havoc & Mercy

Will an assassin and a mercenary find their balance on the thin line of loyalty, or will it snap under the weight of their wary hearts?

CAUGHT IN THE AFTERMATH

Vex & Math

Caught between a looming conflict and the fallout of a brutal betrayal, will they survive vengeance's aftermath?

FEAR THE REAPER

Reaper & Lilith

Two adversaries must navigate a minefield of past betrayals and broken promises to defeat a common enemy before it all turns to hell.

about the author

"This story is an emotional roller coaster, from betrayal, anger, fear, love…" —InD'tale Magazine

Jami Gray is the coffee addicted, music junkie, Queen Nerd of her personal Geek Squad, Alpha Mom of the Fur Minxes, who writes to soothe the voices crammed in her head. Her series combine high-stakes urban fantasy and edgy paranormal romantic suspense into books you don't want to put down. Buckle up and get ready for a wild ride through the fascinating worlds of the Arcane, the Kyn, the PSY-IV Teams, and the Collapse.

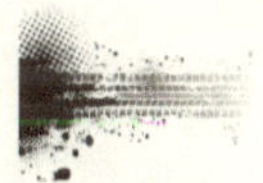

Come visit Jami's website at **https://www.jamigray.com** and stay up to date on what kind of trouble she's getting into and when you can expect to join in.

amazon.com/author/jamigray

instagram.com/jamigrayauthor

facebook.com/JamiGrayWriter

threads.com/@jamigrayauthor

goodreads.com/JamiGray

bookbub.com/authors/jami-gray

www.ingramcontent.com/pod-product-compliance
Lightning Source LLC
Chambersburg PA
CBHW061057190726
48286CB00006B/1778